Pame

C000069221

The Weight of the Crown
Second Son Chronicles - Volume 6

Black Rose Writing | Texas

ISBN: 978-1-68433-788-0
PUBLISHED BY BLACK ROSE WRITING
www.blackrosewriting.com

Printed in the United States of America
Suggested Retail Price (SRP) $19.95

The Weight of the Crown is printed in Book Antiqua

*As a planet-friendly publisher, Black Rose Writing does its best to eliminate unnecessary waste to reduce paper usage and energy costs, while never compromising the reading experience. As a result, the final word count vs. page count may not meet common expectations.

This series is dedicated to the hope that thoughtfulness, compassion, respect, and rational dialogue can triumph over bigotry, greed, mistrust, and self-righteousness to create a world that is truly a better place for all of humankind.

I'm particularly grateful to Linda Kirwin for her help and guidance. Though her project started as a beta read with critique, she quickly grasped what I was trying to do in this series and became a valued editorial consultant. Thanks also to the members of the DFW Writers Workshop who listened to readings and offered their food for thought. And a very special thank you to Jeffrey – himself a second son – who was my first reader and who encouraged me in the early days, when I was unsure if my vision was worth pursuing.

Praise for The Second Son Chronicles

2021 Next Generation Indie Book Awards Finalist – Fiction Series

2020 Eric Hoffer Awards Finalist – Historical Fiction

2019 PenCraft Awards 2nd Place

"A healthy blend of drama, politics, history and action make the story engaging on every level, and the protagonist's journey makes for brilliant storytelling and character progression."
–Pacific Book Review

"A fine-grained and emotionally satisfying medieval adventure."
–Kirkus Reviews

"In the genre of historically inspired fiction, Taylor has done a marvelous job of combining fact, history, and fun."
–IndieReader **"Highest Rated" list**

"Historical fiction lovers will enjoy this tale of knightly adventure."
–Sublime Book Review

"Written in elegant prose, with an intricate storyline that is woven together like a fine medieval tapestry."
–Authors Reading

The Royal Family

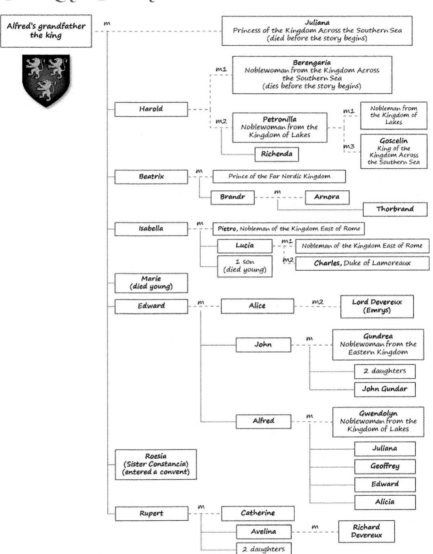

Alfred's grandfather the king — m — **Juliana** Princess of the Kingdom Across the Southern Sea (died before the story begins)

Harold
- m1 — **Berengaria** Noblewoman from the Kingdom Across the Southern Sea (dies before the story begins)
- m2 — **Petronilla** Noblewoman from the Kingdom of Lakes
  - **Richenda**
    - m1 — Nobleman from the Kingdom of Lakes
    - m3 — **Goscelin** King of the Kingdom Across the Southern Sea

Beatrix — m — Prince of the Far Nordic Kingdom
- **Brandr** — m — **Arnora**
  - **Thorbrand**

Isabella — m — Pietro, Nobleman of the Kingdom East of Rome
- **Lucia**
  - m1 — Nobleman of the Kingdom East of Rome
  - m2 — **Charles, Duke of Lamoreaux**
- **1 son** (died young)

Marie (died young)

Edward — m — **Alice** — m2 — **Lord Devereux** (Emrys)
- **John** — m — **Gundrea** Noblewoman from the Eastern Kingdom
  - **2 daughters**
  - **John Gundar**
- **Alfred** — m — **Gwendolyn** Noblewoman from the Kingdom of Lakes
  - **Juliana**
  - **Geoffrey**
  - **Edward**
  - **Alicia**

Roesia (Sister Constancia) (entered a convent)

Rupert — m — **Catherine**
- **Avelina** — m — **Richard Devereux**
- **2 daughters**

The Nobility

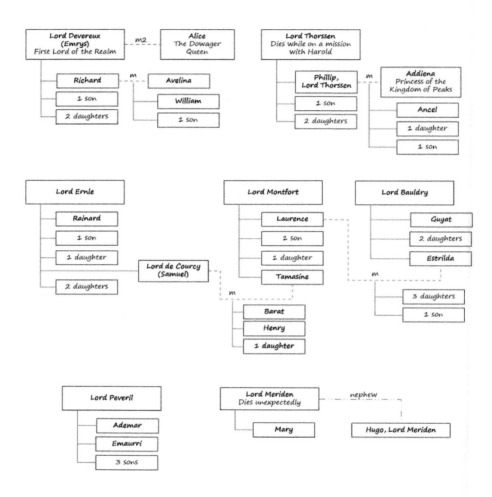

Royal House of the Kingdom Across the Southern Sea

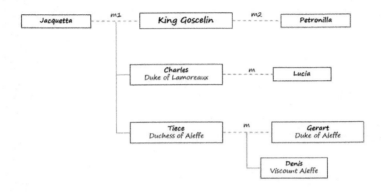

Jacquetta — m1 — King Goscelin — m2 — Petronilla

Charles, Duke of Lamoreaux — m — Lucia

Tiece, Duchess of Aleffe — m — Gerart, Duke of Aleffe

Denis, Viscount Aleffe

Lords of the Unorganized Territories

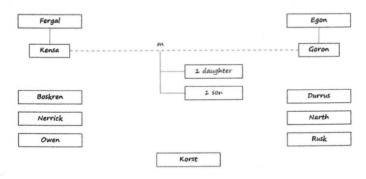

Fergal

Kensa — m — Goron

Egon

1 daughter

1 son

Boskren

Nerrick

Owen

Durrus

Narth

Rusk

Korst

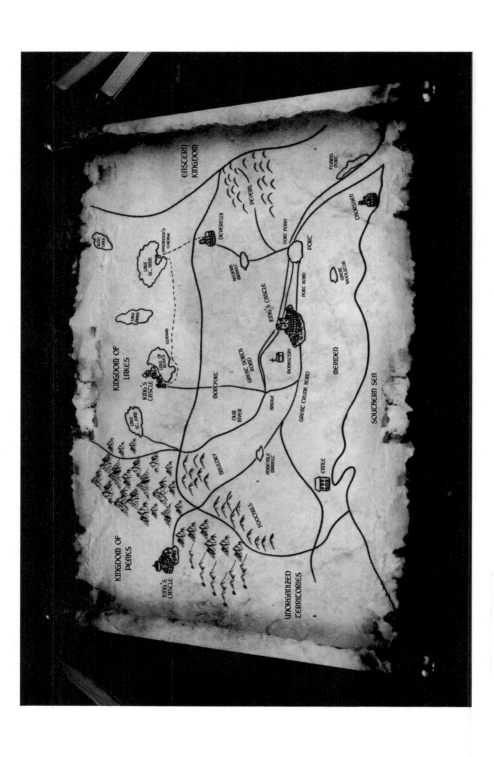

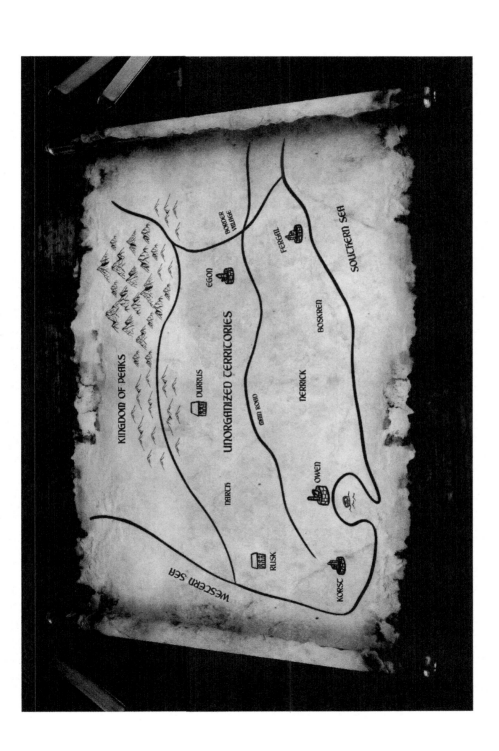

The Weight of the Crown

Sleep eludes me. Though I try valiantly to avoid disturbing Gwen with my wakefulness, it seems I'm unsuccessful, for she snuggles close and lays a hand on my chest in a gesture of comfort. "Thinking about the boy?" she asks.

Since Petronilla affirmed that the lad who'd interrupted our banquet was indeed the young Viscount Aleffe, I've been able to think of nothing else.

Denis, Viscount Aleffe. Grandson of my dear friend and our great ally, the late King Goscelin of the Kingdom Across the Southern Sea. Betrothed to my cousin, Harold's daughter, Richenda. Heir to the throne if King Charles is unable to overcome his aversion to women long enough to produce a son. A pawn in the factional unrest in that kingdom. How did he get here? And how did he get into our celebration?

The joy I'd felt at finally being able to make my friend Samuel a lord as a reward for the extraordinary services he's rendered to me and to the kingdom, many of which must still remain secret but not least of which was winning the war launched against us and driving all of Charles's forces out of the kingdom . . . that joy vanished in an instant when the viscount threw himself at my feet, asking for protection. Matthias, the steward, took him away and put him somewhere to sleep. But the import of the young man's actions has been with me ever since.

"Aye." I put an arm around Gwen, and she lays her head on my shoulder.

"I can't help but wonder why he approached you so boldly in such a public setting," she remarks.

"I've been wondering the same. Was he acting on instructions from someone with a calculated plan? And if so, who? And to what purpose? Someone trying to draw us into the instability over there?"

"Perhaps it was no more than youthful naïveté . . . just a frightened young man, sent away for his own safety and taking whatever opportunity he could find to speak to you."

"Regardless, half the kingdom and all of Charles's spies will know by morning that he's here. And therein lies the danger. If I don't immediately send him back . . ." I let the rest hang in the air.

We lie together in silence, each with our own thoughts. Finally Gwen says, "He has to vanish, you know. Before anyone can lay a hand on him or speak with him."

"What about Petronilla and Richenda?"

"Especially them. They'd be the first ones Charles's spies would pursue. Petronilla would easily recognize and deflect such an approach, but Richenda hasn't the experience."

"I'm glad you agree."

"He *must* disappear, Alfred. Tonight, if possible."

"That's what I've been thinking about as well. And I have a plan that just might work." I explain to her what I have in mind, then climb out of bed and go into my dressing room to wake Osbert.

"Do you know, Osbert," I keep my voice to a whisper, "where Matthias put Viscount Aleffe for the night?"

"Aye, m'lord." He volunteers no details.

"Do you think you could get him and bring him to the Council chamber without anyone knowing it? Without being seen by any guards or any servants that might be about?" I ask, starting to get out of my nightshirt and into some proper clothes.

"I be thinking there not be many folks about, sir. They all be sleeping off the banquet."

"My thoughts too. You'd have to go about without a candle. I don't want anyone thinking they may have seen a light in a corridor and deciding to investigate."

"Aye, m'lord."

"And Osbert, I want you to blindfold the young man. I don't want him to be able to tell anyone where he was taken or how he was taken there if anything should go wrong." He hesitates. Something's bothering him.

"What is it, Osbert?"

"What I be telling the boy? Fer certes he be asking what be happening."

"Tell him to be exceedingly quiet, that I'll join you shortly, and then he can tell me his story in private. That should be enough to reassure him. Tell him the blindfold is for his own safety."

"Mayhap that be enough."

"Do you know if the wagon for the monastery has already been loaded with the leftovers from the banquet?" It's a custom that we donate much of the leftover food from great celebrations to the brothers.

"Aye. Brother Eustace be wanting to leave at dawn, so he be helping the kitchen maids load things up."

"Very well. I'll join you in the Council chamber shortly. There are a couple of things I need to do first. When I get there, Osbert, I'll need you to do one more thing. Wake Brother Eustace and bring him here to my dressing room. I'll find you here after I've spoken with the lad."

Returning to our bedchamber, I light a single candle and sit at my writing desk to compose the necessary note to Abbot Warin.

My dear Warin,

This is the sort of favor I'd much prefer to discuss in person, but I haven't the luxury of time, so I must trust you'll understand the circumstances.

I go on to describe what's happened and the details of my plan, writing quickly to minimize the time this candle must stay lit. It wouldn't suit my purposes for someone to notice a light in the king's bedchamber at an unusual hour and later start imagining a link to the disappearance of the viscount. The moment I affix my seal to the missive, I douse the candle.

It takes a moment for my eyes to readjust to the darkness of the room. Though I can see Gwen sitting up in bed, covers drawn up to her waist, arms grasping her knees, it nevertheless takes a bit of fumbling to find the mechanism hidden in the chimney that releases the latch on the door to the secret passage. As I open the door, Gwen lets out a quiet gasp. She's long known about the existence of the passage, but has never before seen the entrance opened.

Inside on the landing, I use the dim glow from the room to light a torch and then quickly close the door behind me. At the level of the old library, I douse the torch before entering the room where I have no idea if the door to the corridor will be open or shut. Now I have to take the first big risk. When I return this way with the lad in tow, the ruse that we're using servants' stairways means there'll be no time to fumble around searching for hidden latches, so I leave the entrance to the passage slightly ajar. Crossing to the corridor door, I check for guards and pause a long moment to listen for any sound that might be approaching feet. Though my slippers are quiet on the wooden floors, to my ears, each footstep sounds like the clang of hammer on anvil as I hurry along to the Council chamber.

When I open the door, there's no one in sight. How could I have arrived first? Has Osbert encountered something to foil our plan? There's nothing for it but to close the door and wait. And then I see the brilliance of Osbert's planning. He seated young Denis at my secretary's small writing desk in the corner of the room obscured by the open door and is standing there with him. Had a guard opened the door for a casual check of the room, their presence would have gone undetected.

The lad is noticeably apprehensive. "You may remove his blindfold now." I speak quietly, avoiding the use of Osbert's name as a precaution against anyone asking the young man who he came into contact with on his movements about the castle. I take the blindfold, intending to use it again for the rest of this evening's business, and Osbert takes his leave, shutting the door quietly behind him.

The young man had begun to visibly relax the moment he saw my face. Once we're alone, he lets out a deep sigh. "I thought—" he begins, speaking a bit louder than I'd like.

"Shhhh." I put my finger to my lips, then continue in a tone not much above a whisper. "We mustn't risk a passing guard getting curious and listening at the door."

"Of course, Sire. I wasn't thinking. It's just that I thought they were going to send me away, and I wouldn't get to speak with you." His relief is evident in his posture.

"Tell me, Denis, how did you come to be here?"

"My mother sent me, Sire."

"Are you sure? We've been given to believe your mother hasn't been seen in months . . . that she's either left the kingdom or is in hiding somewhere."

"As sure as I *can* be, Sire, though I haven't seen her either."

"Then maybe you should tell me the whole story of how you got here."

"It's true my mother left us, Sire," he begins. "Quite some months ago. I've lost track of just how many. My father wouldn't speak of it. He wouldn't tell me where she was or why she'd left. You know, I suppose, about the conflict in our kingdom. I can only guess her disappearance must have something to do with that.

"But a month ago, I got a message from her. I was to dress myself like a peasant and go to the port. Someone I knew would meet me there. And I wasn't to tell my father. So I sneaked out in the middle of the night and managed to make my way to the port without anyone stopping me."

"You were so sure this really was a message from your mother?"

"I wasn't sure, Sire. But the messenger gave me a piece of paper on which was written just one word – her pet name for me when I was a wee lad – and it looked like her writing. I was suspicious. Someone could have forced her to write it or could have forged it. But I decided I had to find out if it was real. If I could blend in with the people at the docks, then I could look for someone I knew. And if I didn't see anyone, then my plan was to go back home."

"You took quite a risk. What if you'd been kidnapped?"

"I know, Sire. But I had to find out."

"Go on."

"I was lucky, Sire. My mother's maid was waiting by the first ship I came to. She was dressed in peasant clothes too, but I couldn't mistake who she was. She hugged me and carried on as if she'd lost track of me in the town and was ever so relieved to find me again, all the while whispering in my ear to go along with whatever she said.

"A man in the bow of the ship was watching us, looking amused. She took my hand and dragged me up the gangway and straight up to the man.

"'Here he is, Captain,' she said, 'just like I told you. I knew he couldn't have gone far.' The man chuckled and looked me up and down. 'My son,' she went on. 'The lad I want to send to his father.'

"And then she took out a note and pinned it to my jacket. 'This tells him, see, why I'm sending the boy to him. Please, Captain, you *have* to take him.'

"So the captain said to her, 'You say you can pay his passage?'

"And she started fumbling in her skirts and came out with an old worn leather purse. She held it out to the captain. 'It's all I got right now,' she said, 'so I hope it's enough.'

"The captain took the purse, dumped some coins into his hand, and bit on a couple of them to be sure they were legitimate. He took his time putting the coins back in the purse, all the while scanning the dock. I couldn't tell if he was worried somebody might be coming after us or if he just wanted to see if there might be any better passengers. Eventually, he put the purse in his pocket and said, 'Alright. He can bunk with my cabin boy. But he'd best not make any trouble. If he does, he goes in the hold with the animals.' Then he turned on his heel and walked away.

"My mother's maid made a big fuss about telling me to behave myself and obey the captain. Then, when she gave me a long hug goodbye, she whispered in my ear that I was to find you and ask for your protection."

"Quite a ruse!"

"Yes, sir. And another reason I think my mother planned it. She's cunning like that."

"So tell me the rest of the story."

"I kept to myself on the passage. At one point, the captain ordered me into his cabin and made me show him the note pinned to my jacket. He read it – or he pretended to, in any event – and thrust it back at me with a grunt and a wave of his hand to leave the cabin.

"When we docked, I couldn't get off the ship fast enough, and I scurried right out of town as quick as I could. I didn't want to run afoul of anyone who might have gotten wind of the plan and be lying in wait for me. I made my way here, Sire, and then started trying to get an audience with you.

"It wasn't easy. The only clothes I had were what I'm still wearing. So no one would take me seriously when I'd ask to speak with you. The guards kept sending me away."

"I hope no one mistreated you."

"Oh, no, Sire. They didn't treat me rough. Just kept telling me I was too young to have business with the king, so I should be on my way. Sometimes one of them would watch to be sure I was headed down the road back into town.

"Anyway, I tried to get work in the stable. I knew you'd have to go riding sometime. But the head groom said they didn't need any more help. So I was just living on the streets in the town, trying to come up with an idea how to find a way to speak to you."

"What did you do for food?"

"I'd brought a few coins with me from home, so for the first week or so, I could buy bread from the baker and some small ale at the tavern. But I ran out of money a few days ago and was having to scrounge what I could wherever I could. I was getting desperate, Sire, and didn't know what I was going to do next. I thought of going to the bishop and telling him my story. But then it occurred to me he might just send me back home. So when I heard some of the lads from the town were coming to help in the castle kitchen for the banquet, I decided that was my chance. I was thinking they might use us to clear tables or something like that, but all the work was in the kitchen. When they gave us our food and said we should be on our way, I had to take a risk. I waited until everyone was busy loading the wagon and made a dash for the banquet hall. The steward spied me, but I was too fast for him."

He pauses a moment, looking contrite. "I'm sorry, Sire. I truly didn't know what else to do."

"I'm sorry too, Denis. This puts us both in a very awkward position."

The boy looks completely deflated. "Does this mean you can't help me, Sire?"

I don't answer right away. "That note that was pinned to your jacket. You seem to think it was important. What did it say?"

He perks up, reaches into his jacket pocket, and produces the note. "Here, Sire. I think it was meant for you."

I take it from him and walk to the nearest window, but the starlight is insufficient to make out the words. "You know what it says?"

"Yes, sir. It says, 'Dear Al, This be your son Joseph. I send him to you so he don't be taken to be a soldier and get killed.' And it's signed 'Tessie'."

"Why do you think it was meant for me?"

"Well, sir, you're Alfred and Al is short for that. My second name is Joseph, though you wouldn't know that without my telling you. And Tessie is close enough to my mother's name – Tiece – that you could figure it out."

"That could just be circumstantial."

"It's in the second sentence, sir. I've been thinking a lot about that. I think my mother was afraid I was going to be taken hostage by one side or the other. If my uncle Charles took me, I'd be a hostage for the surrender of the opposition. And once he had his kingdom back, he'd accuse me of treason and have me executed so there'd be no one for his opponents to rally around. If the nobles who hold most of the country now and who claim allegiance to our family . . . if they took me, they could force me to ride at the head of their army and make it look like I was leading the rebellion. If the rebels didn't win, then once again I'd be branded a traitor and executed along with all the nobles in the opposition. My father and mother too, most likely, though my father has taken great pains to constantly demonstrate his loyalty to the king."

My respect for this young man has just grown enormously. He seems to have a good head on his shoulders and is far more thoughtful than his rash entry into the banquet hall might have indicated. Don't be too trusting, Alfred, I remind myself. It could still be an elaborate ruse. But if this is a ruse, then Denis is a consummate actor who's been well tutored. I decide to take a chance on him.

"To answer your question, Denis, the manner of your appearance at the banquet greatly limits my options. You'd agree, wouldn't you, that your uncle most likely has spies here in our kingdom? Perhaps even in my court or in my household."

"That makes sense, Sire."

"And since so many people heard your petition tonight, we have to assume your uncle's spies now know your precise whereabouts and what you've asked of me."

The dejected look returns. "I should have thought of that, Sire. I'm sorry. Perhaps I should just be on my way and trust in God for my future."

"You're right, Denis, that I can't openly offer you protection without putting my family, perhaps even my kingdom, at risk. And having only recently driven Charles's forces out of our lands, I'm in no mood to do battle with him yet again. Besides, you'd also be at risk because there'd no doubt be spies from both sides of the conflict swarming all over our countryside looking for you . . . perhaps even bribing people to turn you in.

"However . . ." I take a long pause for effect. Denis looks up, his expression somewhat hopeful. "I think you may be onto something with your idea about trusting God."

"Sire?" Now his expression is quizzical.

"Here's my plan. You have to disappear. When people awake in the morning, there must be *no* sign that you were ever here. To that end, I'm going to take you down to where the monastery wagon is loaded and ready for departure and hide you beneath the baskets and sacks of food. You'll have to spend the rest of the night there alone, as quiet and still as can be.

"The brother who drives the wagon is a man I would trust with my life. But you mustn't speak to him or in any way acknowledge your presence during the journey. If he's stopped for any reason, you have to trust him to satisfy the curiosity of whoever waylays him and remain perfectly still and quiet. Make your breathing as shallow as possible to avoid any sound or movement that might give you away.

"Only when the abbot of the monastery comes to free you from your hiding place may you emerge. His name is Abbot Warin, and he'll identify himself to you when the time is right."

"I can do that, Sire," he says eagerly.

"There's more, Denis. You're going to live the life of a monk. You'll be tonsured. You'll dress in monk's garb and live in a monk's cell. You'll participate in the holy offices. And you will cheerfully undertake whatever tasks the abbot may assign to you. Abbot Warin will provide a narrative for you and for his community of how and why you come to be among them. You must adhere to that narrative in everything you do and say. And you can have *no* communication with the outside world except through Abbot Warin.

"Regardless of what happens in the conflict between your uncle and the rebellious factions in his kingdom, you deserve to live. And this is the only way I can think of to protect your life without putting far too many other lives at risk." I've been rather stern, with the intent of impressing on him the seriousness of the step we're about to take together.

For several moments, he's silent . . . thoughtful. At long last, he says, "I understand, Sire."

"It's not enough that you understand, Denis. You must give me your word of honor as Viscount Aleffe that you agree to the plan and will comply with the conditions."

In an instant, his breeding and his training take over. He stands, his back perfectly straight, every inch a nobleman. He looks directly into my eyes and puts his right hand over his heart. "I give you my word of honor, Your Grace . . . the honor of the Aleffe family . . . that I will do everything you ask."

I hold out my hand and we grasp arms as gentlemen of honor. I take the blindfold from my pocket. "In that case, we should get underway. The night is fast disappearing."

"Sire, before we go?"

"Yes?"

"May I see the Lady Richenda? I wouldn't have her believe that I've deserted her."

"Do you really think that would be wise? Isn't it likely she's going to be the first person your uncle's spies seek out to try to learn your whereabouts?"

"I'm sorry, Sire. You're right again. But will you tell her for me that I still love her and that when all this madness is over, I still intend to make her my bride and one day my duchess . . . perhaps even my queen."

"When the time is right and some of the search for you has died down, I'll tell her. For now, I think it best she truly believe you've disappeared. Now, let me blindfold you again. Even though it's unlikely, if you *were* to be captured, it's safest if you can't tell anyone where you went or how you got there." He takes the blindfold from my hand and ties it on himself. "Take my hand," I tell him, "and walk as softly as you can. There's one set of somewhat treacherous stairs – I'll never understand how the servants negotiate them carrying a full chamber pot – but we'll manage fine if you trust me to guide you."

I lead him down the corridor, into the library, and onto the landing of the secret passage. "Now put one hand on my shoulder and follow me down." I won't light a torch, having no wish for anyone to see an unexpected light in the undercroft when we emerge. My recent experience with blindness – suffered when Charles's cannon exploded during the last war – gives me confidence I can manage, and I begin to count the steps as we descend. When I open the door into the undercroft, I'm gratified by my decision to avoid the torch – much of what's usually stored here has been removed for use at the banquet. We move quickly to get Denis hidden in the wagon before anyone should chance to hear a noise and investigate. As I leave, I tell him, "Trust in God and Abbot Warin, Denis, and you'll be safe." He doesn't reply . . . his way, I believe, of telling me that, from this moment, he's complying with my conditions.

Hurrying back through the undercroft, I prepare a torch for lighting, not wishing to take any risk with securing the entrance to the passage here or at the level of the library. The moment the torch shows the first sign of flame, I shut the door quickly. Not for the first time, I marvel at how well maintained this passage is. The door mechanisms always well oiled so that the only sound is the soft click of the latch as it's released or closed. A plentiful supply of torches always at the ready . . . and though most are old and require priming, I've noticed from time to time a somewhat newer one in the bunch that takes to the flame more readily. There's someone else among us who knows and maintains the secret.

I've sometimes wondered who that might be. Perhaps the steward. But stewards come and go, and if a steward were to be dismissed, he'd have no way of transferring the knowledge to his successor. So this seems unlikely.

Perhaps the brothers from the monastery. André did seem to know about the passage when I asked him to use it to protect the library during John's reign. And the brothers are here from time to time. But this, too, seems unlikely as their movements in unusual places such as undercrofts would elicit comment.

What seems most plausible is that it's our stable master – the endless succession of Mervyns and Elvins who've served our family for generations. The stories say it's an unbroken line of service going back long before my grandfather's grandfather's time. Why would that be? Certainly, they're expert horsemen, but there are equally capable horsemen throughout the kingdom. I remember the account of Sir Cedric's trial, when the man I knew as Mervyn the Elder was asked if he performed special tasks for the king, and he replied in the affirmative. A stable master could move about with a can of oil or tools or torches anywhere on the castle grounds, and his movements would be completely unremarkable to anyone. Perhaps I should ask Elvin one day, as this is knowledge that should probably be passed on to Geoffrey at the appropriate time. Perhaps it would have been passed on to me had the succession from my father to my brother to me not been so violent and unexpected.

My musings have brought me to the library level, where I pause to secure the door and make certain the latch is firmly in place. Then I rush up the next flight, not wanting to keep Brother Eustace waiting any longer than necessary . . . though his monk's training would induce him to be patient for whatever time it might take me to arrive.

Emerging into my bedchamber, I find Gwen waiting. She takes my hand immediately and leads me to the door to the private reception room, causing me to delay closing the passage entrance. Standing on tiptoes, she whispers in my ear. "There shouldn't be the sound of two doors . . . only this one opening and closing as you return. You take this one so your footsteps are heard moving from here to your dressing room." Leave it to Gwen to think of such details. She tiptoes, barefoot, over to the passage entrance and watches as I open the other door. We close both doors simultaneously, and I make a bit more noise than usual walking to the dressing room, grabbing the note to Warin from my writing table on the way, while she scrambles back into bed. I can check the latch on the passage entrance later.

Osbert and Eustace are waiting. We speak quietly, still intent on avoiding being overheard by a passing guard or servant. "Eustace, I once trusted you with my life, and now again I need to trust you with the safety of my family and perhaps even the kingdom."

"Sadly, my friend, I must admit I betrayed your trust on that former occasion."

"Calm yourself, Eustace. André told me he insisted on your confession. There was no betrayal." Seeing a frown begin to form on Eustace's face, I hurry to add, "Never fear. He didn't break the sanctity of the confessional. He told me none of the words that passed between you . . . only the extremity of your distress over the risk I was taking and how I was endangering my life. His revelation was part of a lesson to remind me that I possess a strength of mind for the things that matter most in life."

"Brother André was a wonderful teacher, Alfred. On that occasion, he helped me see that it wasn't necessary for me to bear all the burden of what might happen to you . . . that my task was to fulfill what you asked of me and I could leave the rest in God's hands. I miss him greatly. We all do, in spite of the fact that we love and respect Warin immensely."

"And now I have another task for you, Eustace. This one will be much easier . . . and you get to share the responsibility with Warin." I tell him everything that's transpired tonight, including all the details of the plan, and finish by handing him the letter for Warin. "When you arrive back at the monastery, the hardest part will be convincing the brothers not to begin unloading the wagon before you can speak to the abbot."

"I'll find a way."

"Once Warin has read this, I'm confident he'll know how to get the young man out of his hiding place and into safety among you. Most likely, he'll need your help . . . which is why I wanted you to know all the details of the plan."

"Would it be useful, Alfred, for me to leave now? Before people are up and about? It could be done if Osbert would help me hitch up the horse."

"I think not, Eustace. Everything should look completely normal. We don't want anyone to notice something out of the ordinary and begin wondering why. Depart at your usual time. Denis is prepared to wait patiently in his hiding place. You should be off and try to get whatever sleep you can before your usual waking time. I think you'll have ample time to be safely back at the monastery before it becomes widely known that the boy has disappeared."

"I won't let you down, Alfred. I'm humbled by your trust."

"All men need others they can rely on, Eustace. I'm grateful for what you do for me."

Osbert goes to the corridor door and peeks out. Seeing no one about, he beckons to Eustace, who leaves quietly as Osbert closes the door behind him. "It be almost dawn, m'lord. I be letting ye sleep a mite later than usual, as ye been so busy tonight."

"Actually, Osbert, you should wake me at whatever would be the usual time following a night of such festivities. Like I told Eustace . . . we don't want anything to look out of the ordinary."

"Aye, m'lord. That make good sense."

He helps me back into my nightshirt, and I walk slowly back to bed. Gwen is propped up on her pillows, waiting. "So I take it the lad agreed?" she asks.

"He did. He was growing quite frightened, and I really think last night's episode was one of desperation rather than some carefully orchestrated plot." As I tell her about our conversation, the tension from the drama of the past few hours begins to slip away, and I realize that I'm quite exhausted. I take her in my arms and we snuggle deeply under the covers. I've done everything I can. I only hope it's enough.

The civil war in the Kingdom Across the Southern Sea rages on. Perhaps not so much "rages" as burbles and spits. Rather like a pot of porridge simmering over the fire – steam gently rising – the occasional small burp to let you know it's cooking – but now and then, an enormous bubble forms deep in the pot and rises slowly, finally erupting through the surface and splattering porridge over anything and everything nearby. So goes this conflict.

Those loyal to the Duke of Aleffe hold most of the kingdom – the castle town and the castle itself, the primary port, and the market towns throughout most of the countryside. King Charles remains holed up in his duchy of Lamoreaux, making little or no effort to reclaim his kingdom. From time to time, he'll send a small force to skirmish with the opposition at a town or village not far from the Lamoreaux border. Once in a great while, he's sent a slightly larger force to try to reclaim the nearest market town. None of these engagements have ended in a clear victory or loss for either side – it's almost as if they're simply staging a bit of theater to prove that neither has actually acquiesced.

The Duke of Aleffe still steadfastly refuses to declare for the opposition, leaving his adherents without a titular leader. The whereabouts of the duchess – Charles's sister, Tiece – remain a mystery even after all these months. Some say she's died, others that she's fled the kingdom, still others that she's in hiding because she fears for her life at her brother's hand. Laurence, my spymaster, has a different theory. He thinks Tiece is actually commanding the opposition forces and moving about in disguise among the people and the opposition nobles, never staying in any one place for very long. Samuel agrees it would be a brilliant strategy . . . one that would allow the Aleffes to emerge from the conflict unscathed, regardless of which side ultimately prevails. I'm inclined to agree with them, especially in view of the young viscount's tale of how he came to arrive on our shores.

There being no further indication of a threat to us from Charles, Sir Jasper, who took over from Samuel as Knight Commander, is slowly unwinding our forces following the war. As usual, some of the men discovered they rather like the military life and have begun offering their services as mercenaries in the conflict across the sea. I'm content to let some of them go, particularly as they provide a pool of potential agents for Laurence, who's had real difficulty getting any reliable information since the conflict began. Most of the mercenaries seem to be aligning with the Aleffe faction – not surprising, I think, for men who most recently fought to repulse Charles's invasion of their homeland. Jasper has agreed to find temporary assignments for a number of those who want to remain, allowing the flow of mercenaries to be more a trickle than a river. The last thing we need is for anyone to decide we're surreptitiously taking sides. Samuel chuckled when I told him about the plan. "You have to admit, Alfred, that a steady stream of mercenaries would be a rather effective way to tilt the balance one way or the other without ever having to land a formal fighting force on their shores."

"If," I replied, "I were inclined to meddle in the conflict . . . which I'm not, as yet." I've not even brought the topic up with the Council. Best to let Charles and his rebellious nobles sort it out among themselves so long as we're not threatened.

That doesn't mean we're entirely free of risk. There's still the issue of the missing viscount. As I'd guessed, in the weeks following his disappearance, the population of spies swarming about the kingdom swelled to unprecedented numbers. They seemed to be in every town and village, looking anywhere and everywhere for their quarry. Bribes in abundance were paid to anyone who would agree to provide them information on the young man's whereabouts. Laurence found their blatant openness quite amusing, despite the fact that his agents were stretched thin keeping an eye on all the activity. And the innkeepers had a windfall of profits from the influx of people needing a place to eat, drink, and sleep. So long as they came nowhere near the truth, I was happy to let them wander about and spend their money, knowing they would soon tire of the game and go home to their masters empty-handed. By the end of the second month, the horde was reduced to the usual numbers, though Laurence and I have no doubt those that remain haven't abandoned the search.

I waited six weeks before visiting Abbot Warin . . . any longer would have seemed suspicious given my new habit of regular visits to read my grandfather's chronicle. Rupert often accompanies me on these excursions, but I took advantage of his absence at the country manor to be able to speak privately with Warin. I found him finishing the midday meal in the company of Prior Dunstan. Not long after he became abbot, Warin had told me, "I really wanted to bring Frery here as Prior, just as André did with me. But Frery's doing excellent work in the west, the brothers there love him, and he's quite content. I'm not as comfortable with Dunstan, though. He has difficulty at times mastering his rather zealous ambition, so I don't fully trust him." Remembering this, I kept my conversation to the more mundane topics of family and events in the outside world until Dunstan tired of it all and excused himself.

"That was rather a lot of food we just ate," Warin said. "I feel the need for a walk outdoors. Would you join me?" As we crossed the compound toward the kitchen gardens, he resumed. "I'd like you to see the progress our new brother has made in adapting himself to our community."

"As usual, Warin, you know what's on my mind."

"Just there," he inclined his head, taking care not to gesture in a particularly obvious way. The monk I saw picking beans was approximately the size and stature of Viscount Aleffe, but his hair was dark whereas Denis is blonde with hints of ginger.

"Where?" I asked.

"Just there, picking beans with Brother Eustace." I looked again, but was still unconvinced. "Excellent!" Warin smiled broadly. "I'm pleased our little subterfuge is succeeding."

"How?"

"Black walnuts. One must be careful, as they'll stain pretty much anything they come in contact with, but it's easier to manage after the first application. We kept him in my quarters for a week, to effect his transformation and avoid any obvious connection with your banquet. The brothers believe he was sent to us from a monastery near Rome, where he'd been a bit of a disciplinary problem. I've assigned him to share a cell with Eustace . . . and Eustace is responsible for helping him learn to fit in and seeing that he doesn't stray from any of your conditions. For the benefit of the brothers, Eustace is responsible for seeing that he maintains discipline."

"Have you had anyone snooping around?"

"None so far. But I think we're prepared, should anyone show up. There's really very little snooping one can do in a community like ours. Dunstan is my biggest concern. He's not shown any excessive curiosity, but if someone were to start asking questions . . ."

"I'm sorry to have put you in this position, Warin, but it seemed there was nothing else to do."

"There wasn't. And I'm confident we'll manage. Now, let's get you back to those chronicles so your visit today appears tiresomely ordinary."

Though the civil war and the hidden viscount are worrisome, they aren't what weighs most heavily on my mind. Far more distressing is the new weapon that Teuton belligerence and Charles's ill-conceived invasion have unleashed in our land. Knights from the Peaks and the Lakes – and of course, our own men – saw the destructive power of the cannon and black powder firsthand. That its existence is no longer a closely guarded secret merely changes the responsibility I've felt since Brandr first told us of the Teutons' activity and we verified it for ourselves. Now the burden is one of negotiation with my fellow kings and the Territorial lords to work out how to live with this new style of warfare.

In some ways, perhaps, it's no different from the appearance of new weapons in earlier times – heavier siege engines, the ballista, the introduction of the crossbow – all new and more deadly ways for men to wreak destruction on each other. Over time, each of these has become a normal part of an arsenal, and men have learned to defend themselves accordingly. Somehow, though, this feels more like a sea change. Perhaps that's only because it's happening in my lifetime. But the explosive power of black powder seems more akin to the taming of fire itself. Samuel and I know how the stuff behaves and are convinced men will find an infinite variety of ways to use it once their ability to control its volatility matches their imaginations.

I've spent many hours with my own thoughts and in conversation with those I trust most trying to chart a course. Over brandy with Rupert one evening, I voiced my doubts. "Father and Grandfather always seemed so confident. Why is it, Uncle, that I'm plagued with uncertainty about how to handle this?"

"Have you considered it might simply be a matter of perspective? That what you saw in them as confidence reflects no more than the fact that you were merely an observer, with no responsibility for the results of any decision?"

I couldn't help but chuckle. My uncle has a way of getting to the heart of the matter. "I've asked myself dozens of times what they would do. And before you chide me for forgetting lessons learned, they'd consult those they trust, decide what outcome they wanted, and then go about convincing any skeptics to support that outcome."

It was Rupert's turn to chuckle. "So have you decided what outcome you want?"

"I'm not sure. But I keep coming back to Lord Ernle's advice. 'Don't make the weapons your main priority, Alfred,' he said. 'You've studied history. You know men have always found new ways to wage war. It won't happen in our lifetimes, but something even more destructive than cannons will come along sooner or later. Focus on what you want the kingdom's relationships with its friends to be and then think about how to defend against our enemies.'"

"Sound advice, in my opinion. And do you have a plan?"

"I think so. I just don't know if it can succeed."

"Give yourself more credit, Alfred. No one knew if your plan to make peace with the Territories could succeed. Not only did it succeed, but you've managed to turn former adversaries into allies and partners. Just remember how you approached that."

"I made that up as we went along."

"Then why not do the same now?"

"It feels like there's so much more at stake."

"There was war at stake then."

"Yes, but there's peace at stake now."

"Is that really so very different? Trust your instincts, Alfred. They're good . . . better, perhaps, than you realize." Not for the first time, Rupert helped me past an obstacle that was hindering my progress.

Samuel found the ideal location for our new armory. Just over an hour's ride west of the castle, the Great Trunk Road curves to the south to bypass a gentle but distinct rise in the land. North of the rise, out of sight of travelers on the road, lies a broad meadow, bordered on two sides by dense forest. All in all, a perfect place to store the volatile powder and experiment with the two cannons we captured from Charles's supply train.

It's somewhat puzzling that such a lush meadow isn't leased out to a herdsman. Perhaps it's merely that the seclusion that makes it so ideal for Samuel's purposes makes it inconvenient for access to the wool markets. The bishop would say it's God's plan that the site should be here for us at this time. I find it exceedingly peculiar that God would plan a location for men to experiment with new ways to wage war and wreak havoc. Regardless, Fortuna has smiled on us, and the location is sufficiently isolated to avoid both casual observation and danger to people, towns, or villages when the probably inevitable accident occurs. It's also on royal lands, so I can simply decree its new use, but the boundary of the Montfort estate lies within the forest to the north, so as a courtesy, I consulted Lord Montfort. Knowing what's at stake, he offered no objection.

The site has been constructed with as much haste as could be mustered. Every building is crafted of stone, to minimize the risk of fire. The huts for storing the black powder have iron grates rather than wooden doors. The floor of each is raised off the ground and the doors face away from the prevailing winds, for we've learned that, when wet, black powder is no more explosive than sand on a beach. There are numerous such huts, spread well apart, the better to minimize destruction should something go wrong. Sir Jasper has assigned an elite troop to both guard the armory and learn how to handle the new weapons. Their barracks are on the opposite side of the meadow, well away from the storage huts. A large pond has been dug in the middle of the meadow to ensure an immediate source of water should fire break out. Samuel still hasn't decided where to locate the foundry if we decide to try our hand at creating more cannons. But that decision can wait.

What's more urgent is discussions with our neighbors. As soon as the work on the site was underway, Samuel turned his attention there, beginning with visits to the Peaks and Lakes kings. I insisted the ambassadors go along. That places an extra burden on Peveril and the separate visits to each of the Territorial lords. I long for the day when Egon's vision of a unified Territories is realized, though I'm realistic enough to know that's unlikely to be in my lifetime. "I want the ambassadors' read as well as your own on the reaction to what you have to say," I told Samuel. "They know the subtleties of each court and each Territory and will pick up on nuances you or I might miss."

"You'll get no argument from me," Samuel replied. "How much can I disclose?"

"Everything we learned on our own. But I gave my word of honor to Brandr not to reveal his role."

Samuel chuckled. "You honor's safe with me, Alfred."

It was my turn to laugh quietly. Samuel has been the guardian of my welfare on more occasions than I care to count, though my gratitude is beyond counting. I only hope that creating him Lord de Courcy has contributed in some measure toward payment of the debt. "What do you think about not revealing that we have the formula for black powder until they're all together?"

"Wise, in my opinion," he replied. "My intent is to do no more than plant seeds for how we might all cooperate around this new madness so they have time to form their own ideas before the big gathering."

We plan to bring them all here to see the new weapons for themselves. Samuel and I are both keenly aware of the risks should any of our friends and allies perceive our intent is anything other than preserving the status quo among us. "I think they should all hear about the formula at the same time, lest they start making up stories about our secrecy," he added.

The fateful day has arrived at last. Though not a formal state visit, it has many of the trappings – kings, lords, and their retinues have been arriving throughout the past week, necessitating court dinners and adjustments to protocol every day. Though we've had our differences, it saddens me, in a way, that Charles isn't here. The Kingdom Across the Southern Sea was an ally since my grandfather married one of their noblewomen over half a century ago. The changes wrought by recent events are, I fear, more than unfortunate.

The first order of business is a trip to the armory. The demonstrations begin with the simple experiments Samuel and I tried on the river bank when we first mixed our own powder. Though everyone is at a safe distance – and we've given them assurances of such – the reaction when the cask of powder explodes is not much different from what ours had been. As everyone recovers their composure, the King of Lakes remarks, "Fearsome stuff, indeed."

"My friends," I use this form partially as a courtesy to the Territorial lords, but more importantly today to reinforce my conviction that we have to be united in what to do about the new weapons. "Fearsome as the powder is on its own, what's even more important for you to see is what's already being done with it." I signal to the captain of the troop to demonstrate the cannons.

They've built a wall with a wooden gate, much like one would find at the entrance to a castle – not as strong and fortified, certainly, but sufficient to the demonstration. First, they fire both cannons in rapid succession at the gate, which shatters under the assault. Next, they change the angle at which the cannons are mounted and demonstrate how the cannon-balls can be lobbed over the wall, creating destruction within. Finally, they fire the cannons at the stone wall itself, breaching a hole through which men could easily pass.

At the end of the demonstration, no one says a word, each man alone with his thoughts. At long last, I decide it's time to speak, though I keep my voice quieter than usual. "My friends, this totally changes warfare as we know it. Gates breached in minutes without having to send men with battering rams into a hail of arrows or a rain of hot oil. The ability to create fear and havoc inside a fortress before troops ever advance. Breaching walls from a distance. Admittedly, this wall and gate were not as well fortified as our castles and fortresses. But we were only using two cannons. Imagine an array of these weapons facing your stronghold." The silence persists as everyone considers what the new weaponry might mean to them.

"So tell me." Korst sounds skeptical. "If King Charles had these weapons in the last war, why weren't more men killed by them?"

I defer to Samuel – these men all know his military expertise. "That was Charles's great tactical blunder. He was far too eager to demonstrate what he had, so he began his bombardment with only a single cannon. If he'd had the patience to establish all his firing positions before attacking, we'd have had a far more difficult time trying to disable them . . . and many more lives would've been lost. As it is, his blunder is our great good fortune in that we were able to capture the weapons he failed to use properly."

"Perhaps we should return to the comfort of your castle, my friend," suggests the King of Lakes, "and talk at length about what to do."

"I agree," I reply. "But before we go, there's one other bit of information you should know." I want them to have time to digest this on the ride back rather than have it sprung on them as part of the talks. "We've come into possession of the formula for making black powder."

"Why have you not told us this before?" Nerrick sounds rather belligerent.

"A reasonable question, Lord Nerrick. One I no doubt would have asked, myself, were the circumstances reversed. When we came into possession of the recipe, I insisted on caution. What if it was *not* what was claimed? What if, instead, it was the formula for some noxious poison that would kill anyone who breathed it or touched it?" I see a few heads nodding among the group. "Or what if it was nothing more than some newfangled way for women to change the color of their hair?" I watch the tensions visibly relax.

"I decided we had to test it first." I've chosen to claim personal responsibility for not sharing the formula – or even the knowledge we have it – immediately. I don't want to spread suspicion that the Council is advising me to maintain secrecy. "As it turns out, the formula is indeed what it claimed. What you've seen here today, my friends, is proof. The cannon on the right used black powder we captured in the war. The other used powder we made ourselves."

"And what do you intend to do with this formula, my friend?" Narth is being diplomatic, but there's an edginess to his tone.

"I intend we should decide that together." I signal to a groom to bring up the horses. "Let's go talk about just that."

I've decided we should hold the talks in the new library. Its large windows make it bright and cheerful, and I hope this will influence the mood of the conversation. The usual furniture has been moved to the side to allow for the placement of a large table around which we can gather. Thinking back to the Arthurian legends, I asked that the table be round. The carpenters thought I was mad, but nevertheless managed to create a very handsome table and the requisite number of simple but identical chairs in the rather short time they had to do so. The Territorial lords naturally assume their relative geographical positions. Interestingly, Goron chooses to sit beside Fergal. That's my cue to take the next chair, leaving the remaining two for my fellow kings.

"An interesting innovation, my friend," observes Egon. Subtleties such as this are rarely lost on him.

Peveril, Brother Eustace, and Phillip are present to help with translations. Samuel, of course, is essential to the substance of the meeting.

"So what do you intend to do with these new weapons of yours, King Alfred?" Nerrick has never before shown this level of belligerence. His past behavior has always been reserved . . . often slow to be convinced . . . rarely pushing a point, but letting others express what might also be on his mind. This is an entirely unexpected wrinkle. Just as well, I suppose, that I have experience making it up as I go.

"I acknowledge we're in possession of two cannons, Lord Nerrick. Frankly, there's not much we can do with just two of them other than learn how they work."

"And how to make more." Nerrick again.

"So could we all, my friend. But as we are all friends and allies, my greater concern is with those who seem to already have such weapons in abundance. We know the Teutons have been building these weapons and making the powder for quite some time. And we know Charles was in league with them at some level."

"My spies confirm what your Lord de Courcy told us," the King of Lakes chimes in. "Not only about the Teutons, but also that the Southern Nordics make it a practice to maintain a balance of power with the Teutons – so they no doubt have many of these weapons as well." I'm grateful to him for helping turn the conversation toward mutual defense.

"We know you've been standing down your fighting forces," says Goron. "I assume this means you think there's no immediate threat from King Charles?"

"Frankly, Goron, I don't know what to make of the events in Charles's kingdom. You're right that we believe there's no threat of another invasion any time soon. But I'm very worried about the instability over there right now. Why hasn't Charles done anything serious to suppress the rebellion? It makes no sense."

Turning the focus on the Kingdom Across the Southern Sea has the desired effect. "Could it be that he is simply waiting the rebels out . . . that he is convinced they will eventually tire of the game and capitulate?" asks Durrus.

"We must consider that, Lord Durrus," I reply. "But personally, I'm not convinced."

There follows much speculation as to what's afoot in that conflict and what might be the threat to any of us. All are concerned Charles may be making a deal with the Teutons and is just biding his time until they provide him with the assets he needs. There are various opinions on what those assets might be – weapons, men, armor, horses, food, money – but there's unanimous concern about what he may have agreed to give them in return. No one seems to have any more solid intelligence than we do.

Finally, the King of Peaks says, "You've not had much to say in this discussion, Alfred. What concerns you the most about your erstwhile allies across the sea?"

"The difficulty of getting any information about what Charles is up to. The fact that this civil war seems to be no war at all, but simply ongoing instability with neither side apparently having the will to force a decisive conclusion. What if the Teutons see this as an opportunity? Could they infiltrate and take over villages and territory all up and down that long border? And what if they then move quickly to expand the territory they hold before Charles and his rebellious nobles can effectively coordinate a defense? Truth be told, my friends, I'm not sure which is more worrisome – that Charles might be *dealing* with the Teutons or that he's *not*."

As has always been the case, the Eastern Kingdom and the Northern Kingdom are opaque to us all. The Kingdom of Lakes shares a border with both – quite a lengthy one with the Northern Kingdom – but there's never been so much as a border skirmish in living memory. The same was true of our border with the Eastern Kingdom until Charles used their land as his invasion route in the last war. "How much does that concern you?" asks the King of Lakes.

I defer to Samuel. "We maintain a small camp there for now, since we have no idea if Charles made a deal with them or if he just ran roughshod across their land. But all's been quiet, and Sir Jasper plans to abandon the camp before the first autumn frost if there's no change. We've no desire to signal a threat where none existed before."

As the afternoon wanes, the discussion follows suit, and I observe Nerrick's impatience growing until he can no longer contain himself. "All this talk of threats and borders and what's happening in the world is well and good. But when are we going to get back to the topic of the new weapons?" His frustration is evident in his tone.

"A fair question, my friend," I reply. "And may I suggest tomorrow morning? We've all seen and heard a lot today, and I, for one, am ready for some wine and food and good company . . . and a chance to mull over what I've heard."

Nerrick looks annoyed. "Very well. But will your Lords be joining us tomorrow? Are we to know how they are advising you?"

"All our Lords are at court. They'll dine with us this evening. Some of them still ride in the mornings when the weather is fine. Please . . . speak freely with any of them . . . in groups or in private. I know they'd welcome the conversation."

Nerrick's acknowledgment is little more than a grunt, and Korst breaks the tension by rising from his seat, the others quickly following suit. "I'm ready for that wine, Alfred," he says. "Too bad you don't have some of my ale as well."

"We've ale aplenty, my friend. But I *must* agree, it's not as good as yours."

Korst laughs aloud. "A man with good taste. I like that!"

As I wait to be the last to leave the room, I notice Egon lingering as well. He falls in step with me once we're in the corridor. "Will you walk with me to the stable, my friend? I would like to be sure Polaris is well bedded down for the night."

Just as I'm about to protest that Elvin's grooms will be giving all the horses the best of care, I realize his invitation is more about an opportunity to speak privately than concern for his horse. "Of course, my friend."

Once we're alone on the path to the stable, out of earshot of others, Egon says, "Don't be put off by Nerrick, Alfred. His intentions are not malicious."

"I must admit I was wondering about the difference in his demeanor."

"Nerrick has never liked change. He used to resist it quietly by going his own way and doing things as he always has. I think he knows, deep down, that change is inevitable. But as he sees his own son increasingly aligned with Goron, he feels more and more helpless to stem the tide . . . or even slow the pace. Add to that the fact that he was quite ill recently and is feeling his own mortality . . . he's rather overcome, I think, by the realization that both he and his world are fading away."

"Thank you, Egon. It's far easier to understand his behavior, knowing that." We walk on in silence for several moments. "Do you think he'll try to sabotage what we're doing here?"

"Of late, he's been looking to Korst for support. I think he sees Korst as a symbol of the old ways . . . the tough, strong, self-reliant lord who brooks no nonsense and defends what belongs to him at all costs. Our friend Korst may be crusty, but we all know that is his ancestral heritage. And he thinks the world of you. Give him one or two things with which he can demonstrate decisiveness, and he will bring Nerrick around." He pauses, then adds, "The rest of us are with you already."

Polaris is stabled between Star Dancer and Altair, Elvin's nostalgic gesture to the lineage of these noble beasts. "Polaris is still the finest horse I've ever owned," says Egon, "and I could ride no other to such an important gathering."

"Come with me. I know where Elvin keeps a basket of apples in case I forget to stop by the kitchens."

We return, apples in hand, to find Korst admiring Altair. "I heard that fine horse of yours saved your life in the war, Alfred," he says.

"You know, Korst, I think perhaps he did."

"That was one special horse. I'm just sorry I never got to ride him."

"Young Altair here is his son. He's only a three-year-old, but I'm starting to think he's just as smart as his sire. Elvin thinks he's even better."

"You're a lucky man, if that's the case."

"Would you like to ride him?"

Korst's eyes light up. "Now *that* would be quite a treat!"

"The King of Peaks and I are riding out tomorrow morning. Join us and ride Altair. He's young yet and not as seasoned as Sirius, but I think you'll enjoy him."

"You don't have to ask twice. Tomorrow morning it is."

I steal a glance at Egon, whose face bears a subtle smile of approval. Step one in enlisting Korst to help Nerrick through what's to come.

When the group gathers in the library once again at midmorning the next day, I'm pleased to find the King of Peaks in discourse with

Narth and Rusk. I hadn't anticipated the degree to which deciding how to react to the new weapons might continue to tear down the ancient barrier of distrust between them.

Not wanting to give Nerrick any further cause for frustration, I start the day in a much different way than I'd originally planned. "My friends, let's go straight to Lord Nerrick's question." Nerrick crosses his arms over his chest and nods sharply, as if to say 'about time.'

"He asked what I intend to do with the cannons we possess. The simple answer, my friends, is 'defend our kingdom.' But since nothing is ever that simple, let me tell you what I mean. The sea protects us all, to some degree, from invasion. Whether it's the Teutons or King Charles or anyone else, they must first assemble a great fleet of ships to transport their men and weaponry to our shores. And the cliffs along much of our shoreline or, in some cases, the inhospitable weather of the Western Sea," I nod to the King of Lakes, "limit the number of places where an enemy could land an invasion force. All of which makes our river the greatest vulnerability.

"Our ancient defenses are no longer up to the task. As we discovered in preparing for the last war, the chains that were once sufficient to block the passage of invading ships have deteriorated with time. Ships have become bigger. There's absolutely no doubt that a determined ship's captain, using the wind and the tide to his advantage, could breach those chains with relative ease. And though Sir Jasper's flaming fleece worked once, I'm sure we'd never get away with that trick a second time. If an invasion force ever captured our port, the door would be open for them to run amok in our land . . . and even make their way to yours if they succeed in overwhelming us. So I propose that we agree to make defense of the river our first priority.

"Another thing I think necessary to defending our lands. Our commanders, our captains, our core of knights must all learn new strategies and tactics to use in the presence of these new weapons. Our commanders must learn new ways to anticipate an enemy's battle plan and how to counter it. Our knight commander has already charged his deputy, who was field commander in the east in the last war, to begin devising new training regimens for our own men.

"This is our proposal, my friends. I'm just as eager to hear yours as Lord Nerrick was to hear mine."

"I agree," says the King of Lakes, "that your river impacts us all. We depend on it for trade. And though you would bear the first brunt of an attack, we are all, nonetheless, vulnerable to an invasion using that route. I fully support your plans to use cannons for its defense.

"Despite the fact that our harbor is smaller and less sheltered, my commanders have always considered it the ideal place to land either a diversionary force or the main invasion force if surprise is the objective. Our only defenses have been bad weather or the deployment of masses of men. These cannons would give us something else in the arsenal."

The King of Peaks remains quiet. I know he believes well-placed cannons in the hills on either side of the road from our lands into his would stop an invading army in its tracks. Samuel and I share that view, but all three of us agree that too much discussion of this might damage the fragile bonds of trust that are being forged with the Territorial lords.

Nerrick still has a frown on his face. "Defending harbors and rivers is all well and good, but what about that garrison of yours, Alfred? How many cannons are you going to put there and threaten us with?"

"My friend . . ." I do my best to keep the conversation calm despite Nerrick's antagonism. "I, more than anyone, regret the two unfortunate incidents in which that garrison was involved. But I hope we've shown our peaceful intent. That garrison is important to us. It's a base for defense against a landing at the cove below Ernle Manor. Lord de Courcy and I also believe it's ideal for a reserve force should we need to reinforce the fight against an invasion farther east."

"Three troops aren't much of a reserve," Nerrick's tone is gruff and dismissive.

"Three troops are sufficient for peace time. In case of a war, you would be right."

Fergal tries to help. "Goron, you captained our force at that garrison in the last war. What's your assessment of its defensive position?"

"The cove is small, but an army could be landed there. Not the main invasion force certainly, but a diversionary force or one arm of a pincer. What I would worry about more, my Lord Nerrick . . ." Goron seems to understand how to appease his elder's crankiness. ". . . is that an invader might land an army there and turn immediately west to us . . . to cut us off from going to the aid of our friends or to keep them from coming to our aid. That garrison might well be needed for our own defense."

"What about you, Owen?" asks Narth. "I know your rocks keep the big ships away."

"Aye, that they do," Owen replies. "But I've been thinking. If I were a ship captain and I had all these weapons and men on my ship, transporting them to some war, why not put them to good use along the way? Why not set up some of those cannons and fire them from the ship?"

I steal a glance at Samuel, who's grinning from ear to ear. This is exactly what he had predicted would be the next imaginative use of the new weapons.

"In the right wind and tide, even big ships might be able to get in close enough to lob cannon-balls into my harbor. I wouldn't mind having a few of those weapons to keep the enemy farther out to sea. Maybe even blow one or two of them out of the water." He laughs at his own audacity.

"Well, I, for one, will not have those infernal things on my land." No matter how his fellow lords try to coax him around, Nerrick is intractable.

"So don't have them," says Korst. "In fact, nobody has to have them that doesn't want to."

"But if Owen has them . . ." Nerrick begins.

"Owen doesn't want to fight you," Korst cuts him off. "He wants to sink ships."

"Aye," says Owen, with a big grin on his face. "Make my grandfather proud." It seems Owen, too, is trying to help Nerrick find a comfortable place.

"But if you're worried about that, get your men trained." Korst again.

"And how am I supposed to do that?" Nerrick still sounds grumpy.

"Maybe send them to train at Alfred's garrison. Two birds, my friend. Your men could train, and you could keep an eye on what's happening at that garrison you're so worried about." He pauses briefly. "In fact, I might send some of my own men there too. What say you to that, Alfred?"

"I say it's a splendid idea. De Courcy?"

"Agreed. Men who've trained together will do better in the field, should we be faced with an invader."

Samuel and I have discussed this. The choice is not without risks. At a different time – under different leaders – today's allies could be tomorrow's adversaries . . . and they would be well schooled in our tactics. But we've already opened the door by accepting their assistance to defend the west in the last war. To close that door now carries a different set of risks and reactions – anger, suspicion of our motives – possibly even renewed animosity. Risks that aren't compatible with the outcome I want to achieve.

Nerrick seems somewhat more relaxed. "Very well, Korst. If you send your men, then perhaps I will consider sending some of mine."

"Perhaps I shall consider," says the King of Peaks, "sending one or two of my commanders to observe how you train your men."

"They'd be quite welcome, my friend," I reply.

As we break for the midday meal, I'm increasingly hopeful about what we're achieving.

When we return from our repast, there's a plain piece of paper on the table at each seat. I watch while each man turns his over and reads the words written in his own language. Another decision that's not without risk of unknowable dimensions. But the commitment to mutual defense seems strong, and it's important for me to demonstrate the same trust I'm asking of them.

No one speaks. "What you are reading, my friends," I break the silence, "is the formula for black powder. As you see, it's made of fairly ordinary materials. It's the combination in the proper proportions that makes it explosive."

Nerrick pushes his paper away, toward the center of the table. "I have no need of this."

"That's your decision, my friend," I reply. "But I, for one, would sleep more soundly knowing that, if the unthinkable happened and you were the last of us standing against an enemy, you would have all the knowledge you need to defend yourself."

"If I am the last one standing, Alfred, then all your knowledge will not have done you much good."

"I can't dispute that, my friend, and I have no wish to compel you. Take it or not, as you see fit."

I turn the conversation to how we'll proceed. "Korst, we'll need your tin. Bronze cannons only, for all of us, I think. Why should we risk another incident like what happened to Samuel and me when Charles's iron one exploded?" Copper will come from the Peaks. All agree that our current little armory should be expanded with forges, and that perfecting the skill of casting cannons should happen there. Egon will send one of his master forgers. And so it goes.

As the sun is lowering in the western sky, Narth signals an end to the conversation. "My friends, we have accomplished much that is good these two days. Like Alfred, I will sleep better knowing we are preparing ourselves to keep each other safe against the threat from beyond the sea."

The King of Lakes surprises me. "Alfred, may I be so presumptuous as to request that some of your fine wine be brought so we may seal our pact with a toast?"

As Phillip rushes to the door to give the order, I reply, "It's no presumption at all, my friend. But we have one more decision to make. Our kitchens are roasting venison just in case we have cause for celebration this evening. We must let the steward know if there's to be a feast or if we'll have our suppers separately in our lodgings."

Boskren, who's said little during the day, answers for them all. "I, for one, am ready for a feast." It's hard to tell if he's just hungry or if this is his way of committing to the plan, but everyone chimes in.

The wine is brought, and the King of Lakes begins the toasting. "To good friends and allies!" A few more offer similar sentiments. Though we have no formal treaty, we have a pact of honor that is likely stronger than anything that could be written on paper. As everyone makes for the door, I notice Nerrick quietly take his paper and slip it into the pocket of his tunic. He'll continue to struggle with his preference for the familiar, but he's making a conscious decision not to be left out. It might surprise, maybe even encourage him to hear of my own struggle. Perhaps one day I'll tell him. But for now, I think, he'll listen more to men he's known longer.

It's only after they've all left that I once again have the chance for a late night brandy with Rupert. "I must admit, Alfred, you've gotten quite good at achieving the outcome you want. A pact of mutual defense is quite an accomplishment for a single meeting."

"That was actually just the extra layer on the cake, Uncle."

"Oh? So what was it you set out to get?"

"I came to the conclusion months ago that we have no choice but to update our defenses and our tactics for a new type of fight. Anyone who might come against us is likely going to have the new weapons, so we can't afford to be unprepared. The thing that was crucial in these talks was to get our allies' understanding that our coming actions aren't suspicious – that we aren't planning to turn our new-found capabilities against them. Without their trust assured, we'd have to proceed very slowly indeed . . . too slowly, I fear, for the risk that seems to be brewing across the sea. That they're convinced we should all be in this together is truly the goose's golden egg. Something I'd not dared to hope for so soon."

"Well, well. I must say I'm impressed. And I finally understand why you didn't push for a signed pact."

"Aye. Best we all act out of mutual respect and trust than have anyone feel they've been coerced or cornered into signing some formal agreement. Who knows? The formal thing may come in time. But I think that may be for someone else to propose."

"Alfred, promise me you won't fly into a rage at what I'm about to tell you," says Gwen.

"The only other time you started a conversation like that, it was about Juliana. Should I assume?"

"Nice to know your memory's as sharp as ever." She laughs softly.

Our bedtime talks are still the best part of my day, but I'm beginning to think this one might be rather more intense than usual. "So who's she infatuated with this time?"

"This time it's far more than infatuation. She's decided she truly loves Rainard Ernle and wants to marry him."

"*What?!* I thought you said she was sensible and this was just a passing fancy." And then another thought occurs to me. "Tell me he hasn't made advances."

"She *is* sensible, Alfred . . . and thoughtful. That's one thing you can't fault her for. And no, Rainard has done nothing you can fault *him* for."

"So what's . . . how . . . how has she gotten this into her head? Doesn't she know I intend to find an ideal match for her?"

"She does, Alfred. But she also has a mind of her own. I'm afraid I'm responsible for that."

"No, no . . . there's no blame. We both wanted her to be strong and brilliant and her own person. It's just that this is a lot to take in. Start at the beginning and tell me slowly . . . give me time to figure out what to think."

She pats my hand. "We've raised quite a remarkable young woman. I'm not saying I agree with her yet, but there's no doubt how much she's thought about this. She's spent hours with Petronilla, talking about what it's like to be married to an older man. And from what I'm told, she left *no* issue unexplored."

"Oh, my."

"She also went to your mother."

"Surely Mother tried to talk some sense into her."

"I'm not sure there was much opportunity for that." She laughs softly once again. "It seems your mother was consulted on the political implications of it all. What's the obligation of a king's daughter? Must she accept a dynastic marriage even if she knows her life will be unhappy? What will the world think if she pursues her own heart? What will be said about you if you allow it?

"Mother Alice and Petronilla have both tried to keep her grounded. I know both of them have continued to urge her to consider someone her own age."

"So when did you find out about all this?"

"Juliana finally came to me three days ago, while you were still in the middle of all those talks about weapons. I didn't want to burden you with it then. Besides . . . I wanted to see if I could have any success where others hadn't."

"I gather, since we're having this conversation, that you didn't."

She smiles. "Our daughter's quite determined. She's not denying any of the concerns I've raised. Quite the contrary – she acknowledges them as truths and has her answers ready."

"So I suppose what you're telling me is that it's time for me to talk to her."

"Actually, Alfred, I think you should *listen* to her first. This remarkable young woman is still the tiny baby you held in your arms that first day you came back from captivity. And I seem to recall your saying more than once that the most important thing you wanted for her was her happiness."

It's my turn to pat *her* hand. "Don't worry. That hasn't changed. I'll make some time to talk with her tomorrow."

"A suggestion?"

"Certainly."

"Don't make it such a big deal . . . as if it's a formal appointment to discuss her future."

"What then?"

"She's going to the kennel day after tomorrow to choose a dog for Edward. He's gotten quite tired of sharing Brumby with Geoffrey since his first dog died, and I agree the arrangement isn't working very well. After all, they both want to go about with their own friends. Why don't you offer to ride up with her?"

"I'm surprised Edward doesn't want to pick out his own dog."

"He declared that since Juliana is the patroness, it's her job to choose for him. And he gave her a long list of what he wants."

"Maybe Edward's the one I should be having a talk with," I chuckle.

"Don't worry. It's just a phase. He'll be on to some completely different notion next week. And Juliana doesn't mind."

"Then I'll offer to accompany her on her quest." I pause. "And I promise, Gwen, that I *will* listen."

"Listen with your heart, Alfred . . . not with your crown."

Thus it is that I find myself taking a carriage ride to the monastery instead of my usual trip on horseback. "Your mother tells me you've been doing quite some serious thinking about your future." I broach the subject as soon as we're well away from the castle since I've no idea how much time this conversation will require.

"Oh, Papa, please don't be angry."

"Well, at this point, I don't know if I have anything to be angry about. Your mother wouldn't tell me much . . . only that you have some very specific ideas." She doesn't reply right away. "And that I should listen to them."

"You will listen, Papa? You haven't already made up your mind what my future should be?"

"Only insofar as I want you to be happy and have the future you deserve. I haven't quite worked out the details of how to achieve that."

The carriage moves onward, passing the track that goes west into the woods. I can tell my daughter is gathering her thoughts, working out how best to win me to her point of view. Finally, she begins. "I know you're going to think I'm quite mad, Papa. Sometimes I even think that myself. But I've found the man I want to marry."

She pauses. I remain silent. Best let her take her time to lay it all out for me.

"Rainard is everything I could possibly want. He's kind. He's brilliant – he's read so much, Papa, about so very many subjects. He treats me as his equal. We can talk about anything and everything . . . he never acts as if a subject is beyond my grasp. And he really and truly wants to know what I think about things. I've changed his mind on more than one occasion, and when I do, he's happy for it." She pauses again.

"I know I have a responsibility, as your daughter, to marry well. I would be Lady Ernle eventually – quite high in the order of precedence – and I think that's a station worthy of a king's daughter." Another pause, and this time she looks down at her hands in her lap as she continues. "I know my duty, Papa. And if I *must* marry some foreign prince or noble for reasons of state, then I suppose I have little choice. But I'm certain I'd never be completely happy."

Her silence this time lasts long enough that I'm sure she's waiting for my reaction. "It seems we're both a bit on the horns of a dilemma. The future I've been envisioning for you, my dear, is as a queen. Beloved by your people . . . beautiful . . ." She blushes. "Educated . . . bringing modern ways to your people . . . much like your mother. But in that vision, you're always serenely happy with a husband you adore, who sees you as a true partner in the running of the kingdom. As for you, even though you believe you've found the love of your life, you acknowledge there may be a greater duty, which you would do even if it were joyless." It's my turn to pause. Her attention is still focused on her hands in her lap.

"So let's start with the premise that what we both want most of all is for you to have a happy life." She looks up at me with perhaps the most radiant smile I've ever seen from her. "Now all we have to do is work out *how* you'll be happy."

"Papa, I *know* I would be happy with Rainard. Even now – when he has no idea that I love him – I'm always happiest in his presence."

"You know, I suppose, that I would be remiss in not pointing out that he's old —"

"Old enough to be my father," she cuts me off. "I know. But Aunt Petronilla says being married to an older man isn't necessarily a bad thing, so long as it's the right man."

"It means you would likely have a long widowhood to look forward to. I'm not sure how well that squares with our premise of a happy life for you."

"I've thought about that, Papa. If I were to be widowed, I'd still be the dowager Lady Ernle. And my son would be the new lord. And if he's not yet of age, then I would be his protectress. I could sit on Geoffrey's Council as his representative. And I could do so much more good for our kingdom in that way than ever I could as queen of some foreign land."

"Whoa!" I hold up my hand. "What makes you think you could sit on the Council?"

"Madam Greslet sits on the Assembly."

"The Council is different."

"How?"

"Well, for one thing, the Council makes decisions about how to run the kingdom. The Assembly doesn't. For another, the Assembly is new and was started after it became accepted for a woman to run a business. The tradition of the Council is that it's made up of lords of the realm. The lords consider it their domain."

"But traditions can change. They weren't created by God on the sixth day. They were made up by men."

"Traditions change slowly, my dear. That's why they're traditions."

"In any event, they were made up . . . by men, mostly. Perhaps the time has come for some of them to change. I could be part of that change, Papa. And that's something that could make me happy if I had lost the happiness of having my Rainard with me."

"And why do you think the lords would accept it?"

"Because it would be temporary. I'd be representing my son until he came of age . . . not sitting there in my own right. And maybe if they see that the world doesn't end because a woman is in the room, then sometime in the future, someone like Lady Mary could inherit rather than having to watch her estate go to some cousin she doesn't even know." Until this moment, I hadn't realized how much Juliana had taken to heart the plight of Lord Meriden's daughter who, despite being as good a steward of the estate as her father, won't inherit for no better reason than that she's not a man.

As I take in everything she says, I begin to wonder if perhaps she might be more in love with this future she's painted for herself than with Rainard himself. Time for a small prick to the bubble. "I'm impressed, my dear, at how thoroughly you've thought all this through. Now let me suggest an alternate future for you to consider.

"Let's assume Rainard is healthy and blessed with a very long life. Look forward twenty years . . . to the time when you're about the same age as your mother is today. Your husband would be of an age where he would look and act more like a grandfather. How will you feel at a banquet or a celebration when he's not up to dancing so much and may even want to retire early? Will you feel left out of the things others your age are doing?"

"I can't know for certain, Papa. But Aunt Petronilla says that if you truly love someone, it's more important to have them with you . . . to hold their hand and enjoy the festivities together . . . than to dance every dance. She was truly happy with King Goscelin."

"Then what if he becomes ill? What if it's a long, lingering illness, and you become more of a nurse than a wife?"

"Then I'll be the best nurse I can be. And I'll run the estate as well as anyone, and I'll raise my son and represent him on Geoffrey's Council . . . perhaps even on yours, if this dire scenario you paint should come to pass." She grins at me as she adds the last thought.

"Your mother would never forgive me if I allowed you on the Council and not her."

"There's where you're wrong, Papa. She would be so proud of you. I think she wouldn't even be able to find the words to express the depth of her pride." She reaches out and briefly touches my hand.

"Now," she continues, "as long as we're painting dire scenarios, what if something totally different were to happen? What if I were to die in childbirth and leave Rainard a widower . . . maybe even with a tiny baby to raise? That happens, you know . . . regardless of the age of the man or woman."

"It does. But that's not part of any of the future I've imagined for you."

"But if it did, wouldn't you want to know that I was truly happy for whatever time I was given in this life?"

I don't know if she's consciously trying to wrap me around her little finger, but I do know this. I'll never be able to deny her the thing she's convinced will make her happy. All I can do is show her what's possible and let her choose.

"I do love him, Papa. And my feet are firmly on the ground. I know . . . as much as anyone can . . . what the future might hold and what my life would be like. This isn't some frivolous girl's romantic fantasy about being lady of the manor. After all, I'm a king's daughter already." She laughs softly.

Time for a different tack. "Very well, you've convinced me of your affection for him. But are you *in* love with him?" She looks at me quizzically. "Are you attracted to him as a man?"

"Do you mean do I long for his fingers to brush against mine when we reach for a book or spread a map on the table? Do I want him to kiss me on the lips? Do I want him to put his arms around me and press his body against mine? He may not be quite so handsome as Sir Samuel, but his touch when he kisses my hand makes me tingle all over."

"Does Rainard know of your feelings?"

"I can't say for sure, Papa. Women can sense these things from a man, but I don't know how well it works the other way round. I've said nothing, and you know I'm not one of those flighty girls that would throw herself at a man."

As I've been listening to her, a plan has been formulating in my mind – something I wish I'd conceived in time to discuss with Gwen in advance – but I've little choice now but to plunge ahead. "Very well. I know you're convinced this would make you happy. But *I* still need to know if this would be the happiest you could possibly be. Will you meet me halfway?"

"How do you mean, Papa?"

"I'd like you to experience what some other possible futures might be like. And I'd like for you to give each of them just as much thought as you've put into a future with Rainard."

"How do I do that?"

"I want you to spend some time at the courts of the suitors I've had in mind for you. The King of Peaks believes you would be the best possible match for his heir . . . and he'll consider no other until he has my answer. And King Brandr's eldest son is in need of a wife. Both of these young men are much nearer in age to you. In both cases, in the normal course of events, you'd eventually be queen. What I know of both young men indicates they're cut from the kind of cloth that would value you for the type of woman you are. But the two courts and the two lands are very different.

"I'd like you to spend three months at each court. Three months getting to know each young man. And then, when you come home, you may spend three months at Ernle Manor. Before you go, I'll tell Rainard of our arrangement and that he has my permission – if he chooses to act on it – to behave as your suitor. If he declines, then you'll still have two quite suitable young men to choose from.

"Promise me, Juliana, that you'll take both of these young men seriously. And if you should discover that one or the other of them would give you a better chance to be happy than what you've told me today, there's no shame or dishonor in changing your mind."

"I promise, Papa." Her tone and expression are solemn. "Can we do this soon?"

"I'll need time to make the arrangements, but as soon as they're done . . . I'm sure there'll be all the fuss of new gowns and that sort of thing before you go."

"I'll need a chaperone."

"And perhaps a confidante as well?" She beams. "Would Petronilla and Richenda be suitable? I suspect Richenda could use the diversion since Denis seems to have gone missing."

She clasps her hands in front of her and smiles her warmest smile. "Thank you, Papa. I'll do this for you . . . I promise." For a moment, I see before me the little girl, clapping her hands and dancing with joy, saying "thank you, thank you, thank you" whenever Gwen or I would do something special for her. Then I blink, and there's the astonishing young woman she's become. Though I still have trepidations, I feel calmer that, whatever the outcome of this grand experiment, she will indeed have the happy life she deserves.

Thus it is that I find myself inviting Rainard to share a brandy following this evening's court dinner. As we make our way to my private reception room, we discuss the appeal of a case of murder that's to come before me tomorrow. "There's something not right about this case, Sire, and the magistrate hasn't been able to get to the heart of it. I've even spoken with the man myself, but have gotten no closer."

"Not right in what way?" I ask.

"I'll not prejudice you, Sire. Suffice it to say, it's peculiar enough that both the magistrate and I urged the man to appeal to you. Perhaps you'll have more success in getting to the bottom of things."

I dismiss the servant, who closes the doors behind him as he leaves. Crossing to the sideboard, I pour two glasses of Rupert's special brandy and proffer one to Rainard. "Please, Rainard, sit." He chooses a place near the fireplace where we can face one another.

First things first . . . we both sip the brandy. "This is really quite extraordinary, Sire."

"We have Rupert to thank for that. He found the distillery when he attended Harold's first wedding and has been importing it ever since. Of course, if the standoff that's passing for a civil war in the Kingdom Across the Southern Sea continues much longer, whatever we have left of this stuff will become more valuable than gold." I chuckle, intending to put him at ease.

Another sip of brandy and then I get to the business at hand. "Tell me, Rainard, what do you think of my eldest daughter?"

"She's quite astonishing, Your Grace. Beautiful and an accomplished young lady, of course, but with one of the most remarkable minds I've ever known. As keen an intellect as any woman

– or man, for that matter – in the kingdom. She's also kind and caring and seems to have a special touch with the people. I've watched her in the town on market days. The people love her."

"Have you ever had a chance to see her with the herdsmen and their dogs at one of the competitions?"

"I'm afraid not, Sire."

"You should do that some time. Ever since she was just a little thing – about nine years old, if I remember – she's drawn the herdsmen to her like a magnet. And she has a way with the dogs that even Brother Adam envies."

"She is much to be admired, Sire." He sips his brandy. "And will make a fine match, I'm sure."

There's no way to move on that's not going to be awkward. Best get it over with. "Do you have any feelings for her yourself?"

He's immediately on edge, sitting up straighter, moving ever so subtly toward the edge of his chair. "I've never treated Lady Juliana with anything but the utmost respect, Your Grace, and I challenge anyone who says otherwise to prove it. Even to a duel, if need be, though I'm not much of a swordsman."

"Calm yourself, Rainard." I put as much reassurance into my tone as I know how. "I didn't invite you here for a reprimand." His posture relaxes ever so slightly, but it's clear he's still anxious about what might be coming next. "It's just that I've found out only recently that she's quite taken with you . . . and I've become convinced that it's much more than a girl's romantic fantasy. I believe her exact words were, 'I've found the man I want to marry.'"

"Dear God in Heaven." He relaxes utterly and slides back in his chair.

"As you might imagine, that's more or less what I said," I chuckle.

"Sire, she'll make any man a wonderful wife, but I'm old enough. . ."

". . . to be her father," I finish for him. "And that in no way dissuades her. In fact, she has a plan for every eventuality . . . everything from her death in childbirth leaving you with a tiny baby to your sharing two or three decades of happy marriage to becoming your nurse should you fall ill or just old and infirm. She can't truly know what it all means or if she'll think of it differently when the time comes, but it seems she's spent hours with Petronilla trying to get at least an intellectual understanding of what life with an older man might be like."

"Sire, my word of honor . . . I've done nothing to encourage this."

"If I doubted that, Rainard, we wouldn't be having *this* particular conversation. So let me ask you again . . . do you have any feelings for Juliana?"

For a long moment, he doesn't reply. I sip my brandy and give him time to compose himself. Finally, he downs what remains in his glass in a single gulp and says, "Permission to speak freely, Your Grace?"

"That, my friend, is what I need in abundance at this moment." I walk to the sideboard and retrieve the decanter, refilling his glass as I make my way back to my chair and top up my own.

"Juliana is the woman of my dreams . . . the woman I've been hoping . . . and failing . . . to find for all my adult life. From the moment she first asked me to tutor her in the law, I've known how special she is. And in the time that's passed since, I've developed an affection . . . no, truly a love for her that is deeper than anything I ever thought to feel.

"I think, perhaps, Sire, that's why I've procrastinated so on seeking a wife. The estate is safe with Samuel . . . and the chances of my finding someone who could measure up to Juliana . . . well, it all seems too daunting even to try.

"You can't imagine how painful it is to keep this all to myself, knowing that one day she'll leave and take up a new life with the husband you choose for her. Yes, I could spare myself the pain by staying away from court. But I know my heart is going to be broken anyway whenever she leaves, so I've decided to enjoy whatever moments I can in her company until that fateful day."

He pauses for a rather large sip of brandy, though it's not the whole glass in one gulp this time. "So to answer your question, Sire, I am hopelessly . . . helplessly . . . in love with your daughter."

"Thank you for your candor, Rainard. You know, in a peculiar sort of way, I'm rather relieved. I can't say I really know what to think yet, but it does seem that the quest I've planned for her to find what will truly make her happy wouldn't go well if she went into it with her own feelings shattered." I go on to tell him about the bargain I made with Juliana.

"Actually, I'm quite grateful for that, Sire. If she were to choose me without really considering what else she could have, then I'd always wonder if she might be regretting her choice."

"So, Lord Rainard, from this moment, you have my permission to pay court to my daughter. She knows of my intent to tell you this. But there's one thing I'd like to ask."

"Sire?"

"Until she returns from her two trips abroad, please be as discreet as possible. Let's let court gossip speculate on those two suitors until we know more."

"That's quite to my liking, Sire. As long as she might be returning home with an entirely different future planned out, I'd just as soon not have my motives and feelings dissected by all and sundry."

"And Rainard, on this topic, let's dispense with the 'Sire' and 'Your Grace' business . . . 'sir' will suffice, given how things might turn out. I admit I'm having trouble wrapping my mind around the notion that the son of the man I think of as a second father might one day become my son-in-law."

"There are many strange things in Heaven and Earth, Your . . . sir."

"One thing I know for certain, Rainard. That extraordinary creature her mother and I have created is going to make the coming year unlike anything you or I ever dreamed of experiencing."

Gwen is already in bed waiting for me, but says nothing as I make my way across the chamber to my dressing room. As usual, Osbert keeps up a running banter on events of the day that I may not have heard about. "Young Edward be ever so pleased with his new dog, m'lord. He be fawning all over Miss Juliana. He bring her flowers from the garden, and then he go down to the kitchen where he be wheedling a sweet cake and some berries to take up to her. And Miss Juliana, she be ever so kind to him."

"I'm glad to hear my son was properly appreciative after his insistence that she find him the perfect dog."

"Oh, he be right grateful, m'lord. And then he be off with his mates to show off his new dog. Young Edward be wanting to give the dog a new name, but Miss Juliana say that not be such a good idea, what with him already being two years old and already knowing his name. So the dog still be called Toby."

"We may be in for quite some amusing times, Osbert, with a dog called Toby and the captain of my guard being Sir Tobin."

"Oh dear me, m'lord. I never think of that. That be funny fer sure." He gives a quick tug to the shoulders of my nightshirt to be sure it's hanging to his satisfaction, then says, "There ye be, m'lord. I just be taking yer boots down and shine them up fer tomorrow. Ye be riding in the morning like usual?"

"Aye, Osbert. After everything I've heard today, I'd like to clear my mind before considering this case that's being brought to me."

And with that, he's off and I go to join Gwen in bed. Climbing in beside her, I put an arm around her shoulders and kiss her on the cheek. "Promise me you won't fly into a rage, my dear, at what I'm about to tell you."

She laughs out loud. "And why would I do that?"

"Because I've been making things up as I went along, and I struck a deal with Juliana without consulting you."

She laughs again, more softly this time, then places a hand on my cheek and pulls me toward her for a sweet kiss. "Well, from what I've heard, you did a pretty good job of making it up."

"Then she's happy?"

"Over the moon."

"And you? I really do apologize for not getting your agreement first, but she was so sincere . . . I couldn't just leave her dangling, worrying about what I might or might not decide."

She smiles at me. "Quite pleased, Alfred. And very proud of you." She strokes my hand. "Rainard?" Not surprisingly, she's guessed what our conversation was about.

"It seems he quite reciprocates our daughter's affection. The man is some sort of paragon of virtue . . . or a bit of a fool . . . I can't quite work out which . . . to spend so much time with her and never let on."

"He's a gentle soul, my love, with more respect and warmth and generosity in his little finger than many men can ever command. If

Juliana does wind up with him, I'm certain she'll be cherished every day of their life together."

"Let's not get the cart before the horse."

She laughs again. "Of course not. But speaking of carts and horses, your daughter is already planning her journeys. She's secured Petronilla's agreement to accompany her. And she's asked Mother Alice to help her choose gifts for Beatrix and for Brandr's wife. She plans to ask Addiena's advice on gifts for her journey to the Peaks. It seems my job is to help choose new gowns."

"My God, I've unleashed a whirlwind!"

"It will calm down . . . at least, I hope so. I did ask her for one promise, though."

"Oh?"

"To keep her interest in Rainard secret until she returns from her two journeys. Alfred, you'd have been so proud of her. She looked me straight in the eye and said, 'Of course, Mama. Why would you even ask? I would never want to have the kitchen maids gossiping about him behind my back while I'm gone. Once we're away at Ernle Manor, people can say what they want, but not until then.' She'll no doubt tell Richenda everything, but I intend to speak to that young lady myself and make sure she knows it would be a betrayal of the king's trust if she broke Juliana's confidence."

"So I'm to be the bogeyman?" I chuckle.

"Just a small one, my love. I'm not threatening to accuse her of treason."

"Well, it seems I'll be a much bigger one if I don't get letters sent and arrangements made. Let's hope this appeal tomorrow can be resolved quickly so I have time to give my secretary some instructions . . . and a few moments to speak with Ernle as well."

She snuggles close and lays her head on my chest. "Thank you, Alfred."

"For what?"

"For being a loving father."

"Everything in its own time. Right now, I just want to be a loving husband."

The proceedings today begin as usual. Phillip, Samuel, and Lord Ernle are present, following the practice established by my father that at least a few of the lords should attend any appeal – largely as an assurance to everyone that the outcome is fair and lawful, though they're certainly free to ask questions or express opinions. My father also permitted the common people to stand in the back of the room and listen, though it's rare that many appear unless the case is from the castle town. Rainard is, of course, present in his role of oversight of the magistrates. Once I take my place on the throne, the appellant, the sheriff and magistrate involved in the case, and any witnesses they choose to bring are ushered into the room.

Rainard steps forward, and the hushed conversations go silent. "If it please Your Grace, the man coming before you today is called Tom. He's been accused, tried, and convicted for the murder of a seven-year-old boy and has been sentenced to hang. Tom has, from the beginning, insisted he's not to blame for the boy's death. He appeals his case to you as he claims that he's an innocent man, wrongly accused."

"Thank you, Lord Rainard. I will hear the appeal." The formal response required of me before anyone speaks further, an innovation Rainard introduced that allows me to refuse to hear the case, even at the last minute. I make it a habit, however, to avoid such surprises unless there are extraordinary circumstances involved.

"Magistrate, you may proceed," says Rainard, returning to his position with the lords.

"Your Grace, My Lords, the man Tom who you see before you," he gestures toward the appellant, who stands with the sheriff, wrists shackled in front of him, "was found by the sheriff sitting beside the dead body of the seven-year-old boy. He was taken into custody by the sheriff and was brought before me, accused of murder. I'll describe the case as it was presented to me.

"The boy's father is a butcher's apprentice and his mother makes lace that she sells to the women of the town. It being market day, the mother was attending her stall and had taken her son with her. In the early afternoon, a customer stopped by the stall looking for some lace for her daughter's wedding gown. The mother didn't have anything suitable in the stall, but she did have some at home, so she sent the boy to the house to fetch it.

"The boy should've been gone no more than twenty minutes, but the mother got busy and lost track of time. When the church bell tolled and she realized it had been an hour since she sent him on the errand, she asked the woman in the next stall to keep an eye on her goods and set off to find her son.

"She arrived at the house to find him lying on the floor dead, his head bashed with the shovel from the hearth, the shovel lying beside him with blood on it, Tom here sitting beside the boy, holding his hand, and a flour sack with all the family's possessions in it abandoned by the door. She ran for the sheriff, whom she stumbled across just two streets away. When they got back to the house, the scene hadn't changed. Tom was still sitting there, holding the boy's hand.

"The sheriff took him into custody and accused him of killing the boy. Tom has said from the very beginning that he didn't do it. I believe, Your Grace, that the sheriff's investigation was thorough in every respect. He did try diligently to determine if there was anyone else who could have committed the act. He questioned all the neighbors, not just in that alley, but in all the streets nearby. He talked to anyone who had been out and about that day. No one remembered seeing anything unusual. No one even remembered seeing Tom on that particular day, but as he's a carpenter, people are accustomed to seeing him about his work in all parts of the town, so it's not surprising they might not recall what day or where they might have seen him.

"There being no evidence to show that anyone else had committed the crime, I had no choice but to find Tom guilty. To this day, however, he insists he's not responsible, but will say no more than that. That's the complete case as it stands today, Your Grace."

"Thank you, Magistrate. Do you have anything further to add, Sheriff?"

"Nothing, Your Grace. It's as the magistrate described."

"Very well, I'd like to ask some questions of Tom. If you would, Sheriff, remove his shackles."

"With all due respect, Your Grace, the man is a convicted killer."

"Humor me, Sheriff. I'm certain he's not armed, you're standing right here, and there are guards in the corridor. It doesn't seem we're in much danger." The sheriff produces a key and removes the shackles, though the expression on his face indicates he's still not sure this is such a good idea.

I beckon to Tom to approach, and he falls to both knees in front of the throne. "You may stand, Tom. You've shown you respect these proceedings, and I trust you won't try to run away. Now look me in the eye and tell me truthfully . . . did you kill the boy?"

He looks up and meets my gaze. Never flinching for even a moment, he says, "I swear on the Holy Bible, Yer Grace, I dinna' kill the boy. I swear on the soul of me dear sainted mother; I swear on me own soul; I swear on the souls of me children; I swear on the soul of that poor dead boy. I never harm a hair on his head. That be the truth, Yer Grace. I swear before God it be the truth."

"You seem very sincere, Tom. So now you must help us get to the truth of who *did* kill him. Tell me how you came to be in that house."

"I were just there, Yer Grace."

"Were you just passing by? Did you simply happen upon the scene and find the boy there?"

"I were just there, Yer Grace."

"Why didn't you run away when the mother went to find the sheriff?"

"If I run, Yer Grace, then it look like I be guilty. I dinna' do it, so I dinna' have a reason to run."

"Was anyone else there with you, Tom? Someone who did run away?"

He looks down at the floor but doesn't answer. I notice a faint trembling of his hands.

"Tom, who else was there?"

Again, no answer, but the trembling increases.

"Tom, are you afraid of someone?"

Involuntarily, he hunches his shoulders, his hands still trembling. He's afraid of something.

I gesture to the others to move back. Then I step down from the throne and sit on the edge of the dais, inviting Tom to join me. He's reluctant at first . . . this goes against everything he's ever been taught about behavior in the presence of the king. "There's nothing to fear, Tom. You and I are just going to have a quiet conversation about how you've come to be in such trouble." Finally, he sits, his hands clasped tightly in his lap to get the trembling under control.

"So let's go back to the day the boy was killed. What did you do that day?"

"Just what I do any day, Yer Grace. I work in the morning and then I have me dinner."

"Do you work in the afternoon too?"

"Most days. When there be enough work."

"But on that day, you weren't working after your dinner. How did you come to be at that particular house?"

"I were just there." Some of the tension comes back into his posture.

"Very well, let's not worry for now how you came to be there. You were just there. And then the boy turned up."

"Aye, Yer Grace."

"So I can't seem to work out how the boy came to be killed. Will you help me figure that out, Tom?"

He nods, but not with enthusiasm.

"So it was just you and the boy there in the house. I think we can be pretty sure he didn't bash himself in the head with the shovel. And you swear you didn't kill him. So the way I see it, that leaves just two possibilities – God and the Devil." I pause, but he says nothing.

"From what I've been taught, Tom, if God wants to call a lad back to Heaven, it's pretty unlikely he'd bash his head in to do it." I pause again, but still no response. "So that leaves us with the Devil."

Looking down at the floor, he says under his breath. "'Twere the Devil . . . aye." Once again, he's having trouble keeping his hands from trembling. Whoever or whatever this devil is, is what he fears.

I put a hand on his shoulder. "Tom, you know you're safe here, don't you?" He nods again, slowly, as if he's not completely certain. "So will you tell me what it is you're so afraid of?"

He whispers so softly that I have to strain to hear. "I be afraid me own children end up like that boy." The catch in his voice and the gentle shaking of his shoulder tell me he's struggling to fight back tears.

I think I finally have something to work with. "There's nothing to fear, Tom. Stay right where you are. I'm going to speak with the others now."

I stand and beckon the sheriff, the magistrate, and Rainard closer. It's important that Tom hear this. "Sheriff, I believe this man has a family? Some children at least?"

"A wife and children, Your Grace. They came to visit him straightaway when I locked him up, but they never came back. Not even for the trial."

"I think he's sent them away. He's absolutely terrified for their safety . . . so much that he'll go to the gallows rather than say anything to put them at risk. Do you have any idea where they might have gone?"

"Nay, Your Grace, but my wife might."

"We need to find them and bring them here where we can keep them safe. I'm convinced there's more to this case than what we know at present. But we're not going to get any more help from Tom so long as he thinks his children are at risk. I'm suspending this appeal, Magistrate, until we have them safely under my protection."

I beckon to my secretary. "Send for Sir Tobin, Coliar." Then, turning my attention back to the others, "Tom will stay here. Just in case anyone's watching, we'll keep him under guard. But, Tom?"

He looks up. "If you give me your word that you won't try to escape, there'll be no more shackles. Do I have your word?"

"Aye, Yer Grace, but . . ."

"No buts, Tom. I need your promise."

"Ye have me word, Yer Grace, but . . ." He seems reluctant to finish.

"But what, Tom?" I sit back down with him.

His voice is barely above a whisper. "But ye canna' send the sheriff after them."

"You could make it much easier for us if you'd just tell us where they are."

He hangs his head. I can tell he wants to trust, but he's simply too fearful.

"If you help us, Tom, the sheriff and the magistrate will stay here. I'll send some of the King's Own Guard to bring them back safely."

"No, Yer Grace. No, ye canna'. No guards." All his fear and anxiety are back.

"Calm yourself, Tom. It'll be just a few men, all of them dressed as peasants. But under their peasant garb, they'll be armed to the teeth. They know how to watch for danger and how to stay safe."

He looks at me with pleading eyes.

"I trust them with the lives of my own children, Tom. I think you can trust them with yours."

A flood of emotion is about to overtake him, so I stand and address the room to give him time to compose himself. Tobin has quietly entered the back of the room, arriving more quickly than I'd expected. "These proceedings are suspended until further notice. Sir Tobin, if you'll join us in my private reception room, please. And Lord Ernle, a word if I may when we finish inside."

"I await your pleasure, Your Grace," Ernle replies.

"Gentlemen?" I gesture to the magistrate, the sheriff, and Rainard. "Tom?" He rises. "Come with me."

Once the doors close behind us, I get down to business. "Sir Tobin, this man is called Tom. He's appealing a conviction of murder, and

I've become convinced there's more to the case than is currently known. But getting to the bottom of things requires finding his family and getting them safely back here without drawing anyone's attention to the fact that we're doing so. In the meantime, he's to be kept here under guard, though he's not to be shackled since he's given me his word that he won't attempt to escape.

"Tom, Sir Tobin is captain of my personal guard. I trust him with my life and am asking you to do the same. When he asks, tell him precisely where to find your family. And answer truthfully any question he may have, no matter how odd it may seem. There'll be things you or I may not guess that he needs to know if he's to keep your loved ones safe. Go with Sir Tobin now and help him in every way you can."

Only when I can no longer hear their footsteps in the outer chamber do I resume, this time with the sheriff. "Sheriff, I'm not entirely satisfied with your investigation. The magistrate assessed your questioning of possible witnesses as thorough, and I respect his opinion. However, I want to caution you about rushing to justice. There were things that didn't make sense about this case from the beginning, and at least one sign that I suggest you overlooked – the disappearance of Tom's family."

"With all due respect, Your Grace, justice has to be seen to be done when someone's been murdered . . . even more so when it's just a child."

"I'm not suggesting justice be subverted, Sheriff. What I *am* suggesting is that when things don't add up, it's sometimes wise to temporize . . . to watch for someone to make a mistake or to drop a wrong word when drinking with his mates. It's the rare criminal who can resist bragging about it if he thinks he's gotten away with something.

"And that's exactly what I'm instructing you to do when you eventually return home. Keep your eyes and ears open. Look for the missing pieces. Tempt potential suspects to show their hand. You know who the ne'er-do-wells in the area are. But keep it casual and subtle. The last thing we want is for this devil to be scared off. I'm sure we'll get more from Tom once his family's safe, but then we have to do everything possible to ensure that the whole case doesn't hinge on Tom's word."

"Aye, Your Grace." He bows.

"Magistrate, Lord Rainard, it may yet turn out that Tom's guilty. But your instincts about the case were sound. When this appeal is concluded, I'd like to hear your recommendations on whether any changes to the law or updates to our practices might be in order. That's all for now, gentlemen. We'll resume the proceedings after Tom's family arrives."

As they leave, Lord Ernle walks in and goes straight to the sideboard. "Pour you one too?" he asks.

"I'd be grateful."

The two glasses he brings are generously filled. "That was very well done this morning, Alfred."

"Thank you, sir." I still revert automatically to this form, so much do I value and respect this man.

"One of these days, Alfred, you're going to figure out we're peers now," he chuckles. "And from what I heard last night," he continues, "that day may be coming sooner than later."

"Oh, dear."

"Rainard knocked on my door after the two of you finished. He wanted me to hear it from him and not someone else."

It's my turn to chuckle. "Funny. I had the same idea."

"Rather suspected that might be why you wanted to talk."

"Any advice on how to think about it all?"

"Only that we can never predict the paths of our children. You seem to have hit on a good way for Juliana to make her choice. That's really the best a father can do."

"Rupert's going to have great fun with me, I'm sure. He's never hesitated to remind me of the challenges of finding a match for a daughter."

"Well, he had more than his share. And I remember when Estrilda decided she was marrying no one but Laurence. Bauldry spent months trying to persuade her to the choice he'd already made for her, but she was having none of it. Unless the future of the kingdom is in the balance, the best we can do, Alfred, is make sure they don't make a terrible mistake."

"And if she doesn't choose Rainard in the end?"

"There's no doubt he'll be heartbroken. And he may never marry. But if she chooses elsewhere, at least she won't be at court all the time to remind him of his loss."

I raise my glass. "To our children." He follows suit and we drink the toast.

"One bit of advice I *can* give you, Alfred. Try not to worry about this. It'll turn out as it was meant to be. And there'll be no end of things for you to worry about so long as you wear the crown."

A week later, the guards return with Tom's family. I've ordered they be taken directly to my private reception room and that Tom be brought there as well. I'm surprised that Tobin is one of the men accompanying them. "He wouldn't tell me anything, sir, unless I agreed to lead the party. Don't know when I last saw such fear and mistrust."

"Very well. Stay here then. You may be needed to escort the family to their lodgings."

The woman falls to her knees at my feet sobbing. "Blessed God in Heaven, Yer Grace. Ye be a blessed man indeed. All the way here, I be scared . . . so scared it be a trap. And then we see the castle and now we be here before ye. Please, Yer Grace, please tell me my Tom be safe."

I reach down and help her to her feet. "Tom is safe and will join us momentarily. And you're safe now too. You're all under my protection until we get to the bottom of this."

While she's introducing her children, who all bow and curtsey without uttering a word, there's a soft knock on the door and the magistrate lets himself in. "If it please Your Grace, I heard they were here. May I?"

"Of course, Magistrate. I've sent for Tom."

It's only a minute or two before the guards escort Tom inside. Tobin, the magistrate, and I step aside to allow the family time for their emotional reunion.

For some reason I can't quite put my finger on, it seems urgent to pursue things with Tom here and now. Perhaps it's no more than not wanting him to get cold feet, but I feel compelled to get the rest of the story from him quickly. I invite everyone to be seated and choose my own place directly opposite Tom.

"I think you know now, Tom, that you can trust me." He nods his head. "So I want you to start at the beginning and tell me the whole truth of everything that happened that day and how the boy came to be killed."

"So I be working all morning, like I say, and then I had me dinner. When I finish, I were just sort of hanging round the edge of the market, trying to make up me mind if I go see Maud and collect the littl'un from her or if I go to the tavern and have a mug of ale. I be standing there, just mulling it over, and a man I know come up to me and say come with him . . . he need some help with a job he have to do.

"So he take me to this alley and into this house and he hand me a sack and he say open it. He start going all 'round the house picking up all what they own and tossing it in the sack. I tell him this not be right, but he say, 'Shut up and hold the sack.' He start looking under the bed covers and under the mattress to see what be hidden. And I be just about to drop the sack and run when in come the boy.

"I try to get him to run away, but he say something about lace and his mum and he push past me. Next thing I know the other man grab the shovel and bash the boy over the head. I drop the bag where I be standing and rush to the boy . . . to try to help him, see. The other man, he hiss at me to run. But I canna' leave the boy. See, Yer Grace, I could tell he be dying, and I couldna' just leave him there to die alone. So the other man, he grab me jacket and spit in me face and say if I ever tell what happened, all me children end up just like that boy. And then he run away.

"So I go sit with the boy and hold his hand and talk to him softly and tell him God be waiting fer him in Heaven. Later his mum come, and I want to tell her what I do fer her boy, but she run away and then she come back with the sheriff. And ye know the rest, Yer Grace."

We sit in silence for a long moment, Tom's wife holding his hand and squeezing it gently from time to time. Finally I say, "Thank you,

Tom, for telling the truth. Now we can find the real murderer and bring him to justice. There's only one thing more we need. You said this other man is someone you know. I need you to tell me who he is."

He hangs his head, and I begin to wonder if he's going to answer. His wife whispers something in his ear, and for a long, anguished moment we sit in silence. At long last, he looks up into my eyes again and says, "It were me brother."

I look across the room where Tobin is leaning against the door jamb. "Sir Tobin, send for that sheriff. He must go and arrest Tom's brother."

Almost before I can finish, Tom practically screams, "*Noooo*, Yer Grace."

Looking back, I see that the magistrate's face has gone completely white, and Tom is shaking uncontrollably. "No, Yer Grace," he says again, this time more quietly. Tobin has stopped in his tracks.

"Why, Tom?" I ask him gently.

"Because, Yer Grace," he says, "the sheriff is me brother."

"Tobin, have that sheriff detained and held under guard on a charge of murder."

"I think, Sire, it was the sheriff we saw riding away from the castle just as we were returning. We'll get patrols organized to go after him straightaway."

"Get him back here, Tobin, without delay. We mustn't let him go to ground and escape justice."

The magistrate is now talking with Tom. "Your brother, Tom? How could this happen? I always trusted him. The whole town did."

"That's how he get away with things. He were no crook when he first become sheriff. But a year back . . . mayhap a bit more . . . he come across a couple of thugs from a nearby village. Ye remember, sir," he addresses the magistrate, "when we started having those thefts that ne'er be solved? 'Twere 'cause those men be paying me brother to look 'tother way. And then he decide, why should he just get a pittance – why not share in the loot? So he set himself up as head of the gang."

"Why didn't you come to me with this, Tom?" asks the magistrate.

"I dinna' know until the robbery at the tavern in Brinker Village. The tavern were closed on account of the innkeeper have to take his wife to her da's funeral. I were upstairs fixing a broken door that some drunk kicked in. Me horse were at the smithy on account of he threw a shoe on the way there. So it seem there be nary a soul in the inn. I hear noises downstairs, so I think I peek over the railing to see who it be. But me brother spot me and make me come down. And he make out to the other crook like I be one of the gang and all be well. Then next day, he find me at me work and tell me 'bout his gang and threaten me if I breathe a word, he and his gang have it in for all me children.

"So I stay quiet. But Maud here, she know something be wrong, so she make me tell her. She say I have to tell you . . . it be the right thing to do . . . and I had just about made up me mind to listen to her when it all went wrong. See, me brother . . . when he say I have to help him on a job . . . he say he have to make me help him so I canna' turn him in as a crook lessen I admit I be a crook too."

The magistrate shakes his head. "So many cases that should have been solved."

"How many, Magistrate?" I ask.

"Perhaps a dozen . . . not just in the town, but in several of the nearby villages. How could I not have suspected something was amiss?"

"We'll find him. And then we'll find the others. Until then, Tom and his family will remain here. For your own protection, Mistress Maud, I'm going to keep you all under guard, but your quarters will be comfortable enough, your food will be good, and you'll have the opportunity for fresh air and exercise from time to time. We won't, however, take even the slightest risk you could come to any harm until all this is settled.

"Tom, I'll have to ask you to repeat your story in open court if I'm to reverse your conviction. But have no doubt, I intend to do just that."

It takes three weeks for the fugitive sheriff to be found and returned in custody. Once it sinks in that he's going to hang, he can't reveal quickly enough the names of all his accomplices, where they live, and where they go to ground when they're being pursued. Within another three weeks, they, too, have all been rounded up.

I'd originally thought to have all the trials here, where an abundance of troops and guards could prevent anything from going awry. Rainard reminds me, however, of my father's guiding principle that it's best for the people to see justice done at the place where the crime occurred. And in this particular case, restoring the people's confidence in this magistrate is just as important. Rainard and I both wonder, though, if he'll ever be able to restore his own confidence in himself or if, in due course, he'll resign his post.

Jasper provides troops to keep the peace and ensure the crooks don't escape. The magistrate presides over two trials – one for the murder of the boy and another for all the unsolved thefts. All are convicted. I'm told that, in the end, Tom pleaded for mercy for his brother, but the magistrate ruled that the abuse of the people's trust was so heinous as to override any consideration of a lesser sentence. Justice sometimes follows a convoluted path.

When I sign the affirmation of the sentences, the next thing I find in the stack of documents is a letter. The writing – a cramped scrawl, rather like that of a school-child just learning – tells me the sender is literate but doesn't often practice this skill.

Yer Grace.

It be Tom here. Me Maud say I needs be telling ye how greatfull we be fer all ye done fer us. I were thinking the town people turn their backs on us on account of all the trouble I were in and on account of all what me brother did and that he be the one what killed the boy. But it were not like that. They welcum us back. Even the priest say nice things about us in church and say this show how god look after the ritechus. I be thinking 'twere more yer grace than god what look after me, but I dinna tell him so. Me Maud say we be welcuming a brand new wee one early in the new year. She say if it be a boy, we name it Alfred.

I wonder what they'll name it if it's a girl?

Absent any renewed threat to our peace, I began last month inviting Geoffrey to accompany me when I ride out with one of the regular patrols. On that first occasion, he was somewhat tentative about his behavior as the heir on an official duty. Watching me at the first village, however, he quickly recognized this is no different from when we attend a market day in the castle town together. Because of his position, the people are rather more formal with him than they are with Juliana, but he seems to be developing a knack for putting them at ease.

Our second journey is two months hence. My grandfather often had some specific lesson he tried to impart on these early patrols. Time to give some thought to what the first such might be for my son.

Today, however, we're only going as far as the armory, so I've invited all of Geoffrey's mates to come along. As usual when they're together in my presence, they begin by being all formal and quiet and respectful. But it only takes the right question to get them to act like lads and mates again, and, today, I seem to have hit on it straightaway. "So what does Sir Gamel have you working on these days?"

Geoffrey turns in his saddle to look at the others. "Shall we tell him?" After a short hesitation, they all say "Aye" or "Why not?"

"So, Papa," Geoffrey begins, "we were going to keep this as a surprise and have a tournament and invite you to watch, but it's just *ever* so much fun."

Now, they're so excited they talk practically all at once. "You see, sir," William, "Sir Gamel said we were all such good marksmen that all we really needed was just to keep practicing."

"So he said he had a surprise for us." Ancel. "And we got to start swordsmanship early."

"Six weeks ago." Geoffrey.

"And it's ever so much fun, sir." Ancel.

"The swords are wood." William.

"I remember those wooden swords." I manage to get a word in edgewise. "Sort of heavy, as I recall."

"Yes, sir." Geoffrey. "But Sir Gamel says if we practice with these, then a real sword will seem much lighter."

"At least we can't get hurt." Barat finally has a contribution to make.

"I take it swords aren't much to your liking, Barat?" I ask.

"That's because Geoffrey kills him every time they duel." William laughs.

"Well, I can't help it if he's better at it than me." Barat sounds highly frustrated.

"I'll tell you a secret, Barat." I give it my best conspiratorial tone. "I wasn't all that great a swordsman either. Your father could get the best of me pretty much all the time. But I kept at it. Then one day, a few things started to click. And after that, it wasn't always a sure thing that Samuel would win."

"I'll try, sir, but I'm not having as much fun as they are yet."

"I'll bet there's something you're better at than they are. And it sounds like you're quite a good archer."

"I'm the fastest in a foot race, sir." He seems a bit mollified.

"Guess what else, Papa," says Geoffrey

"I've no idea."

"Sir Samuel has been coming to our training more often." And they're off again in excited chatter.

"Shouldn't we say Lord de Courcy now?" Ancel.

"Anyway," William, "now that he's not commander, he has more time."

"He's tougher than Sir Gamel, sir." Ancel.

"Well, I seem to recall you lads wanted him because he was the best," I remind them.

"Oh, we like it because he makes us try different things." Ancel again. "But he's really tough."

"What about you, Barat? What's it like to have your father as trainer?"

"I don't mind, sir. It's nice to do things with him even though I know I'll never be as good as he is."

"Few of us are, son. As long as we know how to defend ourselves and our families, that's good enough for most gentlemen."

We've arrived at the armory. The boys go wide-eyed when the military village opens up before us as the track rounds the hill. There are only two troops here to guard the fledgling enterprise and begin to get some familiarity with what the new weapons are all about. But with the addition of the forge and a kitchen and men to help tend the forges and make charcoal for both the furnaces and the powder, the place is beginning to feel more like a small beehive of activity.

Our arrival coincides with the removal of a very long object from one of the furnaces. "It's the longest we've made yet, Your Grace," the master forger tells us. "The engineers say the longer the tube, the farther it can propel the ball, so we've made four lengths so the knights can try them out and tell us which ones to make. This last one, Sire, is the longest. It is one heavy beast. You won't likely be carrying that thing around from one battle to the next. Most like, it'll be in some fixed place somewhere."

"I'm impressed at how quickly you've gotten this up and running," I tell him.

"Well, Sire, 'tisn't all that much different from casting a bell. And at least with these things, nobody cares what they sound like when you take them out of the mold." He laughs at his own joke.

"Your Grace?"

"Yes, William?"

"Do you think it would be possible for us to see how a cannon works?"

"I don't know. Let's go find the captain and see if they have a test planned for today."

As we turn to leave the forge, we spy a knight captain hurrying in our direction. I recognize him as one of those who'd been in the command tent during the last war. "Your Grace," he bows as he meets up with us, "if you'd told us you were coming, we'd have arranged to greet you more properly."

"Not at all necessary . . . Sir Evrouin, isn't it?"

"I'm honored you remember, Sire."

"I rather think it might be considered bad form for me to forget the senior commanders who won a war for us," I chuckle. This earns me a slight relaxation of his military bearing and a hint of a smile, as I'd hoped. "I didn't know you were posted here, Evrouin."

"Well, Sire, when we disbanded the camp near here, I guess it was just natural I'd be assigned to set this place up. I won't be here much longer, though. Carew wants me back to work on drawings for the river defenses. Once we work out the distances each of these different length tubes can lob a ball and figure out the best angles to mount them, I'll be back at the castle."

"Then we're fortunate we came when we did. I brought the lads along to see your armory in operation. My son, Geoffrey." Evrouin bows to Geoffrey, who responds with a small incline of his head – the kind of gesture I'm seeing more often as a friendly acknowledgment of the other person without breaking royal protocol.

The other lads introduce themselves in turn, ending with Barat. "We're all exceedingly fond of your father, young man," says Evrouin. "He was a good commander. Now let's show you lads around."

"We were wondering, Sir Evrouin," says Geoffrey, "if you were going to be firing a cannon today. We all really want to know how they work."

"What say you, Sire, to a full tour for the lads? They've seen the forge. I think perhaps next we should go see the cannon-balls."

"They're in your capable hands, Sir Evrouin. I'll just have a look around and join you for the firing." And with that they're off. If young lads trying to be serious students of things military can be said to be dancing with excitement, then all four of them are.

My purpose isn't really an inspection of the site . . . more getting a feel for our progress. I come across one of the masons finishing a row of stones on what he says will be a hut to store the cannons themselves as they come out of the forge. "Nice to be doing real work for a change, Yer Grace," he comments. "Most of what we do be rebuilding those walls so they can blow them apart again with these infernal machines."

"That's important work too, my good man. Best we learn how to use the machines on something temporary rather than on some beautiful structure men like you have poured heart and soul into."

"I never think about it like that, Sire."

He and his companions are going to be building a lot more temporary walls before we learn the right way to deploy and defend against these new weapons. And no doubt this camp . . . like the one at the reservoir . . . will remain a permanent part of our landscape.

Making my way over to the spot where one of the cannons we captured in the war is set up for firing, I see that Sir Evrouin is showing the boys how the powder and the ball are loaded and miming how the fuse will be lit for firing. I arrive in time to hear his admonition, "Now you young gents come back over here with me. We want to be a safe distance away."

I've learned to expect the deafening sound of the cannon firing, but the boys react much as Samuel and I did the first time we exploded a cask of black powder. Almost in unison, Geoffrey and William shout, "Whoa!"; Barat throws himself to the ground and covers his head; and Ancel shouts, "Christ on horseback!"

"Not in front of the king, Ancel," yells William. No doubt his ears are still ringing from the blast. Geoffrey helps Barat to his feet.

It takes all my control not to laugh out loud. Glancing over at Evrouin, I see the same struggle on his face. "So, lads, what do you think?" I ask in the most serious tone I can muster.

"Is it always that loud?" asks Barat.

"Pretty much," Evrouin replies.

"I'm sorry, Sire," Ancel turns to me. "It's just that . . . please don't tell my father."

"I think, Ancel, that a man's entitled to an occasional outburst when what's happened is so completely beyond his imagination. I won't tell your father if you promise to remember that a gentleman watches his tongue in polite company." But of course, I *will* tell Phillip, who'll find the whole thing hilarious, especially as he's always the first in our group with the bawdy remarks.

"Yes, sir. I promise, sir. It was just that . . . I've never heard anything so loud, sir."

Now I allow myself the liberty of a chuckle. "Nor had I the first time I heard one of these things go off."

"Does it always make a hole in the wall like that?" William asks Evrouin.

"Well, the walls we're using aren't as thick as the ones at the castle, so we can breach them more easily."

"But if you had a dozen of these things arrayed before a fortress, Sir Evrouin," Geoffrey this time, "could you bombard even a thick wall enough to make a hole?"

"We think so, Geoffrey. But we don't have enough cannons right now to even try. There's so much we have to figure out. And we're in a hurry to figure it out before an enemy tries to use these weapons against us."

On the ride back to the castle, the boys talk excitedly among themselves. I'm quite astonished at how quickly just a single demonstration has gotten them imagining all the things they could do with the cannons. At their age, naturally, it's the offensive opportunities that come first to mind.

"Sir," asks William, "are we going to be trained with these new weapons?"

"Eventually, I'd think, William. But right now, we don't even have a proper training program for the experienced knights. Sir Edmund is working on it. Maybe by the time you've finished your other skills, something will be ready."

"Papa?"

"Yes, Geoffrey?"

"What if we could help Sir Edmund?"

"Do you have something in mind?"

"What if we could ask questions? Just as if we were trying to learn things ourselves. Maybe that would help him figure out how to teach people?"

"I really have no idea, Geoffrey. But if you boys want to put the proposal to him, I have no objection. Just be sure you have your ideas well thought out before you approach him."

Two days later, Samuel joins me for my morning ride. He now rides a son of Sirius, a half-brother to Altair, foaled in the same year. Since his retirement as knight commander, he's had more time for training a mount. Elvin chose this one for him and gave the colt some early training while Samuel and I were off at war. Samuel has been applying the finishing touches, teaching the youngster his own manner in the saddle, developing that one-ness of horse and rider that all of Star Dancer's lineage seem to understand instinctively.

"I still can't believe I spent my entire career as a knight without one of your fine horses as my mount," Samuel shakes his head as we leave the stable and urge the horses to a trot on the path toward the big meadow.

"It's your own fault, you know," I tease him. "You should have kept Sirius when I gave him to you."

He laughs out loud. "Would've definitely been easier on my backside. I don't know where this smooth trot comes from, but a man can get used to that in a heartbeat."

"Credit for that goes to Gwen's mares, I think. Star Dancer had nice gaits, but nothing as comfortable as these two."

When we reach the meadow, we give the horses their heads and enjoy the kind of romp through the field and over the hedgerows that's the hallmark of a young stallion feeling frisky and energetic on a cool autumn morning. Their first burst of energy spent, we slow the horses to a walk so we can engage in serious conversation. "Barat told me all about your trip to the armory. Sounds as if the boys were suitably impressed."

"Like children with a new toy. Why is it, Samuel, that the young always seem to embrace something new and try to figure out what they can do with it, while we fuss and fret over how it's changing our world?"

"Because they're too young to understand unintended consequences. Besides, it's all a matter of balance. Without them to think about what *could* be done, we might not do such a good job of figuring out what could possibly go wrong."

"Which reminds me. The boys are planning to propose to Carew that they be included in figuring out the new training. What do you think?"

"Actually, I think they may very well be onto something, Alfred. Carew, Jasper, me . . . for that matter, any knight in the realm . . . we've all had current tactics ingrained in us for years. We see a landscape . . . we instinctively know how to deploy. We see an enemy formation . . . instinct, again, tells us precisely how to counter it. We can even anticipate how an enemy might try to surprise us, because we know so well what our own tactics would be. The boys have no tactical training yet. They'll ask questions where we might make assumptions. The more I think about it, the more I like the idea. I'll speak to Carew later so he's not caught off guard when they make their request."

We let the horses have another swift run before settling back to a comfortable pace for talking. "Something else I've been meaning to tell you," says Samuel. "You know Gamel has started them out on swordsmanship."

"They talked of little else on the ride out to the armory. That and the fact that you're dropping in on their training more frequently. From what I heard, swordplay is not much to Barat's liking."

"Poor Barat. I can't even imagine what the burden must be like on a young trainee when your father is – or was – knight commander."

"He seems to take it in stride, Samuel. From what I can tell, he's made his peace with the fact that he's not cut out to follow in your footsteps. He's just frustrated that he's not getting the hang of the sword right away, and the others best him all the time. With other skills, he's been able to do well . . . even excel . . . but this is a struggle for him."

"I'll spend some time with him and give him a few pointers."

"I think he'd like that. What I think he'd *really* like is to surprise Geoffrey by holding his own against him in a practice duel."

"Now *that's* a tall order."

"Really?"

"In fact, it's what I wanted to talk to you about. Gamel told me that, from the outset, Geoffrey's been a natural with a sword. In fact, what Gamel said was, 'It's surprising in a lad so young. He uses his sword like an extension of his arm.' So at the end of last week, I stopped by to watch them practice. It's uncanny, Alfred, how instinctive he is. The way I'd describe it is that he uses his sword as an extension of his mind. If you try to teach him a maneuver by breaking it down into individual elements, he performs each element with skill . . . but the overall maneuver is awkward and disjoint. If you tell him what the objective is and then demonstrate the complete maneuver, he grasps it straightaway. It may take him a couple of times to get the hang of things, but then he gets progressively better every time.

"So when they finished practice, I asked Geoffrey to stay behind. When the others were gone, I put a real blade in his hand and took him through some basic skills. He held his own, Alfred. A novice still, but with the makings of one of the finest swordsmen I've ever known if we can keep him interested."

"This is *my* son you're talking about?" Samuel knows my skill with a sword is sufficient but hardly brilliant.

"Well, from what I've heard, your father was quite accomplished. Maybe the talent just skipped a generation."

"Come to think of it, I'm not sure I remember ever seeing my father handle a sword." I pause, trying to recollect. "So what do we do for Geoffrey?"

"I think we start him practicing regularly with the knights . . . with a blade. Keep him challenged. Let him progress as fast as he can or wants to. I'm afraid if we hold him back at the pace of the others, he'll get bored and lose interest . . . and then, of course, he'll get sloppy and all that talent will go to waste."

"What about the others? Won't they feel left out?"

"Oh, I think Geoffrey should continue practicing with them. It will help all of them improve their skills. Now, I do intend to give Geoffrey some guidance on how to be a good tutor. Last thing we need is for them all to get frustrated and have this ruin their friendship."

"Good. And frankly, I think that advice would be best coming from you. He needs to take this in as a way to use his skill . . . not as some expectation because he's the heir."

"I was hoping you'd say that. So we're agreed?"

"Samuel, is it really safe to have someone of his size and inexperience engaging in swordplay with full-grown men . . . and trained knights, at that?"

Samuel laughs out loud. "Come on, Alfred. Think about it. There's not a knight in the realm who wants to risk being brought up on charges for injuring the king's son."

"Well, when you put it like that," I chuckle.

As we reach the far corner of the meadow and turn to head back to the stables, I finally get to the topic I've been fretting about. "Tobin came to me yesterday to tender his resignation as captain of the Guard. Is that really necessary, Samuel?"

"Alfred, you know as well as I do why the rotation system exists."

"I know . . . the king's safety, minimize the risk of a group with ill-intent, avoid jealousy in the ranks. I know. But I have absolute confidence in Tobin. And he's been rotating the members of the guard. Couldn't that accomplish the same thing?"

"And couldn't a captain with ill-intent use those rotations to get his own men in place to do you harm?" He pauses, knowing that I already know the answer. "I have confidence in Tobin too, Alfred. But too much confidence in your guard captain is itself another risk. You might not see – or be willing to admit it – if something seemed amiss. Fresh eyes in your captain are just as important as fresh men among the guards."

"You're not telling me anything I don't know. It's just that I'm in no mood to go through the whole business of getting to know and learning to trust someone new. Can't I postpone this for a while?" Listening to myself, I realize I sound like a whining child unwilling to let go a favorite toy even though he's long since outgrown it. So I add, "Or are you going to tell me just to take my medicine and get it over with?"

Samuel laughs. "I should. But what if I offered you some medicine that might be more palatable?"

"I'm listening."

"How would you like Carew as your next Guard captain?"

"That, I could deal with. But wouldn't that disrupt his progression to knight commander?"

"Not necessarily. Jasper won't be ready to step down for a few years. A stint as captain of the Guard would be a feather in Carew's cap. But Jasper needs him right now to finish working out the new training program. What if I ask Jasper to leave Tobin in place until he can free up Carew?"

"That would be a feather in *your* cap."

"Let me see what I can do. As long as there's not some other reason Tobin wants to step down right now, I don't think this would be too great a risk."

"What about when the switch is made? Any chance we could give Tobin the opportunity to be deputy commander?"

"I can't meddle that much, Alfred. You know the commander always chooses his own deputy."

"Sorry, Samuel. I just want the best for Tobin. He's a really good man."

"So is Jasper . . . and he'll see that Tobin is taken care of." We walk on for a few minutes before Samuel continues. "This isn't like you, Alfred. What's eating you?"

"Besides not wanting to part with Tobin? The fact that I completely overlooked this. I should've known it was time for a rotation and started planning it. It shouldn't have been necessary for Tobin to have to nudge me to do my duty. Which, naturally, makes me question what else I'm missing." I pause for a long moment. "I suppose it's because finding good matches for my children is weighing so heavily on my mind."

We ride on in silence for quite some time. It's as if Samuel is carefully weighing how to respond. At length, he says, "It seems Juliana's provided you with quite a dilemma. Father told me about it."

"Dear God in Heaven!" I can't keep the exasperation out of my tone. "I thought he'd agreed to keep that a secret for now."

"Calm down, Alfred. He did . . . and he is. But he also thought Rainard might need a confidant closer to his own age no matter how things work out . . . even *while* things are working out. And who better than a brother. It's a secret among the Ernle men. I have no intention even of telling Tamasine."

"Some confidant you'll be. I seem to recall you married the love of your life and didn't have to deal with a loss."

"In the end, yes. But it almost didn't work out that way."

"Oh?"

"Our fathers had already signed the contract when Tamasine decided to object. Said she didn't want a husband who was always away and always at risk of being injured or killed. Apparently, Estrilda's insistence on getting her own way gave Tamasine the courage to speak up. Anyway, do you remember the year that both our families kept Easter on their estates rather than at court?"

"Which one?"

He chuckles. "Well, for me, there was only one that mattered. I had a month off duty and went home to wallow in self-pity, certain I was going to lose my bride. I spent the first week just moping around . . . lots of time sitting on a rock down by the cove, staring out at the sea. I even tried my hand at writing her love poems, if you can imagine that."

I laugh out loud.

He grins. "Well, when I looked back at them after it was all over, they *were* pretty pathetic. Anyway, by the middle of the second week, I'd resolved to leave the knighthood. After all, a man has his wife and family long after he's past his peak as a fighter.

"Unbeknownst to me, Mother had invited Lady Montfort for a visit . . . and that good lady made Tamasine come with her. They arrived a few days after I'd reached my decision. Even still, things were really awkward at first. To their immense credit, my mother and hers allowed the two of us an inordinate amount of freedom to spend time together. It was obvious Tamasine wanted the marriage but just couldn't find her way to cope with what it meant to be married to a knight, so I told her of my decision . . . and was completely taken aback by her reaction."

"What was that?"

"She said she could never be truly happy knowing she'd forced her husband to give up his life's ambition. So we were at an impasse. She wouldn't marry a knight; and she wouldn't marry me if I gave up being a knight."

"Alright, we know how the story turned out. How did you get there?"

"Father stepped in and assured her he'd make arrangements for her to live at court whenever I was assigned there. She insisted that be part of the marriage contract . . . which, naturally, was of no consequence to my father or hers. And the rest, as you say, you know."

We ride on in silence again, the horses seemingly content to walk after their romp in the meadow. As we pass the track leading into the woods, Samuel says, "You've handled this well, Alfred. Just as my mother and Lady Montfort did for me. It will all come right in the end." He pauses and then grins. "And then you can spend all your time worrying about a bride for Geoffrey."

I roll my eyes. "Don't remind me!" As usual, Samuel has managed to lighten my mood and put everything into proper perspective.

We arrive back at the stable to find Laurence just turning his horse over to the grooms. We stick to the usual pleasantries until we're out of earshot of the stables. "So what brings you?" I ask.

"News of a sort. Not quite sure what to make of it yet, but thought you'd want to know. And Estrilda wanted a change of scenery, so the whole family's here to spend a few days at court."

I broke with protocol over the black powder by making Samuel privy to Laurence's role as spymaster. Now, as a hereditary lord, he's entitled to the knowledge anyway, so Laurence knows he's not speaking out of turn. "You should probably hear this too, Samuel," Laurence adds.

Osbert meets us on the path as we approach the castle. "I be coming to tell ye Lord Laurence be here, m'lord, but I see he find ye already."

"He has indeed, Osbert. Do you think you could arrange a midday meal for us in my private reception room? We have things to discuss."

"And ye not be wanting interruptions?"

"You read my mind as always, Osbert."

Once the servants leave and we've helped ourselves to hot potage, fresh pandemaine, and wine, Laurence gets down to business. "Like I said before, I'm really not quite sure what to make of this yet. One of our mercenaries returned a few days ago. He and a mate of his have been with some of the Aleffe forces in the southeast. They've seen absolutely no sign of the king's men . . . not even a patrol or anything that might look like a scouting party. This has to be the strangest civil war in the history of man."

"Amen to that," says Samuel. "And unless Charles just plans to live out his days holed up in Lamoreaux, I fear the violence when he does move against the Aleffes is going to destroy the kingdom."

"So if there's nothing new on the military front, what did your man have to report?" I ask.

"They've been with a group patrolling the villages and a small market town not far from the Teuton border. And they've been running into Teutons in the taverns."

"Is that unusual?"

"According to the local innkeepers, yes. They were quick to point out that, in the past, Teutons only crossed the border to steal horses. They'd come into a village during Sunday services, when most folk were at church, or sneak up on a farm when the family was at mealtime. But they were seen often enough that the local folk are certain who it was. Now they're drinking in the taverns and trying to blend in. My agent says it's too hard for most of them to disguise their guttural accent, so blending is a relative thing. And there's another curious thing . . . not a single horse has gone missing in the last three months."

"Couldn't that just be coincidence?" I ask.

"It could," Laurence replies. "But it's a damn curious one. The locals say there hasn't been a whole month go by in the last two years that hasn't seen at least one horse stolen and sometimes as many as three or four across the area."

"Maybe there've been more frequent patrols, and it's just not worth the risk to the Teutons?" Samuel suggests.

"I asked about that. Whether it was Charles's troops before the war or the Aleffe militia, it doesn't seem there's been much change in the military presence.

"There's another thing," Laurence continues. "There's one man who keeps appearing in all the villages and in the market town where this is happening. According to the innkeepers, the first time they show up in a village, it's this guy with a mate . . . three or four mates in the town. Then he disappears for a while, but the others keep showing up to drink every couple of days. No one knows where they sleep . . . the only guess is that they're sneaking into barns late at night and managing to be gone before dawn.

"Anyway, this other guy shows up again from time to time to drink with the ones he left behind. It seems they always find a corner table where they can huddle together and talk . . . and go quiet if anyone passes too close by. One innkeeper said he brought them another round once, before they asked for it, trying to see if he could pick up on anything. He was sure he heard them speaking in the Teuton language as he approached, but they went silent as soon as he got near.

"My agents say it's like this guy is infiltrating his people into the area and coming back to check in with them periodically. It certainly sounds that way to me. The problem is, we don't know to what end. Are they spying for Charles? Trying to find a place where a Teuton invasion coupled with Charles breaking out of Lamoreaux could create a two-front war for the Aleffes? Are they spying for the Teuton king? Trying to decide if Charles's kingdom is ripe for invasion? Or are they just testing the waters? Maybe trying to figure out if they could infiltrate people into the border areas and slowly peel away Charles's territory, bits and pieces at a time, and make it part of the Teuton Kingdom."

"None of which would be a good outcome," I state the obvious.

"Do your men think that area's particularly vulnerable?" asks Samuel.

"That's the unfortunate part about having to split the mercenaries up in various parts of the Aleffe territory in a broken kingdom where we have no ambassador. The only way I can assemble a big picture is to get disjoint reports and try to piece it together myself. The Aleffes are strongest in the northeast, around Aleffe province. I won't have a report on the long central section of the border until next week. But I thought you'd want to know what we do have right away so we could all start contemplating what . . . if anything . . . to do about it. The rest of the kingdom . . . inland from the border . . . seems to be business as usual – or at least what usual has become these days."

"It will be telling, I think," says Samuel, "to see if they confine whatever this activity is to the southeast border or if they start venturing deeper into the kingdom. Do they want to keep these people where they can pull them out quickly? Or is their object to get as many people into as much territory as possible without any adverse consequences?"

"What if their objective is the port?" I ask.

"Then coming at the Aleffe stronghold from both the south and the east would be almost certain to overwhelm a loosely organized militia," says Samuel. While Laurence and I are mulling this over, he has another thought. "Surrounding them would be even better."

"Much to think about," I sum up. "Keep your men on this, Laurence. I don't want to bring it to the Council until we have more of your big picture. Neither do I want to delay figuring out our position if the instability over there is getting worse. But for now, since all of us are here, what say you to drinks at the tavern later this afternoon?"

"You don't have to ask me twice," says Laurence.

The innkeeper has the first round waiting when we arrive, and we quickly settle into catching up with one another. At some point, Richard remarks, "I hear the boys enjoyed their trip to the armory."

So I regale everyone with the events of that day. When I get to the part about Ancel's outburst, Phillip nearly chokes trying to avoid spewing a mouthful of ale all over the table and the rest of us. The others laugh uproariously. When Phillip manages to catch his breath, Richard raises his mug. "Like father, like son!" And more laughter follows the toast.

"At least, at his tender age, he isn't extolling the delectable charms of the bar maids," Laurence teases.

"Don't you be so smug, my friend," Phillip retorts. "You still have all this to look forward to." After three daughters and a child who died in infancy, Laurence finally has his heir. Given the long lives of the Montforts, it's probably just as well that the little tyke came along late . . . at least he won't be a decrepit old man when he finally inherits the title.

Phillip turns serious. "One thing's for sure . . . we mustn't let Addiena find out. She'd have the poor lad reciting his catechism every day for a month."

"I suppose we shouldn't tell your mother either?" Samuel.

"Oh, Mother would teach him more delightful oaths and get him into even more trouble," laughs Phillip.

Samuel raises his glass. "To Lady Cecily!"

Laurence adds, "And to Ancel!"

When the five of us are together like this, it's always as if we're still young men starting to find our way in the world. The responsibilities of the crown seem to belong to a different man and a different time. And I'm reminded that one of the best things I can do for Geoffrey is to be sure the bonds he's forming now with his mates will last a lifetime.

By the time our wives join us for supper, we've moved on to other things, so Ancel will be safe from his mother's chastisement. We'll never know if the innkeeper was planning to serve guinea fowl to all his clientele this evening or if it's something he concocted at the last minute for special guests. Either way, it's delicious, and Gwen and I make a point of complimenting him as we leave. Osbert will, as usual, add a few extra coins to the payment when the bill is presented the next day. It seems to go without saying, now, that "Alfred's buying."

Walking back to the castle, we let the women go on ahead. Speaking quietly, I tell Phillip, "I gave my word to Ancel that I wouldn't tell his father if he would remember to watch his tongue in polite company."

He chuckles. "Don't worry, Alfred. The king's honor will be protected."

Richard remarks, "I can just imagine the four of them, off in the woods together, debating what's the most daring oath they can try out."

My first reaction is utter dismay at the notion of my son . . . the future king . . . practicing swearing with his mates. But it's immediately replaced by recognition that what they're actually doing is working very hard at figuring out how to become men. So I join in the quiet laughter of my friends while we hurry to catch up to our wives.

Primrose is lonely – if one can ascribe such sentiments to a dog. Gwen assures me that if Juliana were here, she would be quick to admonish me for having any doubt. And therein – the absence of her young mistress – seems to lie part of the source of Primrose's malaise. The other source, I'm told, is the loss of Willow, our long-time nursery dog and Primrose's constant companion since she first came to live with us as a small pup. Willow left us shortly after Juliana's departure and was laid to rest in Brother Adam's little cemetery alongside Morgana and Edward's first dog.

So it's been decided that Primrose will accompany us to the country manor for the harvest festival . . . to which I have no objection whatsoever. It's also been decided that, until Juliana's return, Primrose will share my bed. Though I'm far less sanguine about this prospect, it seems to be non-negotiable and not worth the expenditure of any regal breath. I remain unconvinced.

Our harvest this year is plentiful, and Rupert says we'll make a handsome profit, even after we distribute the portion that we allot to our tenants. Richard reports an abundant harvest on the Devereux estate as well, so there'll be no shortages of food this winter.

It's always a source of amazement to me how quickly this setting works on my spirit. From the moment we arrive, it seems only natural to set aside for a time the worries of daily life. It was thus when we holidayed here with my friends in more carefree times . . . and when it was our refuge from the madness of John's reign . . . and now, the weight of the crown seems far away in the peace and quiet of the countryside.

On the first night here, I stay late in conversation with Richard and Rupert, postponing as long as possible my introduction to the new sleeping arrangements. When I can finally delay no longer, I find Gwen already in bed with Primrose nestled at her feet. As I climb into bed, Gwen snuggles closer than usual, giving the dog space. This might turn out not to be so bad after all. I'll learn later that Primrose's choice of sleeping spot had little or nothing to do with consideration for my sensibilities and everything to do with the fact that a well-worn pair of Juliana's gloves had been strategically placed beneath the bedcovers.

And then something occurs to me. "Am I going to have to put into Juliana's marriage contract that her bridegroom must expect to share his bed with a dog?"

"Oh, dear." Gwen sounds deeply concerned. "You mean you hadn't thought of that?"

Though I think it likely she's having me on, I've had one brandy too many to come up with a reply that isn't certain to be wrong in some way. The best I can manage is, "Well . . ."

Finally, she giggles. "You ninny. Once Juliana returns, life will be properly ordered once again." She pauses before adding, "But it would have been great fun watching you try to negotiate that with a fellow monarch."

We return to the castle to find Juliana home a week earlier than expected. "Winter was setting in early this year," she tells us over a quiet family supper. Gwen has arranged for the boys to dine with Richard's family so we can hear about the visit without interruptions. Juliana is as animated as when she and Richenda returned from their visit to Goscelin's court.

"We'd already seen two snowfalls," she adds, "and the harbor was freezing over. Cousin Brandr and Aunt Beatrix said we should be on our way if we didn't fancy spending the entire winter with them.

"It was extraordinary, Papa. The ice was so thick, you could walk on it. Only the main channel was open, so they took us on sledges out to where the ice was thin, and then we went in row boats out to the ship. The seamen used their oars to keep the ice broken up as much as they did to row."

"Oh, dear," says my mother. "Did you have to climb up one of those rope ladders to get on board?"

"No, Grandmama. They had something like a tree swing attached to the cargo hoist. So we sat on the swing and they lifted us aboard. It was rather fun!"

Richenda chimes in with delighted agreement.

"I'm not sure I'd go *that* far," says Petronilla, clearly less enthusiastic about the adventure than the girls.

"And then, when we were all aboard," Juliana resumes, "they replaced the swing with a cargo net and hoisted all our baggage aboard. The captain said if we'd waited another week, his ship would have been locked in the ice, and we'd have had to wait for the spring thaw. It was a fast journey home . . . we had the north wind behind us all the way. That made it really cold, though, so we couldn't spend much time on deck."

"It must get quite cold there in midwinter," Gwen muses.

"It does, Mama, but everyone has furs for going outdoors . . . and warm boots. And the ladies have fur muffs to keep their hands warm and fur lap rugs for the sleighs. Aunt Beatrix has some of the most beautiful furs I've ever seen. She gave me a muff. You'll have to see it, Mama, when Milla finishes unpacking."

"She gave me one too," says Richenda. "And Mother."

"And they have these marvelous stoves that keep the rooms warm. In the castle, they're ever so beautiful with pretty tiles all over them that get very hot. Cousin Brandr says they don't need as much wood as an open fire, and they warm the whole room – not just the spots close by the hearth. Aunt Beatrix says one can be quite comfortable in the same sort of winter clothes we'd wear here."

"How is dear Beatrix?" asks my mother. "I've not had a letter from her in a while."

"I think Aunt Beatrix is lonely, Grandmama," Juliana replies, sounding somewhat concerned. "The ladies of the court are all fawning over Queen Arnora, trying to gain favor and position with her. Aunt Beatrix is sort of forgotten amid all the drama. No one visits with her. Oh, Cousin Brandr drops in from time to time, but Aunt Beatrix says he's reluctant to intervene in what he considers the women's business, so she always puts on a cheerful manner when she's with him."

"Juliana has the measure of things, Alice," says Petronilla. "Arnora seems to be a bit enthralled with her recently acquired power and isn't handling it well. She favors one lady this week, a different one the next. It's all a bit chaotic with no one ever quite sure of her position and everyone trying something new to garner the queen's favor. I know it was never expected she'd be queen, so she had no preparation, but . . ."

"You had no preparation, either," says my mother, "but you listened and learned."

"And that's the problem," replies Petronilla. "Beatrix could help her if the girl would just listen, but . . . Listen to me, calling her a girl when she's every bit as old as me or Gwendolyn. But when I compare her to Juliana, there's no doubt who's the more mature and the more sensible . . . and the better suited to be a queen. It doesn't help that Beatrix isn't a dowager queen, so she has very little influence at court."

"I don't think the relationship between Beatrix and Arnora has ever been an easy one," says my mother, "so perhaps I shouldn't be surprised."

"Why don't you invite Beatrix for an extended visit, Mother Alice?" asks Gwen. "She certainly wouldn't be lonely here . . . and it's not out of the question there's a young lady who might be rather more interested than Arnora in what she has to say. Speaking of which," she turns her attention to Juliana, "you haven't said a word about the most important part of your visit. What did you think of Thorbrand?"

Juliana becomes more subdued and demure. "Well, he came of age this year, so he's a couple of years older than me, as you know. He seems very kind, and he's well read. He told us some wonderful legends of the Nordic gods. They had a whole different set of gods, Papa, from the Greeks or the Romans. It was all *ever* so interesting."

Richenda nudges her. "They don't want to know about gods, Juliana. Tell them the rest." And then she adds mischievously, "Or shall I?"

"Oh, very well then." Juliana smiles. "He's much like Cousin Brandr, only more blonde . . . like his mother."

"He looks like one of those Nordic gods Juliana was carrying on about," chimes in Richenda. "In fact, I'd be quite happy to take him if she doesn't want him."

"You already have a betrothed," Juliana chides her.

"Who's gone missing," Richenda retorts.

"Anyway," Juliana returns to the topic at hand, "he spent every day with us, and we had so many very pleasant conversations. We went riding several times before the snow fell . . . he's a good horseman, Papa, and he treats his mount well. He told me all about their court and their traditions. He even apologized that his mother paid so little attention to us. He told me he thought things would be better once she got used to being queen, but I'm not so sure."

"So do you favor him, my dear?" asks my mother gently.

"He's really very nice, Grandmama. But it's too early to say. I made a bargain with Papa, and I intend to live up to my part of the bargain in its entirety." She gives me a warm smile then gazes down at her hands in her lap as she adds quietly, "But he did invite me to visit again in the spring."

The next morning Juliana is waiting at the stable when I return from my morning ride. "I think I might have made a mistake, Papa," she tells me, giving Altair the apple she's brought from the kitchen.

"Oh?"

"Taking Richenda on the visit to Cousin Brandr's court. I think maybe it reminded her too much of that time when she was getting to know Denis . . . the time just before their betrothal. And now he's gone, and she doesn't know if she'll ever see him again."

"Did that make it hard for you to get to know Thorbrand?"

"Not at all, Papa. Richenda's always been like a sister, and this time was no different. It's just that, every now and then, I'd catch her looking rather sad. She'd brush it off and say it was nothing. But you heard her last night. I really don't want to make her feel sad because I'm happy. Would you talk with her, Papa?"

"I'm not sure what I can say that would make any difference."

"Please, Papa. I think it would cheer her up just to know you haven't forgotten about her."

"Very well. When's this little talk to be?"

"I asked her to wait for me in the garden. Maybe you have a few minutes now?"

We've just reached that place where a small path leads through the hedge and into the garden. She takes my arm and we pass through to find Richenda admiring the autumn crocuses that are always such a nice surprise after summer's flowers have bloomed their last. There's a single bench nearby where the girls take a seat, leaving me to lounge on the grass lest I appear to be some onerous father figure towering over them. No one says a word. Richenda seems rather ill at ease.

Seeing that it's going to be up to me to break the silence, I say, "Juliana tells me there are some things that might be troubling you, Richenda. Would you like to talk about it?"

Juliana pats her cousin's arm. "It's alright, Richenda. You can talk to Papa."

Richenda doesn't look up. "You know I can't, Juliana. You know Mother expressly forbade me to bother the king."

"You needn't worry, my dear. I promise to protect you from the wrath of your mother. And anyway, unless I was dreaming, it was Juliana who bothered me." She still says nothing, so I keep trying to help. "I gather from last night's conversation you're worried about Denis."

And then it all comes pouring out in a flood of emotion. "I don't know where he is, Uncle Alfred. How could he just disappear like that? Things were ever so good, and I knew what my life was going to be like. And now I don't even know if he's alive or if I should be asking you to find a new match for me or if I do, will he suddenly come back and things will be all in turmoil again. I'm happy for Juliana . . . really I am . . . but it just reminds me what a mess I'm in and that makes me sad and . . ." She hesitates only briefly, but the restraint she's exercised for so long finally reaches its breaking point. "Why didn't you protect him, Uncle Alfred?" Even though, technically, she's my cousin, she's always called me uncle.

I have a brief twinge of conscience, wishing I could speak Denis's message to her and tell her he's safe, but I know the time isn't yet right. "I can't protect someone who's not here, my dear," I tell her as gently as I know how.

"Then why did he leave? He asked for your protection, and then he just disappeared."

How can I bring her some sense of calm without revealing any of the truth? "Shall I tell you, Richenda, a bit about how men think?"

"Will that help me make sense of all this?"

"It might. You see, when women sense danger, they tend to gather their brood together in what they think is a safe place and hover over them. Our mothers do it . . . and so do the animals, for that matter. But men . . . their instinct is to go out and face the danger . . . fight it off . . . and if they can't fight it off, then they try to draw it away from whatever is under threat. It's just possible that when Denis saw you there at the banquet, he suddenly realized he'd put *you* in danger by coming to me so publicly. And since he couldn't fight the danger off alone, perhaps he decided the best way for you to be safe was for him to run away."

"You think that's what happened, Uncle?"

"It's possible. It's how a man – even a young one – would think."

"In that case, then, he's still in danger. He might not even be alive."

"Or he might have found a safe place to hide. You can't be certain of either."

She's regained much of her composure, but the sadness persists. Thankfully, Gwen has educated me on how girls her age can go from dreamily romantic to the heights of joy to the depths of despair in a single afternoon . . . well, morning, in this case.

"Then what should I do, Uncle Alfred? I don't want to be like the story heroine whose man goes off to war and never comes home, and she pines for him for the rest of her days."

"I think you should be hopeful."

"Mother says I should be patient." She hangs her head, sounding and looking terribly dejected.

"That can't hurt, but it's a rather different thing, don't you think?" She looks up, her interest piqued, so I continue. "I wish I knew how the conflict across the sea is going to turn out. I've no idea, but I'm hopeful it will be resolved soon. So I'll make a bargain with you as I did with Juliana. Be patient and hopeful for a bit longer. If things go badly, then I promise you my help. If you want a quiet life with Denis here in this kingdom under my protection, then I'll try to find him for you, though we both know that may not be possible. Or if you think a different life would make you happier, then I'll find you an excellent match, just as if you were my own daughter."

The smile that lights her face tells me things will be well . . . for the time being, anyway. She turns to hug Juliana and then drops to her knees on the grass and hugs me. "Oh, thank you, Uncle Alfred. You've made everything so much better."

I stand and help her to her feet as Juliana rises from the bench. "So you agree to our bargain?"

"I do, Uncle."

"And your part is?"

"To be hopeful. I promise I will."

"Very well. Then off with you both and start thinking about things like Christmas and the New Year and your next journey."

As they link arms and head across the lawn together, I can hear part of their conversation. Juliana: "See, I told you Papa would be helpful." Richenda: "But you mustn't tell Mother. She'd have my hide." Juliana: "Since when have I betrayed a confidence of yours?"

It warms my heart to see how hope for her future marriage has restored Richenda's spirits. I'm far less hopeful, however, about the situation in the kingdom where she's destined to be queen. Laurence's news, when we'd stopped by the port on the way home, was particularly worrisome. The Teutons continue to infiltrate the southeastern province of the Kingdom Across the Southern Sea, and Charles still makes no move to do anything about it. Equally alarming, the Aleffe loyalists have reduced their patrols in the area, seemingly content to let the Teutons take over the territory.

What kind of game is this? One of two parties or of three? Are the Teutons simply using the stalemate between Charles and the rebels to encroach on territory they've long wanted to claim? If not that, then which faction has allied with the Teutons? If it's Charles, why doesn't he simply mount a two-front attack against the rebels, crush them, and reclaim his kingdom? What's the point of this creeping encroachment? To draw the rebels' attention away from their strongholds? If so, it doesn't seem to be working.

If it's the Aleffe loyalists who're in league with the Teutons, what advantage do they gain from allowing a not-particularly-strategic province to be occupied by traditional enemies? Are they trying to draw Charles out? Hoping he'll attack a foreign intruder in a remote location so they can bring all their forces down on him from the north? If so, that doesn't seem to be working either.

And what sort of deal might either side have made with the Teutons? Whatever it might be, I can conceive of no way in which it bodes well for the future.

So far, trade and commerce have remained unimpeded while these players make their peculiar moves around their odd chess board. It seems inevitable the situation will change, but when? That prospect is a gloomy one for us, and I'm perplexed about how to prepare for it. To that end, I've been strengthening our alliance with the Far Nordic Kingdom. We need Brandr's influence on the Southern Nordics if we're forced to open up new trade routes for our goods. But even if we succeed in finding new routes, trade will be more costly. The journey is longer, with more time on the open sea, and the Southern Nordics will rightfully want a tariff for access to their port and their roads. Our merchants and traders, as always, will be disinclined to see their own profits diminished, so they'll pay less for what they buy and charge more for the finished goods they sell, putting the common man in a financial squeeze that will eventually ripple through all layers of society.

Do we make laws to restrict how much the commercial interests can pass on to the people? The Assembly will be united in its opposition to that. Do we raise taxes on the commercial interests so we can provide societal supports for the average man? I'm certain the Assembly would raise its voice against that as well. And, of course, they'd try to push any dent in their profits down onto their customers.

Or do we take up arms to intervene in a foreign conflict for the primary purpose of protecting our trade routes and our own self-interests? No doubt that's what the Assembly will urge, and mankind has been doing this from time immemorial.

I know a decision is looming, no matter how much I might prefer to temporize to see the next move in that strange game across the sea. So I've been spending half my waking hours reading history, looking for guidance, and the other half in deep discourse with the lords, with Laurence and Richard, and even with Abbot Warin. When the new year begins, the Council must take up the matter formally, and we must decide our path forward. I only hope that, by then, I'll have some better grasp of what I think that path should be.

The first week of Advent is normally a joyous time. When the enormous yule log is dragged in from the forest, it signals the beginning of so many festive pleasures. The evergreen garlands beginning to appear in the rooms of the castle, adding that special holiday fragrance. Warm spiced wine. Childhood memories of delicacies from the kitchen that we had at no other time of the year.

This year, our joy is to be tinged with sadness. Lord Meriden has died, suddenly and unexpectedly. The message from Lady Mary arrived only moments ago.

Your Grace,

It is with deep sadness that I must inform you of the death of my father. Two days ago, he suffered some sort of fit, after which he was in a terrible state. He could move neither his arm nor his leg on his left side, and the left side of his mouth drooped, causing him to drool uncontrollably. He was taken to his bed, where he slept deeply but fitfully for the next day and night. This morning, he awoke and seemed to rally, speaking a bit, though his words were quite slurred. Soon after, he experienced another fit, which took his life.

I've dried my tears for a moment to send this message to you and also a letter to my cousin informing him of these events. It will take more than a week for my messenger to reach the mountain principality that Hugo now calls home. But I've exhorted him to make haste in coming to take up his position and swear his loyalty to you as the next Lord Meriden.

I know, Sire, that your generous nature will lead you to suggest a funeral of state for my father. I trust that same generous nature will guide you to take no umbrage when I tell you that what my father wanted was a simple funeral mass in the parish church among the people of his estate, and I would like to honor that wish. We'll hold the service one week hence and lay him to rest alongside my mother in our family plot.

And now, I must see to our people, as we mourn his loss together, for I know they'll be uncertain of the future and will need my assurances.

Mary

My secretary has been waiting while I read. "Is the messenger who brought this still here, Coliar?" I ask him.

"Just outside, Sire."

"Bring him in, please." The young man shuffles in, cap in hand, head bowed, looking at his feet. "It's quite alright, my good man." I try to put him at ease, but it doesn't seem to have much effect. "How long have you been in getting here?"

"It be two days, Yer Grace. Her ladyship say make haste, so I ride as fast as can be 'thouten harm me horse."

"Thank you. Tell Lady Mary that the queen and I will be with her as quickly as we can make the journey. But there's no need to push your horse on the return . . . you'll easily arrive before our carriages."

We're fortunate in the weather, and our party arrives at the Meriden manor on the day before the funeral. Lady Mary seems genuinely touched by our coming. The parish church is overrun with people from the estate paying their final respects. One can see how well Meriden was loved by his people.

As we settle into the carriage for the return journey, Juliana remarks, "It's all so sad for Lady Mary, I think. In the blink of an eye, she loses her father and her status all at once."

"Sadly, it's the way of the world, my dear," says Gwen. "And Mary's not the only one who stands to lose. This is a very uncertain time for their people as well. Who knows what the new Lord Meriden will be like?"

Who knows indeed? It will be longer than is seemly before we find out.

This year, all the lords have chosen to keep Christmas at the castle and go to their estates for Twelfth Night. Gwen invited Mary to join us, and though she first refused, thinking it best to be with her people, she later changed her mind and has arrived three days before Christmas. "I didn't want it to be a sad Christmas, you see," she tells us when she and her husband dine with us that first night. "And everywhere I went in the house . . . every room . . . every corridor . . . I'd see something that he treasured . . . or just feel his presence . . . and missing him would start to close in on me."

"It's no wonder," Gwen tries to console her. "It was all so very sudden."

"We've neither seen nor heard from your cousin," I tell her. "Have you any news?"

"No more than you. I did tell him in my letter, Sire, that he should come straightaway. My messenger returned more than a week before we left, so I know Hugo received my letter. I was most disappointed that he didn't have the proper sense of protocol . . . or even courtesy . . . to send a written reply and a letter to you. I fear I'm becoming quite concerned about his behavior."

"I was inclined to put his initial lack of response down to the suddenness of events and surprise, but as time goes on without any news . . ." I let the thought hang in the air. "You should know that Lord Devereux shares your dismay."

"Be assured, Sire, when he does arrive, I'll do everything I can to instruct him in our customs and his expected behavior."

"And I won't hesitate to encourage him to listen carefully to your advice." I hope the new Lord Meriden will be wise enough to recognize how much Mary can help him.

"What do you know about Hugo?" Gwen asks her.

"When we were children, we played together often. They lived in the large family cottage on the estate, and since neither of us had siblings, we filled that role for each other. But my aunt's husband died when Hugo was about six or seven, and she chose to marry a wealthy landowner from an island in the Roman Sea. It seems she had some sort of romantic notion of an idyllic life of sun and sea air. Father often said he thought good sense in the Meriden women had completely skipped a generation and come in its entirety to me." Her eyes glisten with moisture at the mention of her father. Her husband gently touches her hand, and she regains her composure quickly.

"At any rate, they moved away when my aunt married. Father believed she was never really happy and that was why they never returned. When Hugo came of age, he married into the ruling family of the principality where he now lives, in the mountains south of Charles's kingdom. As I understand it, his wife will inherit when her father dies. So to answer your question, Gwendolyn, I can tell you everything about the six-year-old boy and absolutely nothing about the man."

The Christmas celebrations are among the most festive I ever remember. Mother Nature graces us with a gentle snow throughout the night on Christmas Eve, so we wake on Christmas morn to a magical world covered in white with the sun shining in a blue sky.

When the lords depart, Laurence and his family remain with us, planning to stay through Twelfth Night. His news of events in the Kingdom Across the Southern Sea takes a bit of the edge off my Christmas euphoria. "I'm worried, Alfred," he tells Samuel and me on one of our morning rides. "There are no more patrols going into the southeast province. And it seems people are leaving there if they have anywhere at all to go. A couple of my agents managed to get some of the Teutons drunk enough to loosen their tongues. If they're to be believed, the plan is to use the southeast province as a base to move on the castle town and effectively split the kingdom."

"It's a big risk," says Samuel, "leaving yourself vulnerable on two sides. Maybe they're calculating they can create enough of a wedge before anyone wakes up to what they're doing. Certainly Charles's inactivity and the absence of the patrols might embolden them."

"And all we have so far," Laurence reminds us, "is the word of two or three drunks who might be making it all up to impress their drinking mates. I'd really like to get my hands on that Teuton who keeps showing up with new arrivals. By the way, there's a rumor he was seen in the port a couple of weeks ago, but we haven't been able to confirm it yet."

Twelfth Night comes and goes and there's still no sign of the new Lord Meriden. It's nearing the end of January when he finally appears. Lord Devereux takes him in hand immediately, chastising him severely, so I'm told, for his behavior so far and preparing him to give his oath of loyalty. The court assembles two days later for the formal ceremony.

As he enters the reception room and proceeds toward the throne, I have time for a modicum of observation. He's of medium height, neither fair nor dark, and starting to develop a bit of a paunch. He walks with a mild swagger, which, I'm guessing, he thinks makes him look either important or attractive to women . . . or both. He performs a very formal court bow, then drops to one knee and recites the pledge flawlessly. I can't discern whether he's truly offering his loyalty or if he's simply mouthing the words.

"Rise, Lord Meriden," I tell him. "We've been at pains to understand your delay in coming to take up your position and the utter lack of any insight as to when to expect you."

"Your Grace will forgive me, I'm sure . . ."

I don't fail to note the swagger manifesting itself in his words.

". . . but as Christmas is an important holiday in my family, I thought it best to spend it with them."

"Is writing letters during the Christmas season forbidden in your family, sir?"

"Why . . . uh . . . no, Sire . . . I just . . . well, the time just passed too quickly, Sire."

Devereux speaks up. "I believe what Lord Meriden is attempting, Your Grace, is a rather botched apology for his failure to observe the courtesies."

The reprimand is not lost on Hugo. "Indeed, Your Grace, I have been remiss in my attention to the details and request your pardon."

"Very well. I'm sure you'll see to your duties and responsibilities properly henceforth." I introduce him to Gwen and to Geoffrey. "Lord Devereux, you've met already. As first lord of the realm, he'll introduce you to your peers and be your guide and mentor in what's expected of you." I beckon to Mary. "And I'm sure you'll remember Lady Mary from your childhood days together. She's expert in all matters related to the running of the Meriden domain. You'll do well to learn from her.

"For the moment, I think it best that you proceed to your manor and establish yourself there. Once you're settled and have the running of the estate in hand, I'll have an additional assignment for you. Whether that's to be a member of the Council or some other role, I've yet to decide. By the way, when will your family be joining you?"

"That also has yet to be decided, Sire."

"Do keep us informed of their plans. We're eager to welcome them to court." And with that, I rise, signaling the end of the interview, and all bow as Gwen, Geoffrey, and I exit into the private reception room.

Once the door is safely closed behind us, I remove my coronet and say, "I certainly hope that man is going to have more to recommend him than what I saw here today."

"He did seem a bit full of himself, didn't he?" Gwen replies. "Until Devereux put him in his place. I must admit, I'm rather worried for Mary. I'm not sure how well he'll take to learning things from her."

"What did *you* think, Geoffrey?" I ask. It's not too early for him to start thinking about how to assess people's behavior.

"I didn't like him, Papa. I know we really don't know him yet, and I know he'll be different from the late Lord Meriden. But he just seemed like he didn't know how to be a lord."

"Let's hope he can learn, Son. I'm also perplexed about that business with his family."

"Perhaps Mary can get to the bottom of that," Gwen offers.

My impressions aren't improved by Hugo's behavior tonight at the court dinner. He's just a bit too hail-fellow-well-met and too quick to empty and refill his wine glass. For now, I put this down to the nervousness of being a lord in this court for the first time, but he may bear watching, especially as his attention to the ladies grows more assertive with each glass.

The next day's evening meal is far more pleasant as Juliana regales us with the plans for her visit to the Kingdom of Peaks. She departs a few days hence. "So am I to make space for Primrose in my bed again?" I ask.

Juliana laughs. "No, Papa, not this time. Though I'm grateful for the offer."

"I'm not sure it was an offer."

"Well, I'm grateful for your helping out last time, then."

I perform my best imitation of being mollified.

"Actually, she's going with me. The King of Peaks was quite taken with her, so I thought he might like to see her again. Even though she's growing old, I think she can manage the carriage ride far better than the ocean voyages. And we'll be breaking our journey for a day in Abbéville Market."

"Oh?" asks Gwen.

"Yes, Mama. You see, I've written to Madam Greslet about spending some time with her."

I stop mid-stride, as it were, a spoonful of soup halfway to my mouth, hoping my jaw hasn't dropped and calling on all my self-control to keep the astonishment from my face. "I want to learn how she manages to be so successful among the men there," Juliana continues without missing a beat, so perhaps I've succeeded. "And I've just had a letter from her today accepting my invitation. I'm to send word by the innkeeper when we arrive and meet her at her shop midmorning of the following day."

Regaining my composure, I ask her, "Aren't you learning from your mother how to succeed among men?"

"Of course I am, Papa. But I should think you, of all people, would agree it's best to learn from as many people as possible. Besides, Madam Greslet operates in an entirely different world from Mama."

"Well, you're right about that, my dear. Please give the lady in question our greetings and our anticipation that she'll once again grace our court with her presence at an Assembly meeting." Did that sound too formal? I'm still unnerved by the notion of my daughter and my paramour becoming friends.

"Papa?" Alicia has a small frown on her face, the expression she adopts when she's in deep thought about something.

"Yes, Alicia?"

"If you need someone to sleep with, I think maybe I could let Dog sleep with you sometimes."

Much to Juliana's dismay, my youngest daughter insists on calling her furry companion Dog. "She should have a proper name," Juliana had tried to instruct her little sister. "Dog is just what she is . . . it's as if you were called Girl." Alicia had thought for a minute and then asked, "Does she know she's a dog?" to which Juliana could summon up nothing better than, "I don't know." Alicia then folded her little arms across her chest and nodded her head decisively. "Well, I know I'm a girl, and that's why I need a different name. But if Dog doesn't know she's a dog, then she doesn't know it's not a good name." Juliana had no choice but to accept defeat.

I reach out and take Alicia's hand, bringing it to my lips as if she were a full-grown lady. "What a generous offer, my dear! But I think perhaps since Dog loves sleeping with you so much, it might be well not to deprive her of that pleasure."

Alicia glows. A combination, no doubt, of delight at being treated as a lady and relief at not having to share her nighttime companion, though I rather suspect more of the latter than the former.

Three weeks later, Jasper is explaining his port defense plan to the Council. "We'll deploy the cannons here," he points on a map, "where the river narrows to limit passage to one – at most two ships at a time. It's why that spot was chosen for the location of the chains, and the tactical reasons haven't changed." Heads nod around the table.

"There'll have to be a battery on both sides of the river. It's unlikely that large ships would attempt the passage two abreast. But I can imagine a fleet commander testing our defenses by sending two smaller ships running almost side-by-side before committing his main force. We can't risk letting one of those slip by on the off-side."

"So what's to prevent an enemy from offloading men in the estuary, before they get to the batteries?" asks Guyat.

"Nothing more, nothing less than when we depended on the chains," replies Jasper. "That tactical position doesn't change much . . . for us or for the invader. The marshes are still our best defense on the east bank. We'll still have to deploy a deterrent force on the west. But if we can make landings as difficult and unsurvivable as possible, we can effectively drive an enemy into the maw of our batteries."

He goes on to explain how the cannons will be positioned and how the first target will be to strike ships at the waterline so they take on water. That would be followed by an assault on the sides and the rigging, to disrupt efforts to deal with the crisis below. "In the case of ships in single file," Jasper continues, "the two batteries give us the option to attack the waterline and the upper portions simultaneously."

The discussion continues, with Phillip looking increasingly puzzled. Taking advantage of a brief gap in the conversation, I ask, "What's troubling you, Thorssen?"

"I'm no seaman, gentlemen, and certainly no expert with these new weapons. But it seems to me that, as the tide comes in, the water level will get higher, and the elevation of a ship relative to the river bank will change by a foot or more. Won't you have to change your firing angle to accommodate the rising tide?"

"A keen observation, Lord Thorssen," says Jasper. "In this respect, firing a cannon is no different from shooting arrows at a target. We've devised a workable mechanism to easily raise and lower the front of the cannon. Eventually, we'll need to commandeer an old ship to determine exactly what to expect from the tides. I'd rather not be figuring that out with the first Teuton ship trying to make its way upriver." This earns him a round of nervous laughter from the room.

As the questions and conversation seem to be wrapping up, Lord Devereux asks, "Well, gentlemen, is there anyone among us who thinks we have a choice but to proceed with Sir Jasper's plan?"

Richard speaks up. "I don't see that we have a choice, gentlemen, but I have a grave concern. What effect is all this going to have on trade? When we relied on the chains, our defenses were out of sight when not in use. There's no way these batteries can be out of sight. Will they deter the captains of the trading vessels from visiting our port at all? If so, are we then faced with the necessity to greatly expand our own trading fleet? Does lack of choice in the matter of defense force us into lack of choice in the manner of how we trade?"

"That, Lord Richard," says Jasper, "is the one question for which we haven't been able to devise an answer."

"And the solution," says Rupert, "lands squarely in the lap of Lord Laurence."

"Well, at least I finally know why I was invited here today," says Laurence, which earns him a round of uproarious laughter as the tension in the room breaks.

"It won't be an easy task," Rupert again, "but no one knows those ship captains better than your people, Laurence. We just need to figure out how to use whatever trust has been built between them to dampen the fears that are bound to arise."

"Remember," says Samuel, "it will take time to build the batteries, so some captains may actually see the building in progress."

"I wonder what they're seeing in other ports." I'm thinking out loud. "What about that Nordic captain who brought Julianna home, Laurence? He might have seen what's happening in the Teuton or Southern Nordic ports. Do you think we could get word to him somehow?"

"Better than that, Sire," Laurence replies. "He's wintering over with us. Said that by the time he could get back home, their harbor would be frozen over and likely the straits leading to it as well."

"I'll bet that's making for some rowdy evenings, what with all those sailors in port and nothing to do," Phillip remarks.

"Quite the contrary," says Laurence. "This captain maintains discipline. Has his crew working much of the time . . . says winter repairs have to be done, no matter what port you're in. He posts a watch day and night, just as if they were at sea, so there's never a time when the whole crew has liberty. But he's fair . . . all the men get plenty of spare time . . . just not enough to cause trouble."

I hold up my hand to interrupt him and turn to my secretary. "Coliar, see that we send some food from the castle stores to that ship captain. Enough for the entire crew . . . and for more than one meal. Something better than what they're getting regularly in the taverns. Lord Laurence can help you sort it out." Then, turning back to the meeting, "I'm sure Brandr's paying them, but we should see that they can get whatever they need while they're our guests." Brandr seems to have designated this captain as his trusted conduit between us, and I want to send a clear signal that I respect and value the arrangement.

"Already done, Sire," Laurence replies. "I waived their docking fees after the first two weeks, once we realized they wouldn't be able to go home. They seem to have sufficient funds for food and supplies, but I'll keep an eye on things. And I'll talk with him about defenses in other ports."

"Don't get too specific about our own plans," I tell him, "but you can certainly sketch out the basics and get his reaction. Brandr trusts this man, and I think we can too."

"So, then," Devereux returns to the process of getting a formal decision, "what say we, gentlemen? Do we authorize Sir Jasper to proceed?" Nods and "ayes" all around the table, so he calls for a formal vote. We've agreed in advance that this is such an enormous step, it requires the gravity of a proper and properly recorded Council decision, both for us here and now and for those who follow us to understand. As Devereux goes around the table, calling on each man in turn, there's a great sense of solemnity in the room as we start down a path from which there can be no return.

Letty is waiting for me in the corridor when I leave the Council chamber. She drops a quick curtsey as she says, "Please, m'lord, m'lady say can you come to her sitting room straightaway."

"Do you know what she wants, Letty?"

She falls in step with me, to the left and ever so slightly behind. "I canna' say, sir. I just know Lady Mary be with her for nigh on an hour afore she ask me to fetch you."

"And how long have you been waiting?"

"Not so very long, sir." From Letty, this could mean she'd just arrived or she'd been there a half-hour or longer. So not an emergency, else Gwen would have come herself and interrupted the Council meeting. "But she did look ever so serious, and she did say straightaway, sir." Not an emergency, apparently, but of some urgency nevertheless.

"Then we'd best go find out." I quicken my pace.

From the moment I walk through the door, I can tell the mood is somber. Gwen gestures for me to take the chair next to her, facing Lady Mary, who hasn't risen to curtsey. Mary would never breach protocol on her own, so Gwen must have given her permission in advance. Though she doesn't look up, it's obvious Mary's been crying – something else that's completely out of character for the late Lord Meriden's strong-minded daughter.

"Thank goodness the Council meeting finished early." Gwen touches my hand briefly. "This needs your attention, Alfred." Then looking directly at Mary she says, ever so gently, "Tell Alfred what you've told me."

Mary doesn't look up, just continues to stare at her hands in her lap. "Perhaps you should tell him, My Lady."

Gwen reaches across and places a comforting hand on Mary's forearm. "He really needs to hear it from you, my dear. You were the one who was there. And it in no way reflects poorly on you."

Mary looks up. "If only that were true, My Lady. But the fact that I couldn't stop it . . ."

Something must have gone wrong on the Meriden estate . . . something Mary believes she should have been able to prevent. "What was it you were unable to stop, Mary?" I ask. "It must have been quite serious indeed if you felt the need to bring it to us."

"That may have been a mistake, Sire, but the queen doesn't seem to think so."

"Then tell me from the beginning. Take your time. There's nowhere else I need to be."

Almost as if she were putting on armor to do battle, Mary gathers her courage by raising her head and straightening her posture. Then, looking directly at me, she begins. "It happened just over a week ago, Sire. It was supposed to be a joyous time. The children of two of our most loyal tenants were to be wed. On such occasions, my father had always held a small celebration dinner for the couple and their families on the night before the ceremony; and I encouraged Hugo to continue the tradition. A bit to my surprise, he didn't hesitate.

"It all went splendidly until it was time for them to take their leave. As everyone was saying their final thank-yous at the front door, Hugo sidled up to the bride, put his arm around her shoulder, and said, 'And now, my dear, it's time for you to come with me.'

"For a moment, no one realized what was happening as Hugo turned the girl around and started walking her toward the stairway. I think it dawned on me first that he intended to have his way with her on the eve of her wedding. By the time I'd grasped the idea and gotten my wits about me, her betrothed had come to the same conclusion and started to run after them. Hugo had carefully planned this, because two servants blocked the bridegroom's path as Hugo hustled the bride up the stairs.

"By now both the bride's father and the bridegroom were screaming after Hugo that he couldn't do this . . . screaming for him to let the girl go . . . and the servants were physically restraining both of them. I put my husband in charge of the mayhem and hurried after Hugo.

"By the time I caught up with them, they were near the door to Hugo's bedchamber. I shouted at him to stop, and he turned to face me. I told him, Sire, that this wasn't done in this kingdom . . . tried to reason with him that, even if it was the practice where he came from, he needed to understand it wasn't our practice here. I approached them and reached out to take the girl's hand.

"At that point, he opened the door, shoved the girl inside, and slammed the door behind her. Then he turned on me with what I can only describe as menace. 'I am lord of this manor and this estate,' he said angrily, 'and I'll have no woman telling me what to do. Now be on your way and don't bother me again tonight.'

"I kept pleading with him, Sire, kept trying to reason with him. All the while, I was trying to get past him to open the door. I thought if I couldn't get the girl out, at least I could get inside, and he might not do anything to her in my presence. It was all for naught. He shouted for servants and had me physically dragged away over my loud protests. My husband heard the commotion and arrived about that time. Hugo ordered the servants to force us into our bedchamber and to stand guard the rest of the night. We were not to leave the room before dawn."

I don't need a mirror to know that the expression on my face is grim. Anger and disgust are vying for priority in my mind. "Go on," I encourage her gently.

"The servants found her in the corridor the following morning, lying on the floor whimpering, her dress torn and barely covering her. They brought her to me. My maid and I bathed her and tucked her into my bed while my husband sent for her mother. She wouldn't speak to us at all. It was no better with her mother. She turned away in shame and wouldn't respond even to her mother's attempts to console her. Her mother finally gave up and left in tears.

"She wouldn't eat or drink and refused to talk. From time to time, she'd whimper softly and tears would stream down her cheeks. Talk in the servants' hall was that Hugo had forced himself on her at least three times during the night and made her do things she would never have been told about by her mother. After the second day, I decided she'd never recover in the place where these awful things had happened to her, no matter how kind we were. So I took her to the convent where she could be cared for. They'll do their best, I know, but Sister Madeleine cautioned me not to expect too much. And then I came here."

"What about the families?" I ask.

"Hugo's ruined that too. The bridegroom's father won't return the dowry. He claims it was no fault of his son's that the marriage didn't take place. And the bride's family can ill-afford the loss of such money for no purpose. They have another daughter to provide for, though they're now talking of having her take the veil rather than be subject to Hugo's rapacious appetites. Needless to say, the families are totally on the outs, despite the fact that they had long been good friends."

"You were right to come to us, Mary. Such behavior can't go unchallenged, and I assure you your cousin will be dealt with. Can you be ready to travel with me tomorrow?"

"Of course, Sire, if that's what you wish."

"What I want, Mary, is for you to see how I deal with Hugo. And, perhaps more importantly, I want him to see that you do. I'll give him no opportunity to pull the wool over your eyes about what expectations are set for him."

"Very well, Sire. I'll be ready. The sooner this is dealt with, the better."

"We'd invite you to dine with us privately this evening, my dear," says Gwen, "but as you know, it's a night for court dinner. I'd like it very much if you'd join us."

"If it's all the same to you, My Lady, I'd prefer to take supper in my room. If I join the court, people will ask why I'm here, and I couldn't bear to tell that story again. More than that, I don't want the dishonor to the Meriden name to become part of court gossip."

"I'll have to tell Lord Devereux," I point out. "As first lord, he must know. And I may want to have his counsel on my plan. But rest assured, that will be done in private."

"Thank you for that, Sire." As I rise to take my leave, Mary stands and curtseys, a sign that unburdening herself and knowing something will be done are already beginning to restore her spirit.

As I relate the story to Devereux and Richard later, over brandy in my private reception room, I watch the frowns cloud both their faces. "That's *despicable!*" Richard reacts. "Men treat whores better than that."

"You must, of course, summon him here at once," says Lord Devereux. "He must answer to you and to me."

"I've not ruled that out, but hear me out and tell me what you think. If I summon him here, he can put about any plausible reason for going to court and his people may never know that I'm even aware of his behavior, much less that I've reprimanded him for it. His people deserve to know I'm putting a stop to such things once and for all. It means he won't have to answer to you, sir, but I rather suspect this is just the beginning of the problems we're going to have with Hugo, so I'd like to save something in reserve for the next offense."

Devereux chuckles.

"What's so funny, sir?"

"It's just amusing that you can't bring yourself to call him Lord Meriden. I've suffered from the same problem. His initial boorishness was barely forgivable, but this . . ." He grimaces and shakes his head in disgust.

"What are you planning to do?" asks Richard, so I tell them. They both agree it's a good plan, though Richard has one reservation. "Are you sure it's wise, Alfred, to have Lady Mary present? Won't that be putting her at risk of some form of retribution from Hugo?"

"It's a consideration, I agree. But on balance, there'll be no doubt when I make my appearance as to who's brought the matter to my attention. My thought was that if Hugo knows she's heard all I say to him, he can't misrepresent it later. But if you think the risk is too great . . ."

"With a man who'll behave like that, who *knows* what to think," Richard replies. "Go with your instincts, Alfred. They're usually right."

"It's your discretion, sir," I turn my attention back to Lord Devereux, "as to when and how to inform the lords. Lady Mary is terribly distressed about the dishonor to her family name and her father's legacy, so I assured her we'd try to avoid this becoming court gossip."

"Quite right, Alfred," he says. "I'll speak with Mary myself in the morning, before you depart. And Alfred?"

"Yes?"

"Don't leave Hugo in any doubt as to the seriousness of his transgression."

Three days later, we arrive in the courtyard of the Meriden manor house in early afternoon to a flurry of activity and scurrying about, occasioned, no doubt, by someone having spotted my banner as we approached. The steward is on the front landing yelling at an underling to go find Hugo. "I don't care where he is or what he may be doing, man, find him and tell him to make haste to receive the king!"

I dismount and offer Mary my arm to step down from her carriage and ascend the front steps. The steward bows deeply. "Your Grace, my lady. Your Grace, if we had known you were coming, I assure you all would have been in readiness for your arrival."

"There's no need to fret, Enos," Mary assures him. "A messenger would have arrived barely ahead of us, so there seemed little point. And I'll be quite happy to entertain the king until his lordship's return."

"As you say, my lady."

"I think the same rooms for the king that he used when last he was here."

"Already being prepared, my lady."

"Osbert can see to the horses and then help you to unpack the king's things. His Grace and I will be in the sitting room awaiting Lord Hugo."

"Aye, ma'am." The steward bows to me, to his mistress, then to me again, still rather flustered by our unannounced arrival. I follow Mary down the corridor to the sitting room. During the hour it takes for Hugo to put in an appearance, we reminisce about her father and about my visit here during my progress as the new king. "He was enormously proud of you, my dear," I tell her. "The great sadness of his life, I think, was that he couldn't leave the estate to you. That's something I think we must start trying to find a way to change."

"It wasn't meant to be for me, Sire, but Father would have been pleased to hear your words."

Pounding bootsteps in the corridor alert us to Hugo's imminent arrival, and we both rise to our feet. Hugo bursts through the door, bows briefly, and then extends his arms expansively. "Your Grace, had I but known, I would most assuredly have been here to receive you. As it was, I was in the forest with my warden, so I hope you'll forgive my tardiness. We're really all so honored . . ."

"I'm sure you are. Though I'm less sure you'll be so pleased at the reason for my visit. I understand there's been an incident involving two of your young tenants who were to be married."

Still in his expansive manner, Hugo crosses to the large chair near the fireplace, seats himself, and with a dismissive wave of the hand, says, "*Droit du seigneur . . .* nothing more."

"Manners, Hugo," Mary chastises her cousin vehemently. "Don't you see the king is still standing?"

Hugo slowly rises to his feet as I turn to look out the window into the garden. This is as bad as I'd feared if he can be flippant about his actions. I hope my turned back is making him uncomfortable.

"Hugo," Mary hisses. I can imagine her gesturing to him that he should be offering me the best chair. Little does he know there'll be no sitting this afternoon.

"Shut up, woman," Hugo hisses back.

There's my cue. I round on him in controlled anger. "Tell me, Lord Meriden, that you did not say what I thought I just heard."

"About the lord's right? Really, Sire, that's all it was." It hasn't registered with him yet just how much he has to answer for.

"That practice was abolished in this kingdom over a century ago and has been proscribed ever since."

"How was I to know, Sire?"

"It's your responsibility as a lord of this realm to know our customs."

The obvious anger in my tone seems to be slowly getting through to him. "I've not been here long. How could I be expected to know all your customs?"

I've no intention of letting him plead ignorance in the matter. "It's your *duty* to find out. What's more, I believe Lady Mary herself told you in no uncertain terms that your behavior was unacceptable and that she tried valiantly to prevent you from dishonoring yourself."

"Why should I take the word of a woman? Especially one who was trying to interfere with me."

"Lady Mary knows more about running this estate than anyone here. Your predecessor trusted its management to her whenever he was away. She is in large part responsible for the prosperity of what you've inherited, and she knows our customs well. If you recall, I told you on the day I accepted your pledge that you would do well to seek her advice and counsel."

He's beginning to understand my anger. "Very well, Sire. It won't happen again."

"That's not enough, Meriden. I'll have your word of honor right now . . . this very moment . . . that you will never engage in this *despicable* behavior ever again so long as you live in this kingdom."

"Very well, you have my word." His tone is still rather off-handed, as if he's agreeing to something he may later choose to ignore.

"Not so fast. On your knee. A proper pledge of honor to your king."

He looks around, as if there might be someone in the room who would rise to his defense. Finally, he drops to one knee and bows his head. "On my honor, Your Grace, I pledge never again to exercise the lord's right in your kingdom."

I leave him there for a long moment, in the hope that the import of the words he's just spoken might sink in. Finally, I release him. "Very well. I accept your word." He rises to his feet. "Now we're going to talk about the restitution you're going to make for your actions." I've dropped the anger from my voice, but my tone is still stern.

"You will send word to both families to present themselves here tomorrow morning at my request. Here in this room, in my presence, you will formally apologize to both families for your behavior and for what it's cost them."

"Surely Your Grace doesn't really mean for the lord to apologize to his tenants," he pleads.

"Surely you were not listening if you didn't understand that I intend precisely that."

"But, Sire, I meant no real harm."

"Can you not see the real harm here?" I add the anger back to my tone. "You've destroyed the future of two young people, defiled and spoiled a young woman, and driven a wedge between two of your most loyal tenants. You *will* apologize. And you'll make a *sincere* apology."

I return to the merely stern tone. "I understand the bridegroom's family has kept the bride's dowry. You'll pay the bride's family twice the amount of the dowry as compensation for your actions."

"Twice, Your Grace?" He sounds incredulous.

"Is something wrong with your ears, Meriden? You will pay the bride's family twice the amount of the dowry. One measure is to return to them what they lost in the ruination of their daughter's marriage. The other is to give them the means to visit the convent to help with the girl's recovery."

"But, Sire, surely . . ." He continues to protest.

"*Enough*, Meriden! Keep this up and I'll happily make the compensation *three* times the original dowry."

"Yes, Your Grace." Finally he seems, if not penitent, at least acquiescent.

"Now, in addition to the compensation to the bride's family, you will make an immediate donation to the convent for the girl's care. And you will continue to make such donations regularly for however long the girl remains with the nuns."

"Yes, Your Grace."

"Your gift must be sufficient for all the girl's needs . . . clothing, food, any medicines she may require. And it would be honorable for a man of your means to also include something for the convent itself, to help sustain the good work they do." He makes a slight bow of the head. "Don't think for a moment, Meriden, that you can get away with sending just a few plain coins. Sister Madeleine is among the queen's confidantes, so we will know if you fail in this obligation.

"Finally . . ." Hugo barely restrains himself from rolling his eyes at the notion that there's more to come. I choose to ignore it. "I've charged Lady Mary with restoring goodwill with these tenants and between the two families."

This pushes him over the edge once again. "Truly, Sire, am *I* not lord of this domain? Do I not have authority over what and how things are done within the bounds of my estate?"

"You are indeed lord of this estate. And as such, you have a responsibility for the welfare of your people. You also have a duty to observe and uphold all the customs of this kingdom and an obligation to your fellow lords to act honorably and for the good of the kingdom as a whole. Your actions broke that trust." I pause to let him take this in. "But it can be mended. And there is nothing dishonorable about relying on Lady Mary's willingness to help in the mending. My final charge to you is that you do nothing to impede her efforts."

Time to assume a more normal tone. "Now, if we're finished, I'd like to refresh from travel before the evening meal. But none of us are leaving this room until I have your assurance, Lord Meriden, that you will follow through on these commitments."

"You have my word, Sire." For the first time all afternoon, it seems to have sunk in that his only path forward is to submit to the consequences of his actions.

"Good. I look forward to more pleasant conversation over the evening meal. Lady Mary, will you be kind enough to show me to my room?" A perfect reason not to leave her alone with what will most certainly be a brooding Hugo.

She drops a curtsey and replies, "Of course, Your Grace. If you'll just come with me." To his credit, Hugo offers a proper bow.

Approaching the door, we hear footsteps scurrying down the corridor. Servants eavesdropping, no doubt. Not necessarily a bad thing. Those who were part of Hugo's misadventure will count themselves lucky not to have been called to task by the king. And Mary and Enos will ensure that the gossip stays controlled and doesn't lead to complete disrespect for Hugo's position.

The feast that Enos manages to assemble on such short notice is rather remarkable. Two meats, some fish, root vegetables, pickles, a variety of sauces, three kinds of fresh bread, fruit jams, cheeses, and excellent wine. When I compliment him, he's gracious and self-effacing. "'Tis not at all a royal banquet, Your Grace, but we try to make his lordship's table pleasing for our guests."

Hugo is quite subdued. I turn the conversation to matters of the estate and family in an effort to restore some sense of normalcy. "I'm surprised to see your family hasn't yet arrived."

"It's not an opportune time, Sire."

"In what way?"

"In my homeland . . ." he begins.

"Is this not your homeland now?"

"In my wife's homeland, then, the women are allowed to inherit. My wife will become the ruler when her father dies. But there is a very strict provision that if the heir is not in residence when the ruler dies, that person is passed over and rule goes to the next in line. So my wife feels the burden to remain in the land of her birth."

"Is her father in imminent danger of dying? Is he ill?"

"Not at present, Sire, but he is old. And you know how things are with old people."

"Then perhaps she might come briefly . . . make herself known as the new lady of the manor . . . bring your son. She could then return to secure her inheritance."

"She's reluctant to have her son away until the inheritance is settled."

"Surely you must want your son to take up his schooling here and to make friends among those who'll one day be his fellow lords."

"I will consider it, Your Grace. I'll write to her."

We speak of his progress in learning the ins and outs of his new estate. He's far more casual on this topic, implying at one point that he has little more responsibility than to ensure the tenancies are filled and the rents collected. Though she says nothing, I can see the consternation in Mary's demeanor, so I remind Hugo of his great advantage in having someone of his cousin's competence to assist him.

"In the coming weeks, Meriden, I'll begin to consider what role you should play in governing our land. Have you given any thought to what you might like to do?"

"None, Sire," he replies. "I assumed you would assign something to me."

"Ultimately, that will be the case. But I'd be interested in knowing where your inclinations lie." And thus, I think to myself, try to take a better measure of your motivations.

"Then I'll give it some thought."

"And I'll take my leave of you and retire for the night. I'm more weary from travel than I'd imagined, and this excellent meal has filled my belly and made sleep seem a most enticing prospect."

"Allow me to escort you to your rooms," says Mary's husband. Once we're out of earshot, he picks up the conversation. "Mary told me everything you did today. I'm grateful, Sire. Not just for setting Hugo straight, but for giving Mary back her spirit and showing Hugo a path to allow her to continue in an important role."

"Not at all, my friend. It was the right thing to do. And I'm a great admirer of your wife."

"She's a most extraordinary woman. The great sadness of my life is that we were never able to produce children to preserve her legacy."

"We all have our burdens to bear. Mine was my brother. I only hope Hugo is not going to take his place," I chuckle.

He laughs quietly. "We'll do our best to prevent that, Sire. Now, your room is just down this corridor . . . second door on the right. I'll bid you goodnight and return to my wife."

Osbert is waiting when I walk through the door. "I be thinking ye be coming up early, m'lord."

"It's been a long day, Osbert. One I hope never requires repeating."

He keeps up the conversation as he helps me out of my boots. "The word in the servants' hall be that ye give Lord Hugo a right talking to."

"No less than he deserved, Osbert."

"That be what the servants think too. 'Tweren't right, what he did to that girl."

"Well, tomorrow morning, he's going to make amends. Let's hope he's learned his lesson today."

"Aye, m'lord."

As I pull my nightshirt over my head, something occurs to me. "What else do the servants say about Lord Hugo, Osbert?"

"They say he be not so serious-minded as the late lord. More like he be playing at being a lord."

"Well, perhaps we should give him a bit more time. He wasn't raised from boyhood to this role." But he's lived all his adult life in the ruling family of his wife's homeland. Surely he's had some preparation for becoming the ruler's consort. I'm not entirely sure what to make of this other than that Hugo bears watching for the foreseeable future.

"We be leaving fer home tomorrow, m'lord?"

"Aye, Osbert. Just as soon as the meeting with the families is finished. There's no cause for staying longer, and doing so would just diminish the impact of my reprimand."

"Then I be having Altair ready and waiting fer ye." And with that, he's gone, leaving me to the comfort of a soft bed and Mary's finest linens. There are distinct advantages to being the king.

The following morning, Hugo plays his role perfectly. So perfectly, in fact, that it's difficult to tell whether he's truly remorseful or just performing for my benefit. The families accept his declaration of regret at face value, which is the most important thing in the moment. It all threatens to fall apart, though, when Hugo tells the bride's family of the compensation they're to receive. "That not be fair," the bridegroom's father interrupts. "Why they be getting money and not us?"

Since this plan is of my devising, I step in to avoid the possibility of Hugo's mucking things up. "I'm told, my good man, that you decided to keep the dowry?"

"Aye, Yer Grace. As were my right."

"As was indeed your right," I affirm. "So you've already received compensation for the collapse of your son's planned marriage. Isn't that right?"

"I suppose it be. But they be getting twice as much. I ask Yer Grace . . . be that fair?"

"Would you agree that it's fair for them to get the amount of the dowry?"

"I suppose it be."

"So then it's the extra money that's in question. Consider this, my good man. Your son was not actually harmed in the incident."

"He not get his bride, Yer Grace. He be right upset by that."

"I've no doubt he was saddened that the marriage didn't occur, and it may take some time for him to recover from that sadness. But he suffered no physical harm, and in time, he can easily find a young woman to wed who will make him happy and give him children.

"On the other hand, this family's daughter suffered great harm to her person . . . so much harm that the nuns don't yet know if she will recover. For her family to see her and help tend to her needs, they must travel . . . and travel requires money. And if she does recover, would you still want your son to take her to wife? Would other men shun her as well? Even if she comes home to her family, it may be that her parents have the burden of taking care of her for the rest of her life. Surely that's the greater harm and is worthy of some additional recompense. Wouldn't you agree, good sir?"

The belligerence fades from his manner and his tone. "I suppose it be, Yer Grace. I dinna' think on it that way."

Disaster averted, I let Hugo resume with the proceedings. I wonder if he learned anything from my exchange with his tenant?

When the families have been shown out, I prepare to take my leave as well. "Well done, Lord Meriden. I trust there's no need for me to remind you of the rest of your commitments." Carrot and a light touch of the stick.

"None, Sire."

"And you will write to me with your thoughts on what role might interest you."

"Aye, Your Grace."

"Then I'll be on my way. Lady Mary, perhaps you'll accompany me to my horse."

"With pleasure, Your Grace."

We don't speak until we're outside the house. "I don't know how to thank you, Sire," she says.

"It's I who should thank you for safeguarding the honor of your family and of the kingdom. I'm hopeful we've put this sort of thing behind us."

"As am I, Sire. I can't predict whether anything else you said will influence him, but I'll pray that it does."

"Keep yourself safe and happy, Mary. And know that you and your husband are always welcome at court should things become too difficult here."

When I mount Altair and take up his reins, she waves farewell. "Thank you for that, Sire. And safe journey."

As the guards fall in around me and we ride away, I think back on last night's conversation with Osbert. What if this man has no more skill or aptitude for being a lord than pretense? It may be well to get him to court soon so we can all find out.

It's early afternoon when we dismount in the inner courtyard and I turn Altair over to Elvin's head groom. Uncharacteristically, Coliar is hurrying down the corridor to meet me as I approach the royal apartments.

"Welcome home, Your Grace. An ambassador has arrived, Sire, from King Charles. He's been here two days already and is requesting an audience with you as soon as may be."

"Do you know what he wants?"

"He'll say no more than that it's of utmost importance that he speak with you."

"Then I'll receive him tomorrow."

"With respect, Sire, he's terribly anxious for an audience."

"And I'm anxious to shed the grime of travel and learn what's been happening here while I was away."

By now, we're crossing the public reception room. "Of course, Your Grace." He assumes a penitent posture and tone of voice.

Once we're inside the private reception room with the door closed, I stop and turn to him. "I'm not angry with you, Coliar. It's just that I recall Lord Peveril says that patience is a virtue much to be desired in a diplomat. It won't hurt this man to practice his own for another day."

"As you say, Sire." Coliar's manner is once again that of relaxed efficiency that marks our usual dealings.

"Tell him I'll receive him in open court just after the midday meal. That should be enough to stop him pestering you until then."

"Indeed it should, Sire." He opens the door for me to pass into the bedchamber.

"And, Coliar, make sure the word is spread among the court. I'd like the lords to hear firsthand what it is that Charles wants."

"I think you needn't concern yourself on that score, Sire. There's been talk of little else since the ambassador first arrived."

Osbert is waiting in my dressing room with bathwater steaming in the tub. "I've never understood how you manage this, Osbert. We arrive at the same time, yet the bath is hot and ready by the time I greet a few people and make my way here."

"Well, it be like this, m'lord. I give a kitchen boy a coin afore we leave so he haul the water up and put it on the fire as soon as we be back."

"That still doesn't seem like enough time."

"So the kitchen boy, he bribe the sentries with meat pies and sweet cakes to tell him the very instant yer banner be spotted on the road."

"That's still a lot of water to haul."

"Well, the other kitchen boys be wanting to help haul the water on account of they be knowing when Cook send them to the market, the one with the coin be buying treats fer anybody who help him."

So there's an entire underground economy built around the king having a hot bath. No doubt this is just one example. "Do I give you enough money to keep these little enterprises going, Osbert?"

"Aye, m'lord. Ye be generous like yer father were."

Coliar was right about the level of interest in the mission of Charles's ambassador. Even the ladies are present when the formal knock and announcement of the visitor initiates the proceedings. He walks resolutely to the front of the room where he performs the most elaborate bow I've ever witnessed. Removing his hat with his left hand, he extends his left leg forward, toe pointed. Then as he bends the right knee, he gives four flourishes with the right hand, beginning at the top of his head and ending somewhere near his navel, and extends his right arm behind him while simultaneously bringing his hat to his heart and bending from the waist until his head is halfway to the floor. His performance would be something of a caricature, were he not so utterly serious.

"Rise, good sir, and address our court."

He returns his hat to his head. "King Alfred . . . Your Grace . . . I am Lord Suidbert, Amba—"

I hold up my hand to interrupt him. "The last time that name was heard in this court, good sir, it transpired that the user was not who he claimed to be. I believe my courtiers would find me remiss were I to fail to question whether this might be some similar ruse."

"Ah, yes, Sire. The man our late King Goscelin impersonated was my dear father who, sadly, departed this world some four years past. I am genuinely Lord Amboise de la Fontaine Suidbert, Ambassador at Large for His Most Excellent Grace King Charles."

Surely no one in their right mind would invent a name like that, I think to myself. "Thank you, Lord Suidbert. Do continue."

"My master wishes me to convey his hope that the recent unpleasantness is now behind us and that you might be of a mind to consider the mission for which he has engaged my services."

Recent unpleasantness? Clearly, this man is a diplomat of the first order. This should be interesting. I remain silent and wait for him to continue.

"King Charles wishes me to convey to you his knowledge of a growing presence of Teutons in our southeastern province, though he considers that you may already have learned of this from tales told by your returning mercenaries."

Is he goading me or is this a slip of the tongue? Either way, it can't go unchallenged. "I fear I must take exception to your reference to 'my mercenaries,' for I have none. The loyalty of mercenaries is only to their paymaster. If, at the end of the recent unpleasantness, as you describe it, some who were once part of our forces decided to continue their military lives elsewhere, they did so of their own accord. It's not an unfamiliar phenomenon in the aftermath of a conflict."

"Your Grace is quite right, though the distinction does not alter the fact that tales of the Teuton presence may have reached your shores."

"If I were in your master's position, I would be concerned about such a presence. After all, the aggressive nature of the Teutons and their constant attempts to expand their territory are widely known."

"Your Grace has gone straight to the heart of the matter. This is a grave concern for King Charles. He also ventures to surmise that you, too, may have reason to find the potential of Teuton expansion worrisome. It is on this basis that he has instructed me to put to you his proposal that you should join with him to expel the Teuton presence from his kingdom."

A hush falls over the room. No shuffling of feet or rustling of clothing, no nervous coughs or clearing of throats, no whispered remarks to one's neighbor. Instead, utter silence . . . which I allow to continue for quite some time. Let this fellow worry a bit about what my reaction might be.

At length, with no change of my demeanor or tone of voice, I ask, "And why, good sir, does King Charles think I would have any interest in entertaining his proposition when not so long ago he was intent on removing me from my throne?"

"My master anticipated you might be inclined to raise that very point," Suidbert replies as smoothly as if I were asking nothing more controversial than whether or not the sky is blue. "He instructed me to tell you that he now knows he was ill-advised and that the bearer of that advice has since been removed from among His Grace's counsellors."

"But surely a king makes his own decisions, particularly when the matter is of such great import as waging war on a kingdom that has long been a friend and ally." I'm not letting him off the hook with this feeble attempt to deflect responsibility elsewhere.

"I would not presume, Your Grace, to speculate about the manner in which our king is moved to any action or decision, for he alone knows the inner workings of his mind and of his heart."

"Then let me ask you a different question. Why does King Charles need my help? Surely your fighting forces are up to the task. The force arrayed against us during the recent unpleasantness, as you call it, certainly seemed to be of sufficient strength and preparedness to expel a few Teutons from a small corner of your kingdom."

"There have been developments in our land, Sire, since the time when you observed our forces. There is an ongoing dispute among our nobility between those loyal to King Charles and those who have declared loyalty to the Duke of Aleffe. As our dowager queen is now resident at your court, there can be no doubt of your awareness of this state of affairs."

"May I remind you, Lord Suidbert, that the Lady Petronilla is also *our* dowager queen and is entitled to take up her proper position in our court at any time and for any duration of her choosing."

"As she is equally entitled to take up her position in our court, though she has chosen to absent herself from us these months past. However, my mission does not concern the comings and goings of dowager queens."

"As you have declared that there can be no doubt of my awareness of the instability in your kingdom, then I think you must also acknowledge that the Duke of Aleffe himself remains loyal to King Charles." I pause. Suidbert refuses to be drawn in.

"It seems to me," I continue, "that King Charles and the duke together could assemble a force sufficient to oust a few Teutons. I remain puzzled as to why your master should feel the need to seek my assistance."

"Perhaps." He pauses to put on a thoughtful expression. "But consider this, Sire. If our loyal forces are occupied with the Teuton incursion in the southeast, might not my master's more rebellious nobles see this as an opportunity to expand their influence in other parts of the kingdom?"

"I have no intention, Lord Suidbert, of becoming involved in the dispute between King Charles and his nobles."

"Then consider this, Sire. If the Teutons in our southeast province are not expelled, what is to prevent their moving into the next province along the border . . . and the next . . . and so on until they are in possession of the port? Would they not then be a direct threat to your own kingdom?"

"It occurs to me that uniting against a common enemy might be just the thing King Charles could use to bring his unruly nobles back into the fold."

"I believe that if my master thought such a thing would succeed, he would not have seen fit to dispatch me on my current mission. He instructed me to tell you that he believes time is of the essence if the Teuton incursion is to be stopped."

"I'll need some time to consider King Charles's proposal."

"Then perhaps I could present myself here once again in . . . say, two days . . . to receive your reply."

"I'll not be rushed into a decision, Lord Suidbert. Tell King Charles that he's invited to visit us here one month from today to discuss his proposal with me directly. You may assure him that I'll be prepared to give an answer at that time."

Suidbert almost succeeds in not looking crestfallen. No doubt he's flattered himself he could complete the negotiation in one visit and return home with everything Charles wants. "I shall convey your invitation to my king, Your Grace." He bows, a more conventional bow this time, held long enough to convey that he understands my position.

I'm just about to give him permission to retire when he speaks again. "There is one other small matter, Your Grace. Something you might prefer to discuss in private."

So he's not done yet. Something he's held in reserve in the event I should require further persuasion. "I've no need for privacy, Lord Suidbert. What else is on your mind?"

"It's the small matter of the missing viscount, Your Grace."

"So he's still missing, is he? When the searchers departed our shores, we assumed he'd either been found or returned home of his own accord."

"He is, as you say, still missing."

"That must be a matter of serious concern to his parents and to King Charles."

"Indeed it is, Sire. My master is particularly eager to learn the whereabouts of his nephew and to see that he is once again safely in the bosom of his family."

"And why would your master think I have any knowledge in this affair?"

"With respect, Your Grace, the viscount was last seen here in your very court."

"From which he vanished just as mysteriously as he appeared."

"Again, with all respect to Your Grace's honor, perhaps there is some clue . . . something that perhaps seemed meaningless at the time . . . that would lead us to the viscount."

"Surely if there were such a thing, the searchers would have discovered it. But to satisfy your curiosity, I give you free rein of the castle for the duration of your stay. I'll instruct the steward to allow you access to any space you wish to inspect, and you may speak freely with servants, nobles, guards, and knights alike." The gesture is a formality. Suidbert is enough of a diplomat that he won't want to be seen openly questioning the veracity of the man his master wants to enlist to solve his Teuton problem.

"Your Grace is most generous."

"Not at all. Is there anything else, Lord Suidbert?"

"I have no further instructions, Sire."

"Then you may retire."

"With Your Grace's kind permission, I shall be on my way as soon as my ship is ready to sail. I am eager to carry your invitation to my king, who will no doubt send word of when he will arrive."

No, Suidbert, Charles doesn't get to choose the time and day of our meeting. "One month from today, Lord Suidbert, we will be ready to receive King Charles."

"Your Grace." He once again performs his elaborate bow, then rises and retreats from the room. As his footsteps echo down the corridor, a buzz of conversation arises here inside.

"Thorssen . . . Montfort . . . Peveril . . . a word if you please. Geoffrey . . . Coliar . . . come with me." They all follow me into the private reception room, where I remove my coronet and the formal court regalia.

"Coliar, please let Matthias know that I've given Suidbert complete freedom to search for his viscount. If the man should be so bold as to take me up on the offer, then Matthias and the staff should respond as if it were the queen herself making the request.

"Then send word to Lord Laurence. I need him here as early as possible tomorrow. And tell him to bring that Nordic ship captain with him. I want to see them the moment they arrive, and I'll forego my morning ride so there's no need to send anyone to find me."

"Yes, Sire." He departs to carry out my instructions.

"Now, Geoffrey. Tell me what you observed in the proceedings we just finished." This is a good opportunity to further his education on what it means to be king. He hesitates, unsure of what I want. "There's no right or wrong answer, Son. I'd just like to hear your impression of the exchange."

He takes yet another moment to think before replying. "It all seemed rather like a game, sir. A game where every time the ambassador asked a question or wanted something, you changed the rules on him, so he never scored any points."

"Keenly observed, Geoffrey," says Peveril. "Diplomacy is sometimes very much like a game. And today, your father had a distinct advantage because the ambassador was here in the role of petitioner. You're also right that Suidbert didn't get anything he asked for, but did you notice that your father actually gave him a gift at the end?"

"You mean the bit about looking around the castle?" asks Geoffrey.

"Before that."

"I'm not sure what you mean, sir."

"The invitation to King Charles to visit."

"I thought that was just so King Charles would have to ask in person for Papa's help."

"You're not wrong about that," says Peveril. "And your father will have to play the game very carefully to force Charles to admit he needs help without causing him to feel humiliated, which would just make him resent your father even more. But the gift to Suidbert was in the invitation. Given his recent attack on your father, it would have been terribly provocative for Charles to just show up here uninvited. So your father's invitation allows the ambassador to return to Charles and claim that the mission was an enormous success . . . something that's of vital importance to a flatterer like Suidbert."

Geoffrey looks puzzled. "How do you know he's a flatterer, sir?"

"Partially from his manner. Those two elaborate bows to your father were intended to curry favor. And did you notice how he described Charles as 'His Most Excellent Grace' and repeatedly referred to him as 'my master'?"

"Yes, sir. You said partially, sir. What else?"

Peveril looks to me, eyebrow raised in a question. I answer with a nod.

"The other part, Geoffrey, is something you don't yet have sufficient life experience to recognize. You've probably heard that King Charles prefers men to women in matters of love."

"Papa explained it to me."

"Well, when you have more experience, you'll be able to recognize that Suidbert is cut from the same cloth. So he must either want to ingratiate himself into Charles's intimate circle or do what's necessary to remain there."

"Oh." Geoffrey looks deeply thoughtful again. "So if the invitation to visit was the gift, what was all that talk about the missing viscount?"

"Well, even with the invitation, Suidbert is forced to go home without a decision. So he tried one last tactic to see if he could sway your father by insinuating he had something to do with the viscount's disappearance."

"So Papa lost that move, since he had to give permission for Lord Suidbert to search the castle."

"Actually, I'd say that was more of a draw. Yes, Suidbert put us on notice that Charles thinks your father may be harboring the viscount somewhere. But in doing so, he showed their hand and gave your father the opportunity to be expansive in his denial."

"Papa, does anyone know where the viscount might be?"

"Judging from today's conversation," I reply, "it seems there are a lot of people wondering that very thing. Wherever he went . . . wherever he is now . . . there's no doubt he's safer than he would be in Charles's clutches . . . or even in those of the Aleffe-faction nobles, for that matter. Right now, that young man is the most important pawn in their strange civil war." I wonder if Geoffrey will notice that I didn't really answer his question.

"Diplomacy is hard," says Geoffrey, causing everyone in the room to chuckle.

"Sometimes it is, Geoffrey," says Montfort, "but it's always worth doing well. And my observation today, sir, is that you handled the petitioner with consummate skill. But Peveril is right. It gets trickier from here on. Things must be rather dire for Charles to admit he's lost control of his kingdom and has no choice but to turn to you for help."

"And he'll only be more resentful if you solve his problems for him," adds Phillip.

"Which is exactly why I intend to treat this as our problem. And not just ours, but our allies' as well. Phillip . . . Montfort . . . I need you to bring the Peaks and the Lakes into the picture right away. I want a meeting three weeks hence at the country manor to agree our response to Charles, and they'll need a bit of time to consider their positions. I also want us to meet Charles together when he arrives.

"Peveril, same for you, but with a complication. I'd like to have just a single representative who can speak for all the Territorial lords. I have no brilliant ideas of how to get them to agree to this, but I think it would be a bad idea to have too many people arrayed opposite Charles. He'll either get angry and resentful, or he'll start trying to figure out how to drive a wedge into our alliance, and the Territories would be the first place he'd look to foment disagreement."

"I rather think they might share your perspective, sir. So it may not be as difficult as you think. The risk is in who they choose."

"It's a risk we'll have to take." I pause before adding with a big smile, "Though I have every confidence, Lord Peveril, in your ability to mitigate that risk."

Peveril laughs and turns to my son. "You're right, Geoffrey. Diplomacy is hard. Especially when your father has the outcome already decided." Geoffrey grins.

"So why the country manor?" asks Phillip.

"I want our gathering to look like a country party and hunt, not some great state visit or war council. Charles's spies will know we have visitors, but they won't have time to send word. And when he arrives, they can only speculate on whether there was more to it than just a hunt.

"We'll return to the castle to receive Charles. A gathering of kings, but nothing more. Be sure and convey all this as part of my invitation.

It wouldn't be helpful to have anyone show up with all the trappings of a grand state visit."

I spend the rest of the day composing a message to Brandr. His help will be needed if we're to achieve what I have in mind. Knowing how difficult it will be to get word to him in winter, I have no choice but to put everything into a single message. My usual care in making messages difficult to decode may have to be sacrificed, but at least I can change the key several times throughout the message.

At last Charles awakened to Teuton threat, but cannot overcome internal disputes to assemble army for expulsion. Now asking my help. We know intruder presence in southeast province substantial and signs appearing elsewhere of possible additional incursion. Problem threatens us if not resolved, but will not help alone as would only add to Charles existing resentment of me. Convening allies twenty days hence to agree terms and plan strategy. Must avoid any perception of taking sides in civil war. Your influence with Southern Nordics vital to keep Teutons engaged at their border, else conflict in south could become massive border war. Urgent to know if we can count on this before deciding how to proceed.

Satisfied this is enough to convey both the facts and my sense of urgency, I encode the message and then decode it twice to make sure I haven't made any mistakes. Then I lock it in my strong box to await Laurence's arrival.

The following morning dawns sunny, but the brisk northerly wind means winter cloaks are welcome as Laurence, the Nordic captain, and I go for a walk in the woods.

"Castles have too many ears, gentlemen," I tell them, "for the matters we need to discuss this morning." We speak only of banalities until I'm sure we're out of earshot of the stables and no one is loitering behind us.

"Captain, I have a rather pressing problem that I hope you can help me with," I begin.

"I will do my best, Sire."

"I know your home harbor is still frozen, else you'd no longer be spending time with us. Unfortunately, I have a very urgent need to get a message to your king. Do you know of any way this could be done?"

"Aye, Your Grace. The nearest Southern Nordic port is likely clear of ice by now. We could sail there and then go overland. The straits are probably still frozen, so we could cross on sledges. We could then spend the rest of the winter in the Southern Nordic port."

"Actually, Captain, I'll need a reply back from King Brandr, so what I'm asking is if you could make the trip in both directions."

"I suppose so, Sire. Assuming King Brandr agrees."

"I'll pay you and your crew for your services, so I think my cousin should have no objection."

"My king is a reasonable man, Sire."

I chuckle. "That he is. Tell me . . . how long do you think this journey would take?"

"It all depends on the weather, Sire. If a winter storm blows up while we're at sea, it could take us well south of our course, and we'd have to fight our way back to the port. And storms at sea often bring blizzards on land. It might be two weeks or more before I could even get to King Brandr." He pauses. I have no doubt my expression must be totally crestfallen. "How soon do you need an answer, Sire?"

"Twenty days, Captain. And not a day more."

"Then best we pray to all the gods we know for fair weather, Sire. It can be done . . . barely . . . if the weather holds. But I'll want to be getting back to my ship straightaway so we can sail with the next tide."

"There's just one more thing, Captain. I'm sure I needn't tell you that ports have even more ears than castles." He chortles. "Can you think of a plausible pretext for this voyage that would satisfy those curious ears around my port?"

"No reason I shouldn't check out our winter repairs and get the crew back in shape for when we can sail home."

"Any chance you might also arrange to return with something not quite right that you can be seen to be repairing all over again?"

"Leave it to me, Your Grace. Whoever it is that you don't want to know about this mission won't be getting the truth of it from us."

"I know Brandr trusts you, Captain. And so do I." I reach into my cloak and retrieve the coded message, handing it to him. "No gifts or letters this time – just this message for the king. Godspeed and fair winds, Captain. Lord Laurence will bring you to me the moment you return."

He bows quickly and hurries away, leaving Laurence and me alone in the woods. "Let's go to the hut and get out of this wind," I tell him. "And I'll bring you into the picture on what this is all about."

Three weeks can seem like a lifetime or the blink of an eye . . . or in this case, both. It seems an eternity since the Nordic ship set sail. And we've no way of knowing what the weather is like in the Northern Sea, for I have no pretext for sending one of our own ships into those waters. Meanwhile, it feels like time is quickly running out for Sir Jasper to make his plans . . . plans that must account for our own forces, accommodate our allies and their commanders, anticipate the risks from the divisions within Charles's kingdom, and avert an all-out border war with the massed strength of the Teuton armies. We desperately need some assurance that the Southern Nordics will keep the Teutons occupied in the north. My anxiety grows with each passing day.

Samuel tries to alleviate my worry during one of our morning rides. "Commanders face uncertainties in every fight, Alfred. The good ones are those who can read the lay of the land in the heat of battle and make adjustments in time to avoid a disaster." He pauses before adding, "And Jasper is one of the good ones."

"I know, Samuel. But that's little comfort when I don't know if he'll be facing a handful of renegades or a massive invasion force."

"You can always tell Charles no."

"Don't think I haven't given that serious consideration."

"But you think you can get something else out of it if you play his game."

"Perhaps. But it's tricky at best balancing what we might lose if we don't help against what we might gain if we do. The best would be to see his kingdom reunited and allied with us. But then there's Charles's vanity to consider. I don't know if I have the skill for this, Samuel."

"I trust you've talked it over with Rupert."

"Over brandy most evenings."

"If only *I* had such a serious problem that it warranted Rupert's fine brandy every night!" Samuel laughs, and I can't help but chuckle along with him.

"You can have this one."

"But then it wouldn't be the same. I'm not the one who disarmed Charles in a sword fight."

"Maybe not, but you're the one who taught me how."

"Touché, my friend," says Samuel as he urges his horse to a canter and turns its head toward the stable. And just like that, Samuel has lightened my mood. He has an uncanny ability to know just when and how to do this, which is why I once referred to him as a tonic for my soul.

"He brings this all on himself, you know," says Samuel, referring to Charles, as we dismount and turn our horses over to the grooms.

"That may be," I reply, "but he leaves the rest of us to clean up the mess after him."

Goron arrives first, a day before the appointed time for the meeting at the country manor. I can barely contain my delight at seeing that not only have the Territorial lords agreed to a single representative but that they've chosen Goron. "I have with me letters for all the kings . . . including Charles . . . giving me authorization to speak for the Territories," he says, handing over the one intended for me.

I open it to find that it bears the signature of every one of the Territorial lords. "You honor me by leaving this in your own language, Goron."

"Nerrick felt that gave it more authority," he replies, "and we needed him on board. As Lord Rusk speaks the language of the Peaks, we have translated that one. We've observed that the King of Lakes speaks your language well and are hopeful that this will be sufficient for King Charles."

"He may pretend difficulty and insist that one of his aides makes a translation, but I can assure you that Charles speaks my tongue as well as I speak his."

Goron reaches into his pocket and produces another folded paper. "A letter for you, sir, from my father. He regrets the length of time since his last visit here but understands this is not the right opportunity."

Once Goron is off to settle in, I retreat to the study to read Egon's letter.

My dear Alfred,

I will begin by expressing my sincere concern for the circumstances in which we find ourselves relative to King Charles and the Teuton intruders. Know that I have every confidence in your ability to negotiate a proper arrangement to repel any threat to our trade.

Having said that, I hope you will indulge me in a bit of celebration for the unexpected and fortuitous opportunity this presents for furthering our long-term vision. I have prayed to our gods and searched on my own . . . with utter futility in both cases, as far as I can determine . . . for some cause or event that would require our lords to speak with one voice. And now you have laid it in my lap as a most unexpected gift for which I am deeply grateful.

This may be a solitary event, but my greatest hope is that Goron will acquit himself in a manner that builds further trust in him as one who can speak and act for us all. To that end, I trust that you will offer him whatever guidance he may require to be successful in these negotiations. I can assure you that he respects you and will be receptive to your tutelage.

Your Lord Peveril will tell you the details of how our agreement was reached. As always, he was masterful in his handling of your request and the debate that ensued. His presence removes that burden from me and advances my cause without calling attention to it.

We make progress, my friend. And who would have guessed, on that day we first laid eyes on one another, that we would come so far?

Egon

I fold the letter and return it to my pocket for storing later in my strong box. Who would have guessed, indeed?

Over brandy after the evening meal, I ask Peveril about the negotiations. "Egon's letter was full of praise for you."

"That's easy for him to say in retrospect," Peveril chuckles, "but I must admit I was not so sure we'd get there." He pauses for a sip of brandy. "My initial strategy was to focus on not letting Charles drive wedges between us or among them. That, unfortunately, opened a totally unexpected debate that was completely unproductive."

"So what happened to change it?" Rupert asks.

"At one point Nerrick said something like, 'I'm too old to be leading an army in the field, especially in some foreign land I might never come home from.' And then it came to me. They've always been able to unite around some military purpose. Remember how quickly they reacted to both Harold's and John's threats?"

"Aye," Rupert replies.

"I was thinking how to use this when Narth asked, 'Does Alfred have a plan for this expedition?' It was just the opening I needed. So I told them Sir Jasper and Sir Samuel were creating the outlines of a plan, but I was certain much of the time in this meeting would be spent perfecting that plan and working out who would command which positions. Maybe, I suggested, they'd be best served by having the commander who would lead their forces be part of that planning.

"Frankly, I had no idea if de Courcy was involved at all, but I know the regard in which they hold him, so I tried to use that to our advantage. The new tactic completely changed the conversation. And it didn't take them long to agree that Goron was the best to command, since he'd done just that alongside our men at the garrison in the last war. It left me feeling a little foolish for not having thought of that ploy at the outset."

"Don't chasten yourself, Peveril," says Rupert. "Planting the seeds about how easily Charles could sow discord was smart. I'll wager that by now, many of them have realized that's exactly what happened in that unproductive debate you described."

"Well done regardless of how it was done, my friend." I raise my glass to Peveril. "When I assigned you the Territories, I thought it might be an impossible task. What you've achieved is nothing short of remarkable."

"You started the wheels in motion, Alfred," says Peveril. "I just keep nudging them along from time to time."

My fellow kings arrive the following afternoon. The day after that, our serious conversations must begin if we're to be prepared for Charles's arrival. And still there's no message from Brandr. I'm becoming resigned to the idea that we'll have to give Charles an answer with this great uncertainty still looming over our plans.

We've gathered in the dining hall where Jasper can use the tables to spread out his maps and drawings. Thorssen and Montfort have also done their jobs well, and by late morning we've reached agreement that, despite some lingering uncertainty about Charles's motives, the risk of a Teuton threat to the major port for our trade can't be ignored. "And that's how I want to respond to Charles," I sum up the discussion. "We're acting jointly to protect our own interests. If, in doing so, we render him aid, then we're pleased to have been of assistance. Under no circumstances, though, will we be drawn into the internecine bickering in his kingdom. We expel the Teutons and we're gone; the rest is up to him. Agreed, gentlemen?"

Everyone affirms their agreement.

"Very well. I've tasked Sir Jasper with devising plans with that goal in mind. Let's hear him out. Then we help him work out the rest of the details."

"Come this way, if you will, My Lords," Jasper leads us to the table where he's spread maps of the eastern regions of the Kingdom Across the Southern Sea.

Just at that moment, the door opens quietly and Osbert approaches. Speaking in almost a whisper, he says, "Ye be needed in the entry hall, m'lord."

It takes an effort not to respond with irritation. But I remind myself that Osbert has never abused this privilege. "Is it so urgent that it won't keep until Sir Jasper has finished?" I ask, also in hushed tones. Jasper has paused in his description of his maps.

"Methinks ye be wanting to come straightaway, m'lord." I look at him questioningly, but he'll say no more than, "I be thinking ye'll agree once ye be there, m'lord."

Turning my attention back to the others, I say, "Forgive me, my friends, but it seems something requires my urgent attention. Sir Jasper, do continue. I'll only be a moment."

Once we're out of the room with the door firmly closed, I question my squire again. "What could possibly be so important, Osbert?" But he's marched on ahead, willing me to hurry my own footsteps.

Turning the corner into the entry hall, I halt in my tracks in sheer astonishment, for standing there awaiting my arrival are Laurence, Brandr, and Beatrix. I rush to Brandr and grasp his outstretched arm in greeting before embracing my aunt. "Thanks be to all the gods!" I exclaim. "I had despaired of an answer from you and now here you are in the flesh. How on earth . . .?" I leave the question dangling.

"I've no idea what pact Thorvald has made with the gods of the winds and the sea . . ." Nominally a Christian, Brandr is very pragmatic about religion, believing that no harm, and perhaps some good, can arise from also appeasing the old Nordic gods. ". . . but whatever that pact may be, I'm eternally grateful for it. He got to us in record time, so I had an entire day to spend with the Southern Nordic king before coming on here."

"And?" I simply can't wait any longer for an answer.

"You have his support, Alfred. I'll save the rest for when we join the others."

At least now I can relax and welcome them properly. "How did you get here?"

"As luck would have it, fair winds and no storms for both crossings. And we've had a hard winter, so there's as yet been no thaw to make the roads difficult. Plus, some good advice from Thorvald and the help of your Lord Laurence."

"And Aunt Beatrix . . . such a surprise!"

"I thought a change of scenery would do us all some good," she replies sweetly.

"What Mother isn't saying is that there's been some tension with Arnora."

"Juliana mentioned something of the sort."

"Arnora's still having trouble finding her footing as queen, and she's convinced Mother's judging her every move."

"Which I'm not," interjects Beatrix.

"Which of course you're not," continues Brandr. "But Arnora's belief just makes her more insecure. She'll favor one set of ladies today and a different set next week, so the court always seems to be in turmoil."

"I thought my being away for a bit might help her settle in," says Beatrix. "Or at least let Brandr give her some guidance without her thinking I'm behind it all."

Brandr seems eager to change the subject. "Our ship docked late yesterday afternoon. Thorvald told me of your concern about spies, so we disguised ourselves as ordinary seamen and came ashore with the sailors going to the taverns for the evening. Thorvald took us from there to Lord Laurence's house."

Hurrying down the stairs to welcome her guests, Catherine arrives just in time to hear this description. "Oh, dear!" she exclaims. "That must have been dreadful for you, Beatrix."

"Quite the contrary, my dear." Beatrix kisses Catherine on both cheeks in greeting. "It was all great fun. Certainly the most daring thing I've ever done."

Catherine takes her sister-in-law in hand. "Now, I'll have the servants see to your trunks, and we'll get you all settled in."

"There are no trunks to attend to, Aunt," says Brandr. "Another part of the ruse. We brought only what would fit inside the carriage so it looked to all the world like Lord Laurence was just making a day visit to his king. The rest will have to follow later once the need for secrecy is past."

"Laurence, I'd invite you to join us, but . . ."

"Say no more, Sire." Laurence's formality is for Brandr's benefit.

"Thank you for getting them here without drawing the attention of prying eyes." Then I turn back to Brandr. "Let's go join the others. I'm eager to hear the rest of your news."

As we turn toward the corridor, I look around for Osbert, but he's already disappeared. I must remember tonight to thank him and to make amends for whatever irritation I may have shown.

Back in the dining hall, Brandr greets his fellow kings, whom he'd met at Goscelin's funeral before he became a king in his own right. He then turns to Goron. "I don't believe we've had the pleasure, sir."

"Lord Goron, sir. Representing the Territories."

Well done, Goron, I think to myself, assuming the title you don't yet fully own in order to establish your role. I must remember to share this with Egon. I pick up the remaining introductions. "Lord de Courcy."

"Ah, yes," says Brandr, "the famous Sir Samuel about whom I've heard so much." He nods to Samuel in greeting.

"And this is Sir Jasper, my knight commander."

"I've heard stories of your flaming fleece, Sir Jasper," says Brandr. Jasper bows and lightly clicks his heels together. "That sort of inventiveness is much to be admired in a commander."

"Jasper was just beginning to talk us through his plans for how we'd confront the Teutons," I remark.

"Then my arrival is timely, for my news will surely influence those plans. I'd have been with you yesterday, gentlemen, had I not spent a day in conversation with the King of the Southern Nordics. He's deeply concerned about this new Teuton encroachment. 'We must keep their ambitions directed to the east,' he told me. 'If they discover they can have success expanding to the west, then it's just a matter of time before they turn their attention northward. And that would bode ill for both of us.' So you have his support, gentlemen. He will ensure the Teutons can't turn their backs on his border while your expedition is underway."

Both Jasper and Samuel visibly relax; Samuel has a smile on his face bordering on a grin. No doubt he'll take the first opportunity to chide me for an excess of worry, but only because it was a worry I know he shared.

"His support comes with a condition, though," Brandr continues. "His involvement in this venture must remain completely secret. Their peace with the Teutons is tenuous at best . . . based on mutual threat rather than mutual trust. And he has no wish to give them any excuse to change the status quo. I, uh . . ." he hesitates. "I undertook to agree to those terms on behalf of everyone in this room. I trust I've not violated anyone's prerogative."

"If I may, Your Grace?" Jasper interjects. I nod my assent. "Your undertaking, Sire, is actually an essential part of the plan I'm about to lay out. For us to succeed, your role and that of the Southern Nordics must remain secret even from King Charles and his forces. To that end, gentlemen, I was prepared to ask all of you not to reveal even to your commanders what part they play."

"Can we agree, gentlemen," I step up immediately to Jasper's support, "that this knowledge is not spoken of by any of us outside this room?" There's no hesitation in their agreement.

"I think what that also means, Brandr," I add, "is that you shouldn't be present when we receive Charles a few days hence."

"I couldn't agree more," he replies. "Besides," he adds, "it would be such a waste of the ruse that got us past Charles's spies if the man himself were to see me among you." Brandr's genial manner puts everyone at ease.

The afternoon and all of the following day are devoted to Jasper's plans. We have to be prepared for a full-scale border war while hoping we face nothing more than a clearing-out operation in the southeastern province. To that end, Jasper has divided the entire border into sectors, each sector to be defended by one of our allies. Jasper will be in overall command. I was prepared to insist on this, but the King of Peaks made that unnecessary. "Jasper knows his plans inside and out. We would do well to keep him in charge." I'm relieved when this sentiment is shared by the others.

Our forces and Charles's will deal with the southeastern province under Jasper's direct command. The Peaks commander will be in charge of the central border section, with the insurgent militias adding to the strength of his forces. Goron will take the northern border sector, supplemented by Aleffe's men. The Lakes commander will defend the port.

At one point, the King of Lakes demurs about how many men he can provide. "Unlike you, Alfred, I have a very long border with a potential enemy that I cannot leave undefended."

Brandr speaks up. "That's something I can help with as well."

"I'm listening," says the Lakes king.

"The Northern Kingdom has always looked to us if they need to trade. What you wouldn't know is that they completely deforested their lands several generations ago, so they're entirely dependent on us for fuel. My grandfather . . . and his father before him . . . tried to teach them how to replant the forests and manage them to last, as we do. But there's never been a high chieftain with the strength to compel the clan chiefs to do his bidding. Until recently. The current high chieftain has found a way to get some cooperation from the clans, and we've given them seedlings to replant their forests. But it'll be two . . . maybe three . . . generations before they can even begin to be self-sufficient again . . . and that's assuming the clans can be kept under control.

"The only reason they'd have to turn their sights to the south would be if we cut off their fuel supply and they had to look elsewhere. You have my assurance – my word of honor, if you need it – that we'll supply whatever fuel they require. Perhaps that will allow you to rest more easily about committing men to this venture."

"It does, indeed."

"And just for a little extra comfort," Brandr adds, "it's been our observation that they're far more interested in their ancient clan feuds than anything else unless something goes horribly wrong like running out of wood. So while your vigilance is wise, you might be able to sleep easier at night knowing this." Having Brandr in this conversation is already delivering unexpected benefits.

Toward the end of the second day, it's clear we have not only an agreed response to Charles but also a sound plan for putting an end to Teuton ambitions along their border with Charles's kingdom. The mood in the room is almost euphoric, everyone confident that our joint efforts will succeed. Which means the time has come for me to say what's been on my mind these past weeks.

"Gentlemen." I have to raise my voice ever so slightly to draw their attention, but the hubbub of multiple conversations goes immediately silent. "My gratitude to all of you knows no bounds. We have an excellent plan. And thanks to Brandr, we have our secret strategy. But there's one more thing that must be said before we have our meeting with Charles."

The room is once again all seriousness, with everyone's attention focused on me. "You all know my history with Charles. And you all know his vanity. So I think you can appreciate why I can't shake the feeling that the facts we see before us may not be the entire story. I keep coming back to what possible motivation would drive Charles to come to *me* for help?

"It's possible that the insurrection is far more advanced than we know . . . that he's in imminent danger of losing his throne and this is a pretext to get me to help him win it back. I think we've built safeguards around that both in our plans and in our conditions for agreeing to take on the Teutons. If he refuses our conditions, that will be telling. And it will mean we have to come together again to assess the Teuton threat and what to do.

"But consider this, gentlemen. What if the truth is something far more subtle? Something far more sinister. Allow me to spin a tale for you.

"Almost a year ago, Charles is forced to flee these shores in defeat when his invasion fails. His second defeat at my hands. And yes," I hurry to add, "we had your support in that war. But in Charles's mind, he's been bested once again by the same man in what should have been his redemption for the earlier defeat. He sails home fuming over the outcome, only to discover his opponents have staged a serious uprising in his absence. He's denied entry into his main port, and his castle is occupied by the insurgents. He sails on to his dukedom with the bile of rage and resentment rising in his throat.

"He takes his immediate revenge on the one who plotted with him . . . the one who produced the bastard claimant . . . the one who assured him that right was on his side and lured him into the belief that this action would remove the stain of his previous dishonor. And he takes great satisfaction from knowing that person is my aunt . . . my own flesh and blood. His actions assuage much of his initial fury, for he imagines that I and my family must be suffering from her disgrace.

"But now he has to turn his attention to getting his kingdom back in order. And that's no small task. Except in Lamoreaux province, the cities, the market towns, and the port are all in the hands of the insurgents, who've declared loyalty to the man whose own allegiance Charles snubbed in the run-up to the invasion. Charles's sister has disappeared and is rumored to have thrown her lot in with the rebels. And Charles's own military forces are badly depleted. He lost many men in the war. No doubt he lost many more on the long sail home, for he would've had only meager provisions on his waiting ships, having assumed he'd triumphantly take over everything in my kingdom. And he'd have had nowhere to resupply food or water during the voyage.

"So he sits in Lamoreaux and fumes. And the more he fumes, the more he convinces himself that his entire predicament is my fault. Surely I must have sent Isabella for the express purpose of getting him to disgrace himself once more for my benefit. And the bile begins to rise again.

"When the Viscount Aleffe shows up here asking for my protection, it's the last straw. Charles pulls out all the stops to find the boy and prove I've been harboring him . . . proof that I'd dishonored Charles once again by interfering in the affairs of his kingdom."

The room is completely silent, but the smiles of exhilaration have changed to portraits of thoughtfulness.

"At Goscelin's funeral, Queen Petronilla told me that Charles had grown rather astute politically during his father's last years. What if he's managed to tap into that ability once again when his future looks bleak and he blames it all on me?

"What if he's negotiated some kind of truce with his rebellious lords? What if what looks to us like a stalemate in their civil war is just a façade? What if, instead of commanding the insurgency, the Duchess of Aleffe is now serving as liaison between Charles in Lamoreaux and the faction we assume to still be disloyal?

"What if Charles made a deal with the Teutons? Whether before or after they began to encroach on the southeastern province doesn't matter. Why else would the rebel militias pull out and essentially cede that territory? It's certainly in no one's interest but the Teutons' for them to do so."

The expressions of thoughtfulness have begun to change into frowns.

"So now the stage is set. He sends Suidbert to paint a picture of the dire situation in which he supposedly finds himself. 'My master learned his lesson. Let bygones be bygones.' The ambassador is at his most ingratiating. 'I need your help and will be forever grateful.' When I refuse to reply immediately, the 'missing viscount' card is played, but that yields nothing more.

"Charles can't have been happy that his ambassador returned empty-handed, but he has a plan, so he plays the game. And he'll present himself here two days hence to make his next move." I pause for a moment, but no one speaks.

"So what's his plan? The southeastern province is the perfect setting. It takes my forces as far away from their supply lines and as far away from an escape route as they can possibly be. And once they're there . . . with their attention focused on pushing the Teutons back to their homeland . . . Charles's forces advance from the east, the insurgent militias attack from the north, and the main Teuton force surges over the border. The result will be total annihilation. And Charles's fondest hope . . . the crown jewel of his strategy . . . is that I'm there at the head of my army."

The silence in the room is profound. No one speaks for several long minutes. Finally, the King of Lakes quietly asks what all must surely be thinking, "So how does this change our plans?"

"It doesn't, gentlemen. I think we've accounted for everything in that dire scenario. We go together or not at all. We have conditions Charles must accept before we set sail. No crowned heads will lead their forces.

"I've thought long and hard about how Charles might react and can come up with only two scenarios. The first is that he gets word to the Teutons that it's to be an all-out border war. We're prepared for that, though it won't be an easy fight. The other is that he instructs his own forces and the militias to attack us from within the ranks.

"That's why your commanders have to know about this. They have to be ready. If those of Charles's men who are fighting with them turn on us, the commanders have to act immediately. They must treat their erstwhile allies as the enemy and subdue them rapidly. Only then can they turn their attention back to the Teutons . . . who, I suspect, will withdraw quickly once they see Charles's grand plan falling apart.

"I can't emphasize this enough. Our commanders' actions must be swift and ruthless. Jasper will give his orders as part of the battle plans. But, my friends, I'm so concerned about this risk that I'd be grateful if you'd give your own orders as well."

My fellow kings agree. "I can assure you, sir," says Goron, "my men will be watchful and quick to act should the need arise. You can put your mind to rest on their account."

"Now, gentlemen, it's my understanding Rupert has dug deep into his cellar to find his best vintage of Lamoreaux wine and that it's waiting for us in the sitting room. Let's go celebrate our friendship and what we've achieved here."

"Better yet," says Samuel, "let's plan for tomorrow's hunt." And with that, a lighter mood is restored – the irony of Lamoreaux wine and the prospect of a day spent hunting are lost on no one. But I can see that the thoughtfulness remains, exactly as I'd hoped.

I'm surprised by the anxiety I feel at the moment of Charles's arrival. I have confidence in my allies; I have confidence in our plan; I have confidence in Jasper to execute it well. But I'm equally confident Charles will have something up his sleeve . . . perhaps even something so entirely unexpected that none of us has even contemplated its possibility. And that's what has me on edge as I wait, seated on my throne, for the knock on the door and the announcement that will admit him into my presence.

It's just past midday. The others are waiting inside the private reception room, where the real business will occur once the formalities have been attended to. Most of the lords are here in open court, along with a number of the ladies and several knights. It's important, for what comes later, that Charles perceive he's appropriately welcomed to my court.

The knock. The opening door. The announcement. "His Grace, King Charles, and the Ambassador, Lord Suidbert." So he's brought Suidbert back with him. To make sure I say nothing different than I'd said before? To show Suidbert how it ought to have been done in the first place? To have Suidbert search the castle for the missing viscount while Charles occupies my attention with business? Or perhaps it's nothing more than the fact that Suidbert is the current favorite in matters of the bedchamber.

As they cross the room, I stand to receive Charles, one king to another. Suidbert once again performs his elaborate bow. I've thought very carefully about the choice of words for my initial greeting. "We're pleased you've accepted our invitation, King Charles. My thanks to you, Lord Suidbert, for conveying it to your master." This releases Suidbert from his obeisance.

"I had hoped that Suidbert would be able to succeed in his mission," Charles can't resist the barb at his minion's expense, "but as you were unwilling to relay your answer through him, we are here to finish the business."

"Your ambassador acquitted himself well." I'm determined to give Suidbert back a small measure of his dignity. "But it seemed to me that such a grave undertaking is best discussed between equals. Wouldn't you agree?"

True to form, Charles simply can't bring himself to accept my generosity in giving him a way to dignify the reason for his presence here. "Best we'd get on with that business," is his only reply.

"Then perhaps you and Lord Suidbert will be so good as to come with me." I gesture to the door of the private reception room, and the attendant opens it immediately.

The sight of the two kings clearly unnerves Charles, who turns to Suidbert and hisses, "You didn't tell me this was a state visit."

As Suidbert tries to gesture his ignorance in the matter, I come to his rescue. "That's because it's not. We've all just returned from a hunt at my country estate."

"Quite a successful one, I might add," chimes in the Lakes king. "We brought down a rather large boar and a young stag. I'm told the kitchens are roasting them all day and that there'll be a feast this evening. You're just in time to join us."

Charles is obviously off balance. "And who is this?" he asks, gesturing toward Goron.

"Allow me to present Lord Goron of the western Territories." Goron bows his head briefly in acknowledgment. I had suggested this as a way to appease Charles's pride without diminishing Goron's authority in what's to come. "Goron is often our guest for hunting parties or other festivities."

But Charles has moved on to the last man in the room. "You, I have seen before. On the battlefield, I believe, and as a hanger-on in that ghastly business on my estate."

Samuel says simply, "Your Grace."

"May I present Lord de Courcy," I say, "my trusted counsellor in military matters."

"Lord?" Charles is as surprised as I had hoped. "How does a troop commander become a lord?"

"By way of reward from his king for extraordinary service," I reply.

"Hmph. If I gave a lordship to everyone who rendered me service, I'd have a whole kingdom of nothing but lords. And what good would that do me?" Charles is thoroughly unsettled by the fact that things aren't going as he'd foreseen. Exactly where I want him to be.

He turns to address the room. "And now, gentlemen, if you don't mind, Alfred and I have some business to conduct. We can continue the pleasantries over this feast your hunt has produced."

No one moves. And Charles is unable to keep the surprise from his expression.

"Actually, Charles," says the Lakes king, "the problem you've brought to Alfred is of concern to us all."

"A threat from the Teutons has the potential to disrupt all our lands," says Goron.

"That's why we intend to be part of the solution," the Peaks king puts our stake in the ground.

"It's not such a big threat at the moment," Charles goes on the defensive. "Just one province. That's why I want Alfred to help me nip it in the bud before the Teutons get overly ambitious."

"Be that as it may," the Lakes king, "your kingdom has a very long border with the Teutons. We share Alfred's concern that this small problem in one province could be merely a diversionary tactic and that their real intent is to swarm over the border while your attention is focused in the southeast."

"It would be irresponsible of us," Goron, "to allow your kingdom to be overrun when the result would be so disastrous for your people and ours."

"What do your spies tell you?" the Peaks king.

"Since Alfred seems to tell you everything," there's a sneer in Charles's voice, "I'm sure he's also told you I'm dealing with a faction of unruly nobles. My spies are mostly occupied in staying one step ahead of their next move. But I've had no reports of a build-up of troops along our border."

"Good commanders know how to disguise their preparations," Samuel. "The plan could be in motion but not be obvious to people in your border towns and villages."

"Are you suggesting I don't know how military planning works?" asks Charles, adding contemptuously, "Lord de Courcy."

"I'm suggesting nothing of the sort, Sire. Only reminding everyone of small details."

This is playing out more or less as we'd planned. Charles is off balance. But we don't need him to become belligerent, so it's time for me to step in. "Perhaps, gentlemen, we're getting the cart a bit ahead of the horse." Making my way to the sideboard, I say, "Please, Charles. Sit. Be comfortable. Allow me to offer you some refreshment." While he chooses a chair, I pour two glasses of wine and return to the group, giving one to him and selecting my own seat where I can observe everyone. I leave Suidbert to fend for himself, and he takes his glass of wine to a discreet corner of the room.

"Now, tell us, Charles. Is the Teuton situation as it was when Lord Suidbert first alerted us to your concern?"

"They're still there. And my people are still moving out, abandoning the villages to them. This delay has done nothing to improve the situation."

"And do you still want help to expel them?"

"I wouldn't be here other than to ask for your help, Alfred."

"What's *your* assessment of the risk that the Teutons have something else in mind beyond just encroaching on one province? I'm certain you've given this some thought. After all, you've no doubt studied how your father managed to maintain the peace with them over several decades."

"My father was lucky. He didn't have a bunch of rebellious nobles to deal with."

"It's my understanding the Duke of Aleffe remains loyal to you. I'd have thought you might join with him and find a way to bring the nobles back in line."

"He claims he's loyal. But what am I to think when his wife . . . my very own sister . . . is running around the countryside stirring everyone up over the succession."

"So you know where Tiece is?"

"Who knows where Tiece is? No one that I can find. But I *know* she's behind this."

This fishing expedition isn't yielding much, so I come back to the subject of the Teutons.

"Lord Suidbert was unable to provide any information when I asked if you and Aleffe might unite forces to expel the Teutons without our help."

"As long as Tiece is stirring up trouble, I don't trust him not to turn coat or turn tail in the middle of the fight. That's why I asked you for help, Alfred. I know you're too smart to turn your back on me."

So there it is. In trying to be ingratiating, he's just revealed that he still holds a grudge . . . that he's still thinking about revenge.

"Very well. I told Lord Suidbert you could have my answer in one month, and the time has come for me to give it.

"We will join with you to expel the Teutons because it's also in our interests not to have them overrun your kingdom . . . even a portion of it. But we have some conditions of that engagement."

"Conditions?" Charles looks and sounds annoyed.

"Conditions. All of us will field forces. Everyone in this room. In addition, we expect the insurgent militias to participate, and we expect the Duke of Aleffe to renew his loyalty pledge to you and to contribute his own men."

"And how do you intend to make that happen?"

"I've already dispatched Lord Emaurri to Aleffe to set our expectations, and I have every confidence he'll secure the Duke's agreement."

"You sent an ambassador to my kingdom without my consent?" Charles doesn't even try to restrain his fury.

"You said yourself that time was of the essence and that you didn't trust the Duke. We've merely put things in motion to mitigate those concerns."

"Is that all?"

"Sir Jasper will be in overall command," the Peaks king picks up the next thread. "Our commanders will lead our forces; they are far better at that than we are, especially if this devolves into a border war. Your men, Aleffe's, and the militias will fight alongside our forces and under their command."

"What you're suggesting is insulting!" Charles. "That I should subjugate my men to you in a simple operation to expel a few Teutons? I asked for your help, Alfred, not for you to take over."

I'm determined not to let him sway me from my calm demeanor. "Do you have a battle plan, Charles?"

"Not yet. I've spent a month cooling my heels waiting for your reply."

"Well, we do," the Lakes king. "One that covers all the contingencies you've agreed might arise."

"We will not take the field ourselves as crowned heads in another's kingdom," the Peaks king.

"At my advanced age," the Lakes king, "I wouldn't be helpful in the heat of battle anyway."

"We can't prescribe your actions in your own kingdom," I begin.

"Indeed you cannot!" Charles interrupts haughtily.

"But we ask that you consider the wisdom of taking the field yourself."

"And why shouldn't I ride at the head of my own army?"

"Your standard, Charles," the Lakes king, "would be a beacon to those who oppose you . . . a temptation for them to divert from the task of expelling the Teutons to internecine fighting."

"We will not," I try to sound emphatic without overdoing it, "embroil ourselves in that conflict."

"Best you don't. Is that all?"

"Those are our conditions," I reply.

"Then I expect your forces ashore and ready to march in three weeks."

We had anticipated this as we talked about Charles's determination to deal me a defeat, so fast couriers are already on their way with marching orders. "Then perhaps you could give us the use of some of your ships."

"You forget, Alfred. The port you'll use is not under my control at the moment. So ships will just have to be your problem. Maybe you shouldn't be sending so many men, if you can't get them there."

There's no need to tell him that Emaurri is also charged with negotiating the extra ships – buying the passage if necessary – as his first task, even before seeking out the duke. With any luck the ships will be on their way soon. Regardless, we'll arrive on our own time line. Charles's could be at the heart of one of his schemes. And in any event, I refuse to leave half an army like sitting ducks, waiting a week or more for the rest to arrive, subject to whatever mischief Charles or anyone else might cook up on the spot.

At the banquet, Charles is an entirely different person. Expansive, genial . . . conversing with all and sundry about art, music, the new pope, the two stallions he'd brought from across the Roman Sea to enhance the bloodlines of his own stock. He compliments the ladies and remarks on the new fashion of headdress being adopted in his kingdom. He's polite to Geoffrey, and even engages him briefly in a discussion of horsemanship.

All of which naturally makes me more than a little suspicious. Is it nothing more than the rather surprising amount of wine he's drinking? Or has he already figured out his next move? Is Suidbert co-conspirator as well as companion of the bedchamber? Or is he merely trying to charm my court into believing he has only the best of intentions and that his villainy is something I've invented for my own purposes?

At one point, after the sweets have been served, he broaches the topic of his rebellious lords with Devereux. "Surely such disrespect would never occur in this kingdom," he remarks casually.

Warily, Devereux replies, "Well, our lords are advisors to the king. We do have a responsibility to guide him."

"But all this fuss over the succession. It's becoming quite tiresome. At some point, I suppose I shall simply have to go to war with my own lords to put a stop to it."

"Why don't you just name the Viscount Aleffe your heir?" asks Devereux. "Bring him to court. Give those lords a role in training him for kingship. Surely that would alleviate their concerns and restore harmony."

"Name a missing boy my heir? Why would I ever do that?"

"Don't you think his mother would produce him straightaway if she thought his safety and his future were secure?"

"What do you know about where Tiece and the boy are?" Charles's tone has taken on a darker edge. Devereux is on dangerous ground without even knowing how treacherous it is.

"Nothing at all. Just speculating on how a noblewoman with ambitions for her son might behave."

Time to turn the conversation in a different direction. "If the viscount can't be your heir," I remark casually, "then perhaps it's time to think about getting a son on your queen."

"That barren cow?" Charles replies indignantly. "I'd sooner name Suidbert here as my heir." He pauses, seeming to mull over the idea. "Hmmm . . . King Amboise de la Fontaine of the House of Suidbert. Has rather a grand ring to it, doesn't it? I might just do that . . . teach those unruly bastards a lesson." And just like that, his jovial mood is restored. God help us all if he actually follows through on the idea. The simmering pot would boil over in an instant, plunging the kingdom into total mayhem.

And then a truly frightening thought occurs to me. What if he just unintentionally revealed his next move? What if he's planning to stir up an all-out civil war for our forces to land in the middle of? The possibility none of us had contemplated now seems very real indeed.

My father once said a king wasn't required to surrender his sense of humor at his coronation. But of late, I've begun to wonder if perhaps he does have to surrender the assurance of a good night's sleep. Much as I try not to disturb Gwen, I can't seem to stop tossing and turning. Finally, there's nothing for it but to get up and wake Osbert.

"Boots and a cloak, please," I tell him. "And then go fetch Samuel and ask him to meet me in the garden."

I'm pacing back and forth along the path when Samuel arrives. "This better be good, Alfred. It's cold out here." Between the pacing of my feet and the racing of my mind, I hadn't really noticed. He sits on a nearby bench and pulls his cloak closer around him while I recount the conversation about the succession, ending with my worry about what our troops might be sailing into.

He doesn't answer right away.

"You know, another possibility, Alfred, is that Charles just wanted to throw you off balance like you did to him this afternoon. And from the state you're in, I'd say he's succeeded admirably," he adds with a chuckle.

I stop my pacing and turn on him, my immediate reaction one of irritation . . . and then I realize he's right, so I join him on the bench. "So what do I do? Wake the others and share this new risk with them . . . make sure they're still committed to the expedition?"

"Why? And anyway, there's no way for you to get Brandr's affirmation." He can tell I'm still uncertain. "So you've now imagined a new possibility we might encounter. Who's to say if Charles might not drop some other offhand remark as he's leaving that will conjure up yet another risky scenario. Would you call them all back for yet another consultation?

"Going into battle is always fraught with uncertainty, Alfred. Remember the tough decision we had to make about where to commit our forces in the last war? But we made it, and we stuck with it."

"And we were lucky it turned out to be right."

"Every good commander knows luck also plays a part – good luck and bad. So he's always thinking several steps ahead about 'what will I do if . . .'" He pauses to let me take all this in.

"You know, Alfred, you remind me so much of your father. He had a remarkable ability to envision all the possible outcomes of a situation."

"Which always stood him in good stead."

"Unless he got paralyzed by it. Remember how he got stuck with his plan for the magistrates? You're at risk of getting stuck right now.

We have an agreement. We have a good plan. Send to Emaurri to stay there, watch developments, and meet Jasper's ship. Then all you need to do is be sure Jasper understands the risks and give him the authority to act." Again, he pauses.

"The only alternative," he adds quietly, "is for you to take the field yourself and make the decisions. And we've already agreed that your being in Charles's kingdom where you could so easily become his prisoner is not a risk worth taking."

Hearing his reassuring words, I begin to feel a sense of calm return . . . and with it, a realization that he's also right about how cold it is out here. I clap him on the shoulder. "Thank you, my friend. Father was right to encourage me to listen to the advice of my mates. Now let's get back to those warm beds."

As we start down the path, Samuel says, "Something just occurred to me. If Charles was really trying to throw you off balance, it might be a good idea to let him think he succeeded. You should be seen prowling the corridors, including those near his room so people tell him you were restless in the night. The last time your strategy was to make him over-confident, it worked exceedingly well. Why not try it again?"

"Funny. That same idea just occurred to me. And we can get Osbert and Timm to make it known in the servants' hall."

· · · · ·

Charles lingers after the other kings leave, his excuse being that his ship has to be made ready. That leaves me no choice but to extend him the hospitality of joining my morning ride. He's in high spirits when he appears at the stable in the company of a couple of what appear to be his guards – which makes me glad I didn't lapse into my usual habit of telling Tobin his men can stand down when I ride with a fellow king. Joviality and guards at this hour of the morning? My gut says he's up to something.

As we start across the meadow, I find out what. "Alfred, I've never seen that famous kennel of yours, you know. I'm told it's at a monastery not far from here. What say we ride there and you can show me around?"

So, his spies haven't been able to snoop around Warin's enclave, and he thinks he's found a way to do it himself. His cleverness in springing this at the last minute leaves me stuck with no choice. Sending a guard to alert Warin we're coming will just make Charles suspicious. Showing up unannounced leaves everything to chance . . . but it's the only option I have.

Dismounting just inside the monastery gate, we leave the horses in the care of the guards, and I lead the way to the kennel. "Brother Adam, King Charles wanted to see your operation. Perhaps you could show him your latest litter and explain how you train the dogs." Charles only gives half an ear to Adam's enthusiastic discourse, repeatedly diverting his gaze to look around the compound, trying to avoid my noticing his keen interest in the monks tending the gardens nearby.

To my great relief, Warin hurries out to greet us. "If I'd known you were bringing guests, Alfred," he says when I introduce Charles, "we'd have been better prepared to offer you hospitality."

"Charles suggested it while we were out riding, so a message wouldn't have arrived much before we did." At least now Warin will grasp what's in play.

"Your gardens are quite extensive, Abbot," Charles walks away from a rather befuddled Brother Adam and heads toward the nearest rows of the garden.

Warin stays at his side. "We grow for both medicines and food, sir." He stops beside a row where two monks are crouched over some young plants. "The foxgloves seem to be growing nicely, Brother Eustace, but I'm worried about the lavender over behind the kennel. Take a look at them if you will." Eustace rises and turns to face us. "As you wish, Brother Abbot," then he taps his companion on the shoulder and they make their way to the far edge of the garden. Though I keep my expression neutral, I'm smiling inside at how deftly Warin has managed to get Denis almost out of sight without Charles catching a glimpse of his face.

Of the monks working in the garden, about half of them have their backs to us and a few of the others have the hoods of their habits raised. Charles will have to make a spectacle of himself if he thinks to study every man's face. About halfway down the rows of the garden, Charles suddenly stops. "This is not many monks, Abbot, for a compound this size."

"Those of our community who aren't assigned to gardening today will have started gathering in the chapel for Sext. In fact, I'd be there myself if we didn't have such honored guests." He pauses. "Would you like to join us for the service, sir? All are welcome."

And in an instant, jovial Charles turns to grumpy Charles as he realizes his intentions have been thwarted in ways he hadn't anticipated. "With respect for your calling, Abbot, I've never found all that kneeling and chanting to be a particularly worthwhile use of my time." He turns on his heel and heads for the horses. I hesitate long enough to mouth "Thank you" to Warin before catching Charles up.

Once outside the monastery gates, Charles kicks his horse to a gallop and calls over his shoulder, "Let's get back. I have a ship to catch." The best thing I've heard all day.

Three weeks later, the port is a frenzied beehive of activity. Supply ships are being loaded first, to wait in the broad estuary at the mouth of the river for the rest of the fleet to be assembled. The first two ships from across the sea arrived within the week, with more arriving each day. The Lakes forces came first, in greater numbers than we'd thought, thanks to Brandr's assurances. Then came Goron's forces, followed quickly by those of the Peaks. As each ship was filled, it moved to join the others at the mouth of the river. The horses will be loaded last — no one wants to clean out a hold where horses have been waiting for days before they ever set sail.

Sir Evrouin is at the port to oversee the loading with much help from Laurence's people, so Jasper is still at the castle. Most of his time is spent huddled with Samuel and Carew, going over their plans again and again looking for the smallest things that could be improved. Evrouin will go with Jasper as his second in command. Carew will remain here as commander in Jasper's absence. I can do little but fret until the final morning before Jasper prepares to depart.

I've invited him to join me on my morning ride – there are things I want to say that are best not overheard. He sounds confident and reassuring as he tells me how he plans to manage the disembarkation. "If Emaurri reports a serious civil war underway, we'll take him on board and sail for home. Otherwise, we offload the Lakes forces first.

Only when they've fully secured the port and we know we have an escape route will we proceed."

"I'm confident you have things well in hand, Jasper." I'm as convinced as I can be of the thoroughness of the preparations. "But there are two more things for your ears only before you leave. The first is straightforward. I want it absolutely understood that you act with my full authority. Whatever decision you need to take, do so without question. And don't think I'll question or second-guess your decisions, no matter what the outcome." I hand him a folded piece of paper bearing my seal. "This should remove any doubt if someone challenges you in the field. Anything you do, short of a blatant act of treason, has my approval in advance."

"Thank you for that, Your Grace. It gives me peace of mind. And the paper might prove necessary in dealing with King Charles's troops."

"The other thing, Jasper, is something that may fly in the face of your training and your sense of honor. So I'm giving you an order. We all hope Charles won't take the field with his troops. But given the fact that he has other motives . . . and especially given his vanity . . . I think it's safe to assume he'll disregard our wishes. Under *no* circumstances are you or your men to take any responsibility for Charles's personal safety. You'll leave that entirely to his own troops."

"Even if he's under attack, Sire?"

"Under *no* circumstances, Sir Jasper. If you think some danger to him might be imminent, my recommendation is that you busy yourself and your captains as far away as possible. You can't intervene in what you don't observe. I can defend you for that. But if you intervene and it goes pear-shaped in any manner, Charles's rage . . . the rage he wants to release on me . . . will be directed at you alone. And I can only imagine what form that rage might take."

"I understand, Your Grace."

"I repeat. That's an order, Sir Jasper."

He stops his mount, looks directly at me, and bows his head. When he looks up again, he says, "You have my word of honor, Your Grace."

There's no doubt I'm concerned for the safety of Jasper and his men. Left unspoken is the decision I've made to leave Charles to his fate. I spared him once for his father's sake and because there was no reason to do otherwise. But now – in these circumstances – I think even Goscelin would reluctantly agree with my choice, for he'd be deeply saddened by what's happened to his beloved kingdom.

So the waiting begins. Jasper will send regular dispatches, but unless the circumstances are dire, he won't waste a ship for routine reports, so we'll only hear from the expedition when resupply is needed. Three ships will stay in port here, one of which will be loaded with supplies and ready to sail whenever a ship returns from across the sea. A cursory report arrived with Emaurri, who came home on one of those three ships. The civil war is still just a simmering rebellion, troop positioning has begun, and the Duke of Aleffe seems to be adhering to our terms. Beyond that, we must simply wait for news.

I try to busy myself with other business of the realm, but it's hard to keep my mind from wandering to the battlefield. Juliana will return in a couple of weeks, so that will provide a pleasant diversion. She'll have celebrated her sixteenth birthday while she's been away, but I suspect there'll be another celebration here. Phillip, Richard, and Samuel do their best to distract me, but I know they're as concerned as I am.

One evening, as Gwen climbs into bed, she remarks, "I wish you had come to the market with us today, Alfred."

"I'm sorry, dear. I just wasn't in the mood."

"No, I really mean it, Alfred. I wish you had come. I wish you had seen the mood in the town."

"What mood is that?" I ask casually, thinking she must be referring to some sort of festivity.

"It's not good, Alfred. The people were polite to us, of course, but there weren't the usual pleasantries or sense of joy at our being there." She pauses and reaches for something from her bedside table. "And then there's this." She hands me a rough, much-used parchment on which something is written. "The first one I saw was at the baker's shop. Then I started seeing them all over. I took this one from the church door. The children were chanting it as they played in the square . . . but of course, they went quiet as soon as they saw us. Read."

I turn my attention to the words scrawled on the parchment in an unpracticed hand.

It seems our king's gone off his head
And many a man will soon be dead
King Charlie come with cap in hand
A beggin' us to save his land
That self-same king what we just fought
He's not our friend, we owe him naught
Our king he say we'll fight with you
That's not the king we thought we knew
Don't make my pa go off to war
Don't know what he'd be fighting for
And so we pray to God above
To bring us back the king we love

Saying nothing, I climb out of bed and go into my dressing room to retrieve something from my strongbox. Back in bed, I hand her a folded piece of paper. "Phillip brought this to me yesterday. He says it's quite popular in Great Woolston."

She reads aloud.

Oh, what's the king thinking?
This war is fair stinking.
King Charles is no friend.
Won't thank us in the end.
So keep our men home.
That's where they belong.

"This seems to have been written by someone well-educated," she says, folding the page and handing it back to me.

"Phillip says the talk is, it was written by a curate." We're both silent with our own thoughts for a few moments before I add, "Richard says they're keeping it much simpler in Neukirk Market. How did he tell me it goes? 'I be not off to fight; there be nary a reason. Just pray that the king dinna' hang me fer treason.'"

"Oh, dear."

"What's up, I wonder? We didn't have this kind of objection to the last war."

"I'm sure that's part of it," she says. "Two wars in as many years. But you know, I've been thinking. Last year they were fighting for hearth and home. And we took great pains to prepare them for what was to come. But this time, you've been so consumed with the planning and the worry about Charles's motives . . . Alfred, you haven't even been out with a patrol in nearly half a year. And I can't remember when you've been to the market with us. The only time you've been seen in the town was that meal at the tavern when Laurence and Estrilda came for a visit.

"I think maybe the answer is actually in the jingles. They don't know why we've gone to war again. And they especially don't know why the man who was their enemy last year is suddenly being treated as a friend. So they're confused . . . frightened that they're going to lose their loved ones . . . and more than a little disenchanted with you for putting them in that state."

I can't argue with anything she's said. "I wonder if the discontent is in the west as well."

"I've not heard from that quarter," Gwen replies. "But Juliana will be passing through Abbéville Market on the way home. I've sent a messenger to the innkeeper with a letter for her, asking her to spend enough time there to get a sense of what mood the people are in. So we'll know soon enough."

"Regardless, this needs attention."

"Well, it will give you something to think about besides pacing and fretting over what you haven't heard from Jasper." She reaches over and pats my hand lovingly. "I have an idea. We're going to the market again tomorrow. I got so distracted by all this that I forgot half of what we went for. Come with us. Mingle with the people again. Answer their questions."

"It's as good a starting place as any."

We go first to the baker's shop. I make a point of stopping to read the handbill. The baker is very polite, but as Gwen said, unusually reserved. I've known this man for years, and it's completely out of character. "I promised the children sweet cakes, Will. You have something nice?"

Alicia has already made her way over to where the honey cakes are on display. Will follows her. "That be what ye want, missy?" he asks.

"One with lots of honey, please," she says.

Will picks out the largest, stickiest, gooiest one of the lot and hands it to her. Nurse won't thank me for bringing her home with honey all over her clothes, but I doubt she can eat it without getting covered in the sticky stuff. She grins at the baker as she bites into her treasure. Edward takes a fruit pie, but Geoffrey demurs. He's picked up on the fact that there's more afoot today than just a treat from the baker.

"That's quite a poem on that handbill there, Will," I remark as I pay him for the treats.

"I be sorry ye see that, Yer Grace, but . . . well . . ." He leaves the thought unfinished.

"Come now, Will, we've known each other too long for you to shy away from telling me what's on your mind."

"Well, it be like this, Yer Grace. It's just that lots of people think mayhap this war not be such a good idea."

"I'll tell you what. I was on my way to visit my father's tomb for a few minutes. What say I wait for you on the church steps? You and anyone you know who wants to talk about it. You can ask me anything that's troubling you."

"I don't know, Sire."

"Let's say half an hour. I'll be there for anyone that wants to come."

"I'll put the word about, Sire," is all he'll commit to.

I hadn't initially planned to visit the tombs, but now it doesn't seem like such a bad idea. Those visits, rare though they are, have always left me with a sense of calm certainty about the path I've embarked on . . . something I could use at the moment.

When I emerge from the church, the square is as always on market days . . . crowded with vendors and a bustle of activity . . . but there's no sign of Will. I sit down on the top step to wait. He finally appears, emerging slowly from a row of stalls, as if unsure he really wants to do this. Seeing me sitting there, he quickens his pace, as if my very presence makes up his mind.

"I dinna' know if t'others be coming, Yer Grace," he says with a little bow, "but I did put the word about like I said."

"Then we'll just have to wait and see, won't we? In the meantime, why don't you tell me what's troubling *you*, Will?"

"Well, mayhap it not be my business, Sire, but I just dinna' understand how we be fighting against King Charles last year and now we go fight with him."

"That was hard for me too, Will." Just then, I catch sight of the blacksmith and the butcher coming toward us from opposite sides of the square. "Looks as if we're about to have company." I point the new arrivals out to Will. "Shall we wait for them?"

"Aye, Yer Grace." He waves and calls out to them. "Rob . . . Loys . . . over here."

The newcomers bow and mumble, "Yer Grace."

I gesture to the steps. "Sit, my friends. Be comfortable. Well, as comfortable as anyone can be sitting on a block of stone."

Loys, the butcher, remains rigidly upright, so Rob and Will hesitate. I gesture to the steps once again. "Beggin' yer pardon, Yer Grace," says Loys, "me ma teach me a man never sit in the presence of his king."

"Did she perhaps forget to mention the part about it being quite acceptable to sit if the king invites you to?" He makes no move to sit down.

"Well, Loys, you may do as you wish, but I think it would be ever so much easier for us to talk if we're all seated." Rob and Will choose a step and sit. Loys hesitates, but eventually follows suit, though he sits stiffly straight, as if there were a stone wall at his back.

"Will was just telling me how he didn't understand why we've joined up with King Charles when we were fighting him just last year."

"That be the truth of things," says Rob.

"Truth be told, my good men, I had the very same misgivings. Why would we do a thing like that? I almost just told him 'no' outright."

"Mayhap ye should've," says Loys.

"I don't deny that. But then I began thinking about what it would mean if the Teutons started running amok in the Kingdom Across the Southern Sea. And the first thing that occurred to me was that they might capture that port. And I thought about all the trade goods we sell and buy there. That's where we get the spices you use in your baking, Will. Not just you, but every other baker in the kingdom. And Rob, what about the horseshoes you sell? If we have nowhere to ship them to, you couldn't make the money you do now. Then there's our herdsmen. They suffer terribly when there's no one to buy their fleeces.

"The queen reminded me of something else. That's where we get fine laces and ribbons and the finest cloth. What happens when your wife needs to make a christening gown for a new baby or a first communion dress for your daughter? Those items would be sadly plain without a bit of lace or ribbon. Young brides would have to settle for a plain gown without any decoration when they should be having the finest dress of their lives."

As I've been speaking, a half-dozen more people have wandered near to listen. The three men sitting with me are beginning to look thoughtful.

"With respect, Yer Grace," says Will, "couldn't we just use the Southern Nordics port instead?"

"That's a fair question, Will. One I asked myself. And the answer is, 'yes, we could.' But not without some hardship. The sea voyage there is longer . . . not to mention that the Northern Sea is stormy for half the year so there's more risk of ships being lost in a storm than with a crossing of the Southern Sea. The overland journey is longer too. So it would cost more to transport goods to and from market. You'd have to pay more for what you buy, and it would cost you more to sell. And we don't know what the port fees might be on top of the transport cost.

"Could you raise your prices to make up the difference? Maybe. That would be for you to decide. But what if you lost custom because people couldn't afford the new prices? Would you then be forced to absorb the extra cost yourself? How much less money would you make?"

The cluster of listeners near the steps has drawn closer, and their numbers are growing.

"'Twouldn't be good," says Rob. "But what makes ye so sure the Teutons be after the port?"

"You've hit on the heart of the issue, Rob. There's no way to be sure. And there's another worry. Our friends in the Lakes and the Peaks trade through that port and ours, just like we do. If their trade were cut off or became more expensive, would they blame us? They're our friends now, but would that change? And there's an even bigger worry. If the Teutons had that port, it's an easy sail for them to send a fleet to attack us. That, my friends, would be a catastrophe.

"So what to do? Wait and see what happens? What if they take over the port and then we have to try to take it back? I've seen that port my friends. It's not an open town like ours. Yes, there are the usual establishments down by the docks for the sailors' entertainment. But it's dominated by a rather impressive fortress. And if the Teutons gained control of that fortress, it would be a horrible, bloody business to win it back." I pause to give them a moment to think.

"Or do we do something to prevent their taking it in the first place, despite the fact that we've no way of knowing if that's their intent?"

"I think mayhap that be a hard decision, Sire," says Will quietly. "I never think of all those things. But do we have to go to war? And why with King Charles?"

"Right now, the Teutons have already taken over a small part of Charles's kingdom. And Charles can't muster enough of an army to kick them out, since he lost so many men invading us and dealing with the rebels in his own kingdom. So if we want to prevent all the terrible things that *might* happen, we don't have much choice but to go help push the Teutons back inside their own borders."

The group of listeners has become a small crowd by now. Someone shouts out, "So how come *we* have to do it, Yer Grace?"

"We're not doing it alone, my friends. The Lakes and the Peaks and even the Territories have armies there equal in size to our own."

Another man near the front of the group speaks up. "So ye be saying that fer ribbons and laces, ye be sending me son . . . me only son . . . to be Charlie's soldier?"

"Absolutely not. Sir Jasper is in charge of everything. None of your sons or husbands or fathers will lift a finger to fight unless Sir Jasper gives the order." I pause to let them take this in. "I would *never* put our men under the command of someone who so recently thought of them as his enemy." Once again I give them time to think.

"But I'll tell you something else. It wasn't easy to decide to fight another war. The queen will tell you I spent many a sleepless night wrestling with that decision." A ripple of laughter runs through the crowd. "What finally made up my mind, though, wasn't ribbons or laces or spices or fleeces. It was the specter of a more terrible and bloody war with the Teutons. I don't want to ever fight another war in my lifetime. I don't want to send men to risk their lives. What I want is peace and prosperity, just like it was in my grandfather's reign and in my father's reign. So I decided the only way to do that was to teach the Teutons a lesson . . . to push them back into their kingdom and do it so convincingly that they'd find it easier to look elsewhere to satisfy their ambition rather than risk taking us on again."

"So why ye not be leading the troops yourself?" asks Rob.

"Truth be told, Rob," I reply conspiratorially, "Sir Jasper is better at it than I am." Another ripple of laughter. "But you know, there's another reason the Peaks king and the Lakes king also decided not to go. If we were there, there'd be four kings, counting Charles, in the field. How could the men put all their effort into pushing out the Teutons if they also had to be thinking about protecting the lives of all those kings? The battle would be more chaotic, and more men would be killed. So we stayed home to stay out of the way."

There don't seem to be any more questions. "You know, my friends, it's been too long since I was last here for market days, but you'll see me again soon. First, though, I need to visit Great Woolston and Neukirk Market, because I've heard the people there are just as concerned as you've been about why we're fighting again.

"Right now," I stand, and Loys is on his feet in an instant followed by the others, "I need to browse the market stalls. I'll be in enormous trouble if I don't find a nice gift for Lady Juliana's birthday."

The crowd parts as I descend the steps, but a number of people follow along, inviting me to their stalls to examine their wares. I wind up buying several trinkets, less for Juliana's amusement than to continue to spread some of the goodwill that I'd let lapse through sheer negligence.

Over the next few days, I send Osbert into the town on some contrived errands to assess the people's mood. He reports that most of the handbills have been removed. A few remain, and there's still some grumbling, but the overwhelming, dark, angry mood has been replaced by something closer to the usual day-to-day business. Real cheerfulness, of course, won't return until our men are home once again, and even that will be tinged by the sadness of some losses.

Geoffrey accompanies me to Great Woolston and Neukirk, where I hope we can achieve the same result. It's a good lesson for him about the value of investing in the people's trust and goodwill.

Juliana has just arrived home as we return. So have the first dispatches from Jasper. I give Juliana a quick kiss on the cheek and rush off to read the dispatches, promising to hear all her news this evening. The first few are nothing more than cursory reports on a successful offloading of men, animals, and supplies, coordination with the other commanders, organization for the march south, and the assorted details necessary to get the expedition underway. I'm pleased to read that the insurgent militia in the port put up no resistance and, in fact, were eager to be blended into the Lakes commander's force.

A report dated a few days later confirms the Duke of Aleffe's men successfully incorporated into Goron's force. The duke himself seems to have acceded to our request to remain at home. I can't help but believe that's a signal to me that he may, at some future time, request a quid pro quo. All in due course.

There's then a gap of several days before the next and final dispatch, which is longer than the others.

Your Grace,

It required a full two weeks to complete the organization and the march south, and it will be at least another week before this is actually in your hands. I'm happy to report that, in addition to the port being secured, both Goron's force and the Peaks force are successfully deployed in their respective sectors. They've taken up positions a half-day's march from the border. The intent is to avoid an immediate provocation while also choosing strong positions from which to prosecute the battle should the Teutons cross the border. Each of the commanders is instructed to give my courier additional dispatches should their situation have changed from my own report. So if there are no such messages, you can be assured that each of those sectors remains calm.

King Charles's forces are here with my own, according to plan. As you predicted, the king himself is leading them. He's already put me on notice that he won't hesitate to countermand any order I give to his troops if he doesn't agree with it. That will be a challenge in the heat of battle, but I took the opportunity of the sea voyage to brief my captains on this possibility and have given them the authority to act on their own to deal with whatever may arise should Charles choose to be meddlesome.

We're as yet just inside the borders of the southeastern province, but already we have clear evidence of a substantial Teuton occupation. As reported, it's more in the form of their men having moved into the villages and farms and simply living there than any sort of organized army preparing for battle. My scouts have seen no evidence of cannons in their forays so far, but they haven't yet penetrated as far as the Teuton border. We're still piecing together the full picture of what awaits us as we move through the province.

We begin our advance tomorrow morning, uncertain of how much resistance we'll meet, but well prepared, I believe, for whatever we may encounter.

Jasper

By now, he's already in the thick of things, and I can do no more than speculate on what might be happening. This seems far more difficult than when Samuel and I were waiting at Peveril Castle for news from the last war. I tell myself it's because there are so many more unknowable factors in this conflict and it's farther away, but I have to wonder if perhaps I was distracted last time by worrying about my own injuries and Samuel's.

After asking Coliar to deliver the dispatches to Samuel, I join the family for the evening meal to hear Juliana's account of her latest adventure – a distraction of an entirely different sort.

The first thing I want to know is what she observed of the mood in Abbéville. "It wasn't the kind of anger Mama wrote to me about. More like uncertainty is how I think I'd describe it. They'd seen the Peaks army pass through, of course, so they knew the Peaks were in it with us. But they're still fearful for their men who are off fighting."

"That's better news than I'd even dared to hope for."

"Still, Papa, I think it would be good for you to visit. Their mood might change if they came to believe they're being left out."

"I entirely agree. Now tell us about your trip."

"Well, of course, I'd been to the Peaks court before, so I already knew a bit about it. The king was ever so happy to see Primrose again and was delighted with my gift of a puppy. And Lady Thorssen could not have suggested a better gift for the queen than the lengths of lace I took to her. We struggled at first to communicate, but eventually managed reasonably well. She really is quite delightful. I know I'd enjoy her company."

"Well, you wouldn't be marrying the queen," chides Gwen. "Tell us about Dafydd."

"Well . . ." she hesitates. "He's very nice and very handsome. He has the dark brooding looks of the highlanders, but there's always a smile in his eyes."

"He's handsome if you like that sort of thing," chimes in Richenda, "but I prefer a man who's fair. I liked Thorbrand better."

"Oh, but Papa, you should see his sister. Eirwen is astonishingly beautiful, and she sings ever so sweetly and plays the lute. And she's smart and knows Latin and loves to read poems and history. She practically swooned when I told her about our library and all the books we have. She would be perfect for Geoffrey, Papa."

"Well, perhaps I'll have to look into that when the time comes, but for now it's *your* future we're talking about."

"I liked Dafydd well enough, Papa, but I'm not sure how much he liked me. I think maybe my ideas for women are too progressive for his taste."

"I hope you weren't too pushy, my dear," says Gwen.

"Oh, no, Mama. Whenever he seemed reticent, I changed the subject. But that does worry me a little."

"He's very serious," says Richenda. "I never quite worked out how he has fun."

"Well, he loves his horses." Juliana. "He seemed happiest when we were with them. And that's when he was the most talkative, telling me all about their bloodlines and how he's planned each year's breedings and about the horses he's heard of that come from across the Roman Sea that are so very fast and agile and how he wants someday to have one or two to breed with his stock. So I think that's his greatest pleasure."

After a bit more conversation about Juliana's time at the Peaks court, Gwen brings up a different topic. "You haven't mentioned your visit with Madam Greslet. Did that go as you'd hoped?"

"Oh, yes, Mama. She was ever so kind. She showed me everything about how she manages her shop and how she runs her wool warehouse."

Mention of the warehouse conjures up memories of the last time Amelia and I were together. Can it really have been more than a year?

"Did you learn anything from her about how she succeeds among the merchants?" asks Gwen.

"She said much of it was a matter of luck. Her husband left her a thriving business, so she had a place to start. But she said it almost fell apart. No one wanted to sell to her . . . they didn't think a woman would know how to pay them the best price. And the men merchants encouraged that . . . kept telling the herdsmen and traders she wouldn't know how to deal with them. So the first year was pretty bad.

"That's when she decided to open the shop, since people thought that was more appropriate for a woman. But she didn't really care if it succeeded or failed. She was going to put all her energy into the wool trade by winning over the herdsmen. And she did. She won over their wives first, then started doing small things to help out the families. The herdsmen brought her all their best fleeces, so the traders had no choice but to deal with her.

"The men in town were furious at first. Mama, she said, 'I'll never forget the looks on their faces, Juliana. They'd never been bested by a woman before, and they simply didn't know what to do.' It wasn't long before they were treating her with more respect. And the women were so delighted to see her outwit their husbands that business at the shop more than doubled the next year. She's never stopped visiting with the herdsmen from time to time, though, and doing little kindnesses for them now and then.

"So to answer your question, Mama, I did learn something. Figure out how to use what people expect you to do in an unexpected way, and then they might be willing to admit you can do just as well as any man."

Gwen smiles broadly. It's exactly what she's done with the infirmaries, so she's happy our daughter is learning how to apply the lesson in different ways.

"You didn't tell them about the boys," prompts Richenda.

"Why don't you tell them?" says Juliana.

"Well, Madam Greslet had us to her home for a lovely meal, and we got to meet her wards. The younger one is just a toddler, but the older one is about Geoffrey's age and is ever so handsome and ever so polite. He treated us all like ladies, bowing and kissing our hands. And when it was time for us to return to the inn, he walked with us to show us the way and make sure we got there safely."

"Wards?" I ask.

Petronilla fills in the details. "It seems Amelia's sister died recently. Her husband had died and she had no other family, so there was no one else to take the children. The youngest is not yet a year old."

My mind is racing, counting the months backward to that last time we were together. Could it be? It's not completely out of the question, depending on how old the baby really is.

Petronilla continues, thankfully unaware of my angst. "So Amelia has brought a wet nurse into the house to see to the baby's needs. She doesn't know if the woman will want to stay on once the little tyke is weaned, but she'll need a nurse for certain so she can continue running her business. At least she has the means to give the children a better life than they might otherwise have had."

"Oh, and I almost forgot." Juliana again. "Lord Guyat was there too, staying at the inn. We had supper with him the night we arrived. He said he had estate business in town, but the innkeeper told us later he thought Lord Guyat's business had more to do with a prominent lady shopkeeper than with the Bauldry estate."

It's been an evening filled with surprises . . . something that seems to have become the normal course of things where Juliana is concerned. She lingers as the others make their way to bed. "So you'll be off soon on the final journey of our bargain?" I ask her.

"Not right away, Papa. I'll be here until Whitsuntide. That's when Aunt Tamasine—" she stops short. "Maybe I should call her Lady de Courcy now. Anyway, she wants to go down about then to plan the furnishings for the new house, so I thought I'd ask her to be my chaperone. She'll be staying at Ernle Manor, and I could help her with the decorating and such. That should help keep the gossip here in check."

"Here perhaps," I chuckle, "but Ernle Manor will be an entirely different story. Will Richenda go along?"

"Not this time. Aunt Petronilla says with all that's going on across the sea, Richenda will be safer here."

"A wise plan. And I'm glad you'll be here for a few weeks. I miss you when you're away. Not sure I'm quite ready for that to become a permanent state of affairs."

She smiles and kisses me on the cheek before heading off to bed. But she's smart enough to refrain from reminding me that sending her off to the Peaks or the Far Nordics would mean her absences would be very long indeed.

About halfway through the journey to Abbéville Market, which Geoffrey and I make together, one of the guards departs as a fast courier to let the mayor and townspeople know we'll be arriving. There's a sizable crowd in the market square – and not just the townspeople. A number have come from nearby farms and villages. The mood is still much as Juliana reported.

There are a quite a few children in the group, so I invite them to ask Geoffrey questions. He's not expecting this. Predictably, most of the children want to know when their papa or their elder brother is coming home. Geoffrey's heard me answer this numerous times for the adults, but I'm actually rather astonished with how he makes it simple for the little ones. "Just as soon as the army makes it safe so he won't have to go off to war again," he told a little girl who was almost in tears.

"But when will that be?" she asked again.

"Well, I can't say for sure. But don't forget that to get home, he has to get on a boat and sail across the sea and then make his way back here. So it might take him a while to do all that. But if you'll be brave and do what your mama tells you, it won't seem like so very long."

When the crowd begins to disperse, the mayor lingers behind. "I'm grateful you came, Your Grace. People hereabouts have been trying to put a good face on things, but of late there's been a bit more grumbling about the men being gone. I think perhaps they understand things better after what you explained today."

"I do hope so, Mayor. Perhaps I should have come sooner."

He bows his head, a silent acknowledgment, I suspect, of agreement with that sentiment, though he won't say so openly. "Unless you plan to leave straightaway, perhaps you and your son would be my guests for a bit of supper this evening?" He frames the invitation as a question.

"We'd be delighted."

"At sundown, then. I believe you know the way."

"I do indeed. And in the meantime, I'd like to pay a visit to one of my favorite bakers."

"Ah, Master Ros, I presume." He whistles to the boys loitering on the steps of the church, and one comes running over. "Show the king the way to Ros's bakery, son."

"Aye, sir," says the boy.

"And not through the back alleys," the mayor adds. "Stay to the main streets."

When we arrive, I give the boy a plain coin for his trouble, and he dances away with a big grin on his face. There's a new sign hanging outside the door: Ros & Hutch, Master Bakers. I couldn't be more proud of these two if they were my own children.

At the sound of the door opening, the man arranging cakes on a table turns to greet his customers. His mouth drops open, he whips off his cap and drops to one knee, then he calls, "Hutch, stop what ye be doing and come quick." Hutch hurries from the back of the shop, wiping his hands on his apron, and the minute recognition dawns, he's down on one knee beside his partner.

"Rise, my good men. I'm here once again as a customer." Hutch scrambles to his feet and offers a hand to Ros, who makes a fuss of not needing help but accepts it just the same. "Ros, Hutch – my son Geoffrey. I think he might want to choose some of your confections to take home to his brother and sisters." Geoffrey nods his head to Ros and Hutch in turn.

Hutch takes Geoffrey around the shop, pointing out the very best of their wares, which Geoffrey graciously selects for his purchase.

"You've done well by the boy, Ros," I tell the older man. "I was pleased to see the new sign."

"I can tell ye now, Yer Grace, I were fit to be tied when ye say I have to take him on as a kitchen boy. But ye be right. And now he be a fine baker. Not quite so fine as me, yet, but better than most. And ours be the best shop in town. So I be proud of him."

While Hutch wraps up Geoffrey's purchases, I place two silver coins on the counter. "I canna' take those, sir. These be a gift fer yer children."

"Then let those coins be a thank-you gift from me to you and Ros."

As we leave the shop, I glance up at the sign again and relish a moment of self-congratulation for my part in making it happen.

Not surprisingly, the mayor has invited the other leaders of the town to his "bit of supper," which, equally unsurprising, is more of a small feast. It's good for Geoffrey to be seen by these people, though one of their number is conspicuously absent. "I'm sure Madam Greslet will be sorry to have missed you, Your Grace," the mayor remarks. "She and her wards are, at the moment, visiting Bauldry Manor at the invitation of Lord Guyat."

Well, well. So Guyat is a bit of a dark horse. It shouldn't be a surprise. His wife's been gone for what – three years now? And I certainly can't fault his taste in women, despite the fact that his choice tugs a bit at my heartstrings.

●　　●　　●　　●　　●

We return to find a new dispatch from Jasper. "It arrived yesterday, Sire," says my secretary as he hands me the folded page. "I took the liberty of showing it to Lord de Courcy in case there was anything that required immediate action."

"Thank you, Coliar. Just as I'd have expected. Any idea where de Courcy might be at the moment?"

"Most likely with Sir Edmund, I should think."

As the dispatch is relatively short, I read it while I go in search of Samuel.

Your Grace,

With our forces on the north and Charles's to the south, we've cleared the Teuton intruders from all the towns and farms in this province. Fortunately, Charles agreed that a pincer movement was appropriate to prevent any of them from escaping farther into the interior of his kingdom. As we dispatched each group across the border, none of them seemed interested in returning to their homes but instead began creating a camp just on their side of the border. Thus it is that we are now established in our own camp opposite them.

We've observed the arrival of supply wagons, some camp followers, and, from time to time, small groups of horsemen, but nothing as yet to indicate the presence of the new weapons. I'm operating on the presumption that these are early arrivals and that a more substantial military presence will appear at some point. So we've arranged our own dispositions with this likelihood in mind.

King Charles once again made it crystal clear to me – this time in the presence of his captains – that he's in sole command of his sector. We therefore function, not as a blended force, but as two distinct units. Hardly ideal should we find ourselves in a pitched battle, but perhaps not undesirable for a protracted stalemate.

Though it's yet early days, my scouts report that some people are beginning to return to their homes in this province. As always, if no additional messages accompany this one, the situation remains calm the full length of the border.

Jasper

I find Carew and Samuel huddled over drawings of the new port defenses. Construction began in earnest once the masons declared the weather was warm enough to work the mortar. Carew jumps immediately to his feet as Samuel makes to rise from his chair. "No need for that." I wave them back to their seats and pull another chair up to the table to join them. "Coliar tells me you've seen this." I put the dispatch on the table. "You too, Carew?'

"Aye, sir."

"Any thoughts?"

"Too bad they didn't just go home like good little children once they realized we'd caught them in the act," says Samuel. "Not enough yet, though, to tell just how strong the Teuton ambitions are or what's motivating them."

"A lot will depend on whether they reinforce that camp," adds Carew, "and how much. One possibility is that they just want to wait us out and hope we give up so they can get back to whatever they were up to before. Until they show their hand, Sir Jasper has to bide his time."

•   •   •   •   •

A week later, Lady Mary and her husband arrive at court, which serves to remind me that I still haven't settled on a suitable role for Hugo. "You said we were welcome any time, Sire," Mary says when Gwen and I greet them at the court dinner.

"I did, and you are. To what do we owe the pleasure?"

"We . . . I, I suppose . . . just thought it had been too long since the Meridens were represented at court."

"Any word on when Hugo's family might join him?"

"I ask now and then," Mary replies, "but he's always evasive. So I really don't know. In any event, I've decided to enjoy myself and not worry about such things while we're here."

"As well you should," laughs Gwen.

A week after that, following the next court dinner, Gwen turns our bedtime conversation to Mary. "Have you noticed, Alfred? She seems . . . actually, I'm not quite sure how to describe it. Not quite herself."

"She seems cheerful enough to me, but then I only see her at times like dinner this evening."

"That's just it, though. She's just a bit too cheerful. Even among the women. It's rather like she's trying to take her mind off something unpleasant by being overly pleasant herself."

"Or maybe she's just glad to be away from Hugo for a while," I chuckle.

"I'm not so sure, Alfred."

"No doubt you'll find out soon enough."

"I'm sure I'll have more time to spend with her after Juliana and Tamasine leave."

"Oh my, it's almost time for that, isn't it?" Time seems to crawl while I'm waiting for Jasper's reports, and yet, somehow, Whitsunday's just two days away. "When are they leaving?"

"It depends on the weather. They're taking the tapestries Tamasine bought for the new house and fabric for the bed hangings, so she doesn't want to set off in the rain. But we'll have a nice private supper with Juliana – just the three of us – the night before."

The next morning, all thoughts of Mary's merriment and Juliana's journey are banished. When I return from my morning ride, Coliar is waiting at the stable – something I don't think he's ever done before. "I didn't want you to tarry, Sire," he explains. "A messenger from Sir Jasper arrived barely a quarter-hour after you'd departed. Says his ship docked with the morning tide and he galloped all the way here."

I dismount and give Altair into a groom's care, wondering what the messenger could have said to make my usually calm and astute secretary risk starting gossip among the stable boys about what's up across the sea. I get my answer as we walk briskly back to the castle. "I suggested he leave the message with me," says Coliar, "but he said Jasper had ordered him to put it immediately into your hands and no one's hands but yours. Nothing would satisfy him but that I go in search of you, else he'd do it himself."

When we enter the private reception room, the messenger jumps up from his seat, bows sharply, reaches into his pouch, and hands me a sealed message – all so quickly that it seems like a single movement. "Your Grace. Sir Jasper said I was to wait for a reply."

"Was there anything else you're to tell me?"

"No, Sire. Everything's in there." He points to the document.

"And how long have you been on your journey?"

"I rode from dawn to late at night every day, Sire. Changed horses three times a day. Then the miserable time on the ship. Just over four days in all, Sire. I couldna' get here any faster."

"Thank you, my good man. Now go get some food and rest. I'll send for you when my reply is ready."

I take the message into the bedchamber to read it uninterrupted.

Your Grace,

My courier has been exhorted to make the utmost haste, so I hope not many days have passed after the events recounted here. Since my last dispatch, the size of the Teuton camp has steadily grown, with the arrival of groups of horsemen and men on foot every two or three days. Some of those arriving most assuredly have military training – one can tell by their demeanor – but the camp hasn't been reorganized to give the appearance of an army preparing for engagement.

A week ago, King Charles decided to stage harassing raids against the opposing forces each day – his way, I suppose, of showing me what he thought a commander should be doing. So far as I can discern, the raids were little more than a show of bravado, producing some noisy clashes of swords, but no casualties on either side.

Oddly, each time one of these raids began, the Teutons would initiate a skirmish at the far north end of our lines, drawing our attention away – intentionally, I now believe – from what was going on among Charles's forces. The skirmishes never amounted to much and were easily defended – and invariably, as the Teutons began to withdraw, the fighting at the south end also came to a halt. All of which suited my purposes.

This morning Charles launched his raid at dawn, and his luck ran out, as he was taken captive and carried away from the Teuton encampment. His commanders waited almost five hours before informing me what had happened. Their tale was a hodgepodge of contradicting stories that seemed contrived to absolve them of any and all responsibility for the capture of their king. I allowed them to prattle on, but made sure they remembered Charles's insistence that his troops were his and his alone to command.

Their next ploy was to demand we immediately organize a massive rescue operation to pursue the captors and bring Charles back – an utterly pointless exercise that would, rightfully, be interpreted as an invasion of the Teuton Kingdom – not to mention that it would leave this province only lightly defended and vulnerable to being reoccupied, this time by military forces.

I managed to convince them that Charles had most likely been taken as a hostage and that, in due course, an offer to ransom him would be received. I hope, Sire, that my interpretation is correct. This is a most peculiar situation, as there's been no real aggression from the opposition nor, it seems, has there been any escalation of the factional conflict within this kingdom. For now, we remain at readiness, though for what remains to be seen. Be assured, however, Your Grace, that I will not allow Charles's troops to embark on any aggression against the Teutons, even if I have to take them all prisoner to prevent it.

Please send my courier back with your guidance on my actions should the expected ransom request be received.

Jasper

Just as I finish, Osbert pokes his head in from my dressing room. "Ye be needing something, m'lord?" There's a hint of apprehension in his voice – he's unaccustomed to finding me here at this time of day.

"Actually, there is, Osbert. Find Lord Rupert, please, and ask him to meet me at the stable."

"Ye be going riding again?"

"Just to the hut. I don't think the boys will be going there until later in the day." While Osbert goes in search of Rupert, I read Jasper's missive one more time, then consign it to my pocket.

Sensing my mood, Rupert says nothing on the short ride to the hut. Once we're inside, I hand him the dispatch, which he reads through twice before returning it. "So what do you make of it?" he asks.

"What's he up to? Did he really allow himself to get captured? Are his troops *that* incompetent? Or did he stage it?"

"To what purpose?"

"To join up with his allies? To come back at the head of a massive force that we're not prepared to contend with? To force me to play into his hands as a duty to rescue a fellow monarch who's supposedly an ally in this business? To lure me into the hands of the Teutons?"

"What if the Teutons really *have* taken him hostage?"

"Whatever his game is, I'm tired of it." I stop my pacing and settle on one of the stools. "The jingles have one thing right – even if I *do* save his lousy arse, he won't thank us for it. In fact, he'll probably find some way it's *my* fault his arse needed saving in the first place."

There's a touch of amusement in Rupert's eyes. "Can't remember the last time I've seen you vent your spleen like this."

"Who better to vent it to?"

"Laurence?"

"He's two hours away and my spleen needs venting *now*."

Rupert chuckles. "Alright. Charles is a supercilious cox-comb and a complete cumber-world. So what are we going to do about him?"

I can't help but chuckle myself. "Better still, what are the Teutons going to do with their prize?"

"I think we have to leave the military options in Jasper's hands."

"Agreed. I'll speak to Samuel, of course, but I'm not inclined to land more troops in a foreign kingdom purely on unsubstantiated speculation."

"Which leaves us with the question of a ransom."

The germ of an idea – first conceived when I initially read Jasper's words but pushed aside by my frustration at being forced into this position – returns to the forefront. An idea that could either restore our world to reason and progress or plunge us into an even deeper quagmire than where we find ourselves now. A huge risk for what could be an enormous reward. The reason I wanted to talk with Rupert in the first place. He waits patiently as I collect my thoughts.

"If . . . or rather, when . . . the ransom is demanded, it must *not* be paid."

The expression on my uncle's face softens to something resembling fatherly approval – perhaps even parental pride. I need nothing else to tell me my instincts are right.

"How would you achieve that?" he asks. "I rather suspect Lucia will think it appropriate to raise heaven and earth to collect the money, no matter the amount. Given the peculiar nature of her marriage, it's even likely she'd feel the need to set the example by contributing huge sums from her personal fortune, just so she'd be in Charles's good graces on his return."

"My thoughts exactly. Which is why we can't leave it to Lucia."

"You have something else in mind?"

"More like some*one* else."

He nods. "Will she do it?"

"I don't think I have any choice but to convince her."

"It's not without risk to her person."

"Neither is the alternative."

Once back at the castle, I head straight for Gwen's sitting room. "A word, my dear, if you don't mind?" She joins me immediately in our bedchamber.

"I need a conversation with Petronilla as soon as can be, away from prying eyes and ears. Could you contrive a way to end your little gathering gracefully and then the two of you join me discreetly in the old library?" With its solid stone walls and heavy oak door, this room is the most secure in the entire castle, and the women can make their way there without drawing attention to themselves.

"Of course, Alfred. May I ask—"

"It'll be easier if I tell you both at the same time."

"Very well. We'll join you as soon as it's prudent."

They arrive separately, and I lower the iron bar across the door to ensure we're not disturbed. I've no wish for Osbert's presence in the corridor for that purpose to signal something important is happening inside.

They both know enough of how we've deployed to flush out the Teutons that I can quickly update them on Jasper's earlier reports. Then I produce his latest dispatch for them to read. I watch each of them furrow their brows in thought as they take in the import of Jasper's words.

"Do you think Sir Jasper's right," Gwen speaks first, "that there'll be a ransom request forthcoming?"

"It seems the most likely among several possibilities. The others would be within Jasper's existing authority to respond to as he sees fit."

"Lucia will be completely out of her depth," says Petronilla.

"I know. And I also know a ransom demand might be just the catalyst for the factional rivalries to boil over. That's why we have to control where the demand is delivered and what the response is." I pause to let that sink in. "And that, my dear, is why I need your help.

I need someone there, in the castle, with high enough rank to control the situation."

"Do you know what you're asking, Alfred?" Petronilla's tone is quiet, her demeanor calm, but I can imagine the turmoil inside.

"I'm asking you to help me forestall an all-out catastrophe in Goscelin's kingdom. And, yes, I know," I add as gently as I can, "that I'm asking you to put yourself at risk. If there were any other way . . ."

Petronilla rises from her chair and walks slowly around the room, pausing for a look at the irreplaceable volumes we still keep here for safety, but I know her mind is not on the books or scrolls she fingers lovingly. When she resumes her seat, she says, "What is it you want me to do?"

"I want you to return to the kingdom and take up residence as dowager queen. I want *you* to be the one who receives the ransom message. If there's any way you can keep it from becoming known that the demand has been made, then it ends there. But I must tell you, I think that's highly unlikely. If it's delivered to one of the commanders in the field, then word will spread among the troops. But Jasper will have my orders that any such message is to be delivered only to you, placed directly in your hands by the courier. If an attempt is made to deliver it directly to Lucia, then you have to be prepared to intercept it before she can read it – but, of course, the entire castle will know that a messenger arrived and speculation will be rampant.

"The most important thing is that you quietly ensure that the money can*not* be raised. We'll help you. We still have agents in place who can sow mistrust among the factions such that neither side is willing to contribute until they see signs that the opposing faction is already doing so. You'll have to give them leeway to operate. But you have my word they'll do nothing to foment an actual clash of arms. The longer you can delay any progress toward assembling a ransom, the more likely the Teutons will change their tactics."

"That's quite a lot to ask, Alfred," says Gwen softly. "Is there really no other way? What if we just let things play out . . . let Lucia raise the ransom?"

"Think about Charles's state of mind when he gets back. He won't be grateful for his release. He'll have weeks – perhaps months – of pent-up fury ready to unleash. He won't remember he intentionally spurned Jasper's command. He'll turn on the very forces he invited to help him in the first place. He'll turn on Lucia for taking too long to raise the ransom, regardless of how quickly it's done. And I wouldn't put it past him to slaughter every man of the Aleffe affinity who's joined forces with us."

"He's right, Gwen. One more humiliation would most certainly be more than Charles could take. His temper would overtake his judgment." Petronilla pauses for a moment. "But, Alfred, what if I fail?"

"Then we're no worse off than if we'd made no attempt." We both know, though, what this means.

"When do you need my answer?"

"That may be the most difficult part of my request. For all we know, the ransom demand may have already arrived while Jasper's courier was on his way here. So there's no time for delay."

"May I have an hour?"

"Of course."

"Gwen, will you come with me?" Petronilla asks as she rises to leave. I spring up from my seat to unbar the door.

"I'll come to your private reception room," Petronilla says as the two of them step into the corridor.

While I wait, I compose my reply to Jasper, hoping that I don't have to conceive an entirely different strategy an hour hence.

Sir Jasper,

In the hope that there's been no change in the situation from what was contained in your last dispatch, I've considered our strategy should the Teutons demand a ransom for King Charles's return. The Dowager Queen Petronilla has returned on the same ship as your courier and will take up residence in the castle alongside Queen Lucia. If a ransom request is received by you or by any of the commanders in the field – including Charles's captains – it's to be delivered immediately to the dowager queen and to no one else. It must be placed directly into the dowager's hands by your courier and must not, under any circumstances, be given to Queen Lucia, to any servant or man at arms, or to any cleric who might offer to be of service to complete the delivery. Beyond delivering the message to the dowager queen, you and your commanders – including Charles's captains – are to take absolutely no action relative to the ransom.

I'm inclined to agree with your assessment that Charles has been taken as a hostage. But I've also considered the other possibilities implied in your dispatch, particularly that Charles may have arranged his own abduction for his own purposes. Since those possibilities all point toward some military scenario, your response to any such events remains in your hands as commander in the field.

Know that you have my full trust and confidence and my appreciation for your success so far in this mission.

Having signed and sealed the message, all I can do is wait.

At the end of the hour, Gwen and Petronilla surprise me by arriving through the door from our bedchamber, where they'd apparently been deep in discussion.

"Despite the risk, Alfred," says Petronilla, "I know there's no one else who can do this. Besides, I can't bear to think of how many lives might be lost if it were all to go wrong. But there are two things I must ask of you."

"Name them."

"Richenda will stay here for now. But if anything should happen to me, I want you and Gwen to look after her as if she were your own."

"Have no doubt of that, my dear. And since Harold named Rupert as her official guardian, she'll have everyone in this family to care for her."

Petronilla squeezes Gwen's hand. "I had Gwen's assurances, but I wanted yours as well."

"And the other?" I ask.

"I want one of Sir Tobin's best men to go with me."

"Of course you can have some protection."

"It's not protection I have in mind, Alfred, though I must admit that might not go amiss. My concern is that intercepting a message intended for Lucia will require some serious subterfuge. So I need someone I can trust beyond any doubt who can masquerade as a servant but who has the intellect and the strength – whichever may be needed – to coerce a courier to surrender his message. Someone who'd have the courage to do whatever was necessary in the moment."

"I'll speak to Tobin straightaway."

"Then I'll be ready to set sail on tomorrow afternoon's tide. I agree with you – there's not a minute to lose."

I go to her, embrace her, and give her a gentle kiss on the cheek. "Gratitude seems an inadequate word. But you have all that I possess. Know that we have agents there. We *will* take care of you. And we'll bring you home straightaway if things should deteriorate."

"I'll do my best, Alfred. I hope it's enough."

Gwen leaves the room with her. After I speak to Tobin and summon Jasper's messenger, I make my own preparations to accompany her to the port tomorrow to bring Laurence into the picture. He'll need to send his own messages. Once she sails, there really is nothing else I can do but wait. Wait and pray to every god ever invented by man for her safety and success.

What to everyone else feels like the normal routine of the court feels to me like an interminable stint in purgatory, waiting for word from across the sea. I sent our ambassadors to apprise our allies of the latest events and included a coded message to Brandr along with Beatrix's latest letter to her son. She's staying with us for the rest of the summer.

Rain delayed Juliana's departure for several days, but by now she should be settled in at Ernle Manor. I'm still not sure what I think of this experiment, but a bargain is a bargain.

My visits to the monastery have been less frequent than is my usual custom, in part to avoid drawing attention to the place but also to be close by should any news arrive, but I did ride up right after Petronilla's departure to apprise Warin of what's afoot. As long as he's responsible for the young viscount, it's essential he know what's playing out. Laurence says there's been little interest in the boy of late, but with these new events, that could change in the blink of an eye.

As Midsummer's Day passes, I can only assume that no news is not bad news.

Lady Mary and her husband are still at court. I asked Gwen about that last night. "I don't remember her ever staying so long. She's usually impatient to be back on the estate. Don't you find this a bit strange?"

"Combined with her continuing cheerfulness, yes. But I've had no luck getting to the bottom of it."

"Do you think there's any possibility Hugo's actually running the estate well so she can relax and enjoy herself for the first time in years?"

"Do *you*?" All I could manage was a grimace and a deep sigh. "Anyway," she continued, "it occurred to me she might just want to be more directly involved with the new infirmary at the convent. But if that were the case, why wasn't she spending the time with Sister Madeleine?"

"Why indeed."

"I think your mother may have the clue. She told me the other day that Mary's had several rather long conversations with Lord Devereux. He wouldn't give Mother Alice any of the details of what they'd talked about – just said, 'Mary's having a really difficult time with the changes on the estate. She's doing her best with Hugo being in charge, but it isn't easy for her.' Maybe *you* need to have a conversation with Devereux as well."

"I'll have a word with him tomorrow."

And as if he were some sort of diviner, I find Devereux waiting in my private reception room when I return from my morning ride. "A word, if I may, Alfred?"

"Of course." I settle into a chair facing his.

"It can't have escaped your attention – even with your focus on the situation in Charles's kingdom – that Mary's been at court for several weeks now. She came to me not long after they arrived. Hugo's management of the estate weighs heavily on her mind, and she's been at a loss to know whether she should say or do anything. At first, I thought it might be little more than just lingering grief for her father. But the more she talked, the more I became concerned. So I've done some investigating of my own, and I don't like what I've discovered. I think you should hear her out, Alfred."

"Why don't you tell me now?"

"I'll add what I've learned to her story, but she deserves to speak for herself. From what I can tell, she's exercised remarkable restraint and only brought this to me once she became convinced it wasn't just a Meriden matter but something that could harm the kingdom."

"Then let's ask Coliar to arrange for us to talk this afternoon."

"Excellent. And is Rainard still here?"

"I think he's planning to leave tomorrow for Ernle Manor. Why do you ask?"

Devereux chuckles. "Ah, yes. Alice told me about your bargain with Juliana. I'm ever so grateful the whole business of finding husbands for daughters is long in my past. In any event, we should have Rainard with us this afternoon. I think you may find yourself wanting advice on the legalities of certain matters."

Knowing I don't stand on ceremony in private conversations like this, he rises from his chair. "Now I'd best be going and leave you to whatever that pile of papers is on your desk. I'll speak to Coliar on my way out – save you the trouble."

There's no hint of a smile on the three faces that join me this afternoon, so we get straight down to business. "I really didn't want to trouble you, Sire, but Lord Devereux assures me you need to know," Mary begins. "You asked when we first arrived if I knew anything more about Hugo's family. I have to apologize, Sire, for being evasive. The truth is, he told me some weeks back – before Easter, in fact – that I should quit asking. I believe his exact words were, 'This is my estate to run as I see fit, and they have no business here. So I'll thank you not to mention them again.' That's when I realized he had no intention of ever bringing them here and began to see that lording it over our people was his way of getting out from under the thumb of his wife's family – and his resentment of being subject to their demands.

"You won't be surprised that he neither tells me nor consults me about anything he does on the estate, so I've had to piece things together from our tenants and the villagers. At least they still trust me – for now, anyway. It seems that as the annual renewal of each tenancy comes due, Hugo's been increasing the rent by a third or more, depending on how valuable he thinks the crops or the herds may be. I know it's the lord's duty to manage the land to the benefit of the estate, but that's absurd!

"If a tenant dares to object, he offers them a choice. They can work the land for him for whatever wage he chooses to pay, or they can leave so he can find a more agreeable tenant. I'm told the wages he offers are barely enough to feed a family with just two children but insufficient to buy wood for cooking or cloth to replace worn-out clothing or even candles."

"Can't they just get wood from the land?" Rainard asks.

"Oh, no," Mary replies. "He's declared all wood – even fallen dead branches – as property of the lord and that taking even a twig is considered poaching. So they have to buy their wood from him. Most of them have little choice. They and their forebears have lived their entire lives on Meriden lands and have nowhere else to go – nowhere to turn. A few of the younger tenants have actually left. And quite a number of the children old enough to do so have decided to try to find a way to make a life elsewhere.

"What's happening, in effect, Sire, is that he's turning our domain into his personal fief and the people who live there into his serfs. And with the younger people leaving, that puts a greater burden on the older ones to work the land and manage the herds. It doesn't bear thinking what might happen when those people can no longer produce to Hugo's satisfaction. I finally couldn't stand by and let that continue without seeking Lord Devereux's advice."

Every face – mine included, I suspect – looks grim.

"When Alice and I were at the country manor a week or so ago," says Devereux, "I took the opportunity to go to Great Woolston and speak to the mayor. He confirmed that quite a few young people – men and women – began arriving in town just after Easter, and they've been coming ever since. All the newcomers are looking for work of any sort, and almost every one of them is from a Meriden farm or village. The estate manager at the manor hired one of them to help around the stable. Some have even made it as far as Thorssen's. He's had two families asking about available tenancies – one just after Easter and the other around May Day."

"That would also explain the letter I had from our steward some weeks back," says Rainard. "A man with a large family looking for a vacant tenancy. He told me he'd sent them on to Abbéville as he knew we had nothing to offer."

"Tell him the rest, Mary," says Devereux gently.

"Sire, I felt like I owed it to you to try one last time, so I ventured to tell him what he was doing was unlike anything I'd ever seen in this kingdom and you might have some objection. I hoped – rather foolishly, I suppose – that after the upbraiding you'd given him over the previous incident, he might think twice about incurring your anger again. I was stunned by his reply. 'If the king thinks he can tell me how to run my domain,' he said, 'then I'll simply withdraw that loyalty oath and go my own separate way. Then we'll see how he likes having a big chunk of his precious kingdom stripped away.'

"I was mortified, Your Grace. And utterly speechless. He took that for my acceptance of his declaration and ordered me out of the room. That's when I knew I had to do something."

Needing time to collect my thoughts, I go to the sideboard and pour four glasses of wine, return with two – one for Mary and one for Rainard – then retrieve the other two for Devereux and myself before settling back into my chair. "I have to admit, Mary, to being as much at a loss for words as I'm sure you were. You've had longer to think about this, Devereux. Any idea for how to control his behavior?"

"Montfort, Ernle, and I have talked about it. You could put him on the Council, give him some role that requires him to stay at court and to act for the benefit of the kingdom and not himself, and we could all monitor everything he does. But that's not without a different set of risks." He pauses for a sip of wine. "Not to mention that he'd undoubtedly leave detailed orders for his estate manager to enforce whatever he wants done there.

"The three of us could have another talk with him about expectations, but so far, he's taken no notice of any guidance anyone has offered. I'm inclined to think we'd get polite acknowledgment of our words and nothing more.

"The fact that he's already threatened to leave the kingdom removes most of our options."

"Do you think he's serious, Mary," I ask, "or was he just brushing you off? I know how much he resents a woman meddling in his affairs."

"There's no way I can know for certain, Sire, but it didn't sound like a remark made on a whim in the moment. It seemed calculated – as if he'd given serious consideration to his options if anyone objected to the path he was taking." She too takes a sip of her wine. I wait, sensing there's more she wants to say. "May I offer my opinion, Sire?"

"Please."

"I think it's quite possible he sees any expectations for his behavior as the same kind of dominance his wife's family must have held over him. He feels like he can brush off advice from the lords because they're his peers. But you, Sire, hold real authority over him. So he's transferred his resentment of his wife onto you. I think it quite likely he'd withdraw his oath in a fit of pique."

For the next few moments, we all commune with our wine in silence. "Rainard," I ask at length, "is there some charge on which he could be brought before the king's justice?"

"Based on what I know so far, no matter how egregious his behavior may be, he's as yet committed no crime. If you wish, I can certainly look deeper into the matter and see if there's anything to justify a charge." He pauses for my reply.

"Why do I sense there's more on your mind, Rainard?"

"Sire, even if he *has* committed a crime and is subject to some sort of punishment – even imprisonment for some period – he's still Lord Meriden. And when he completes the term of his punishment, he's still Lord Meriden. So unless he has some miraculous change of heart as a result of whatever happens to him, the problems we're wrestling with now will still have to be faced. But I think you know that, Sire."

"I do, Rainard, and I know I'm trying to catch at a straw." For something to do, I go to the sideboard to fetch the pitcher of wine and bring it back to the low table beside my chair. "Which brings me to the real question – is there a way we can be rid of him?"

I know Devereux knows the answer – as I do – but he defers to Rainard. "The other hereditary lords can come together and petition the king for his removal. It would likely be quite an acrimonious process and the aftermath is difficult to foresee. To my knowledge, it's never been done before."

"Nor to mine," adds Devereux.

"The best would be if we could identify a senior claim," Rainard continues. "Someone from the late Lord Meriden's – or even his father's – lineage and in a line older than Hugo's mother. If such a claimant came forward and the claim could be verified, you'd have no choice but to displace Hugo in favor of the legitimate heir."

"Mary," I ask, "was there anything in your father's papers that might point in that direction?"

"Truth be told, Sire, I've been remiss about going through them. When he died so suddenly, I couldn't bear to deal with them. And then it was Christmas. And then when Hugo finally arrived, he was so impatient to make my father's study his own that I simply stuffed all the personal papers in a box and stashed it away in my dressing room. With everything that's been happening since, I've just never gone back to them. I know Father had been engaged in some sort of new correspondence last autumn, but he never told me what it was about."

"Perhaps it's time to find out."

Suddenly, she furrows her brow and studies her wine. "There was . . . something strange . . . on his last day. He could barely speak, and when he did, it was difficult to make out what he was trying to say. But in one of his more lucid moments, he seemed quite agitated and grasped my arm and said something that sounded like it might be 'Find Clarie.'"

"Clarie?"

"I don't know, Sire. I remember, when I was a very small child, hearing odd bits of servants' gossip about the lord's disgraced daughter . . . that would have been my grandfather's daughter. It didn't mean anything to me at the time other than that anyone caught speaking of it was chastised severely. I couldn't have been more than four years old, so I don't remember more than that."

"If that daughter was older than Hugo's mother . . ." Rainard ventures and then pauses. "But at the moment, that's still catching at straws."

"Well, it's one more straw than we had when we started this conversation. Mary, can you get those papers out of the manor without Hugo knowing about it?"

"It should be easy enough when he's out hunting. But no doubt one of the servants will tell him I carried away a box."

"You need to retrieve those papers and bring them back here. Rainard, until this is sorted out, I want you to help Lady Mary turn the

Meriden family inside out, looking for any possible solution to our dilemma. For that matter, turn the entire kingdom inside out if you have to." I pause, then add, "But do it discreetly" with a little chuckle.

"If I might suggest, Sire," says Rainard, "it might be far more discreet if we do it from Ernle Manor – that is, if Lady Mary is willing to spend some time there. Here, too many people would be aware we're doing something, and word might get back to Hugo."

"Whatever you think best – just don't delay."

"When should I arrive at the manor, Lord Rainard?" asks Mary.

"As soon as you can retrieve the papers. I'm leaving here tomorrow, so I'll be there before you in any event."

"Very well," I say. "Do this as quickly as you can . . . but more importantly, be thorough. Leave no clue unexplored." I rise and offer to pour more wine for Mary.

She declines and rises from her seat. "I should go, Sire. My husband will need to start organizing our journey. And, Sire . . . thank you. You too, Lord Devereux. I think perhaps tonight I'll have my first decent sleep this year."

The others rise as she leaves, closing the door behind her. "Rainard, I know this is an enormous burden to place on you, particularly at this juncture, but it can't wait – and it needs to be done at arm's length from the sitting lords and at great remove from me."

"Say no more, sir. That's why I suggested we do the work away from here. As for the other matter — "

"Don't worry," I interrupt him. "I'll write to Juliana and tell her she can extend her visit by whatever time this matter takes to resolve."

"I think I can predict her response, sir. She'll say this is just part of a nobleman's life that she needs to experience."

"Well, just to be on the safe side, I'll give you that letter anyway. I wouldn't want her to think I'm meddling with the terms of our agreement. Pick it up from Coliar before you leave. Now I think maybe you, too, have travel preparations to attend to."

Devereux remains. "Nothing in all my tutelage has prepared me for anything like this," I tell him.

"Nor mine, I have to admit. Montfort and Ernle were equally perplexed."

"You should probably tell them what we're doing. But let's not spread the knowledge any further at this point. Rainard's right about the importance of nothing getting back to Hugo."

"I couldn't agree more."

"Sir . . . are we doing the right thing?"

"We can't stand by and see him destroy the Meriden heritage. I just hope they turn up something. Even if it's a junior claim and we have to fall back on the petition process, at least you'll have someone to install in the lordship. God help us if they turn up nothing."

As June comes to an end, my restlessness grows. It's quiet across the sea. Too quiet? And the fact that I can't even inquire about progress in the Meriden matter just piques my curiosity. I only hope Hugo doesn't do something spectacularly stupid before Rainard finishes his work.

Richard tries to distract me with updates from the recent Assembly meeting. "An entirely new group this time," he says, "so they've had to spend more time than usual getting to know one another and figuring out how the Assembly functions instead of conducting actual business."

"What do you make of that?"

"I'm not sure whether to worry they're all new because people think the others were ineffective or if our familiar faces just decided it was time to give someone else the opportunity. I must admit I wish there was at least one experienced head in the group so that the guidance doesn't all have to come from me. At least they were all cordial . . . and so far, they seem sensible. Unlike that lot Phillip had to contend with in your first year on the throne."

"Did you get any business done?"

"Hard to say. Some pretty serious conversations about the issues at the mill and hiring a new manager. And, surprisingly, not a word about taxes . . . not one single word."

I laugh. "Give them time."

The distraction I've been hoping for finally arrives in the form of Laurence and his family. Laurence is still in his traveling clothes when he finds me in the new library and asks, "Fancy a ride?"

"Nothing I'd like better."

"Then put away that book. Samuel's meeting us at the stable."

We head for the hut in the woods, where Laurence gets straight to the point. "The message came with a ship that docked last night. Sir Jasper's courier placed the ransom demand in the dowager queen's hands five days ago."

There's been no dispatch. Good man, Jasper – reading between the lines of my instructions to do nothing more than deliver the missive to Petronilla. I want no trail of clues that can be followed back to me.

"So now we wait?" Samuel voices what we're all thinking.

"At least now we have some idea what we're waiting for," I chuckle.

"Don't worry, Alfred," says Laurence. "My people know what to do."

"Let's just hope no one realizes what they're doing. Samuel, how will the troops be faring? They've been deployed for a long time now."

"Some of them will be restless. But Jasper made sure going into this that all the captains understood the mission wasn't intended as an all-out war – just as a deterrent. It's summer and they can eat off the land, so no one will be worried about going hungry. If his captains can keep up morale, then we have a little more time. That said, you're right to be concerned."

"Should we be thinking about swapping out some of the troops with fresh men?"

"Let's concentrate on how we get everyone home rather than on making this mission a permanent one."

"That's what I'd prefer, but . . ."

"We have to let it play out a little longer, Alfred. Be patient. Jasper and Carew had many long conversations about this before the army departed. Carew knows what to do and when."

And so the waiting continues. It's nearly the end of July before the next dispatch arrives.

Your Grace,

The news that reaches us here in the field is that there has been little or no progress on raising the ransom for King Charles's return. My growing concern about the Teutons' reaction was answered last week when they launched an all-out attack on the border with Aleffe province.

Goron's scouts had reported that people living near the border were fleeing their homes, so he had warning that something was up. He moved his positions up to the border before the Teutons could invade and fought a series of short battles over two days after which the enemy retreated into the interior.

We suffered some casualties in the engagement. Some of the injured could be patched up in the field. The others have been taken to the monastery north of Aleffe Manor to be cared for by the monks. We've kept a careful record of the dead. Thankfully, there weren't many.

As a precaution, Goron's forces remain deployed along the border. Neither of us knows if the retreat is merely to regroup, if an attack is being planned somewhere else, or if this was merely a test of our strength. Everyone is now on high alert.

There is one other thing you should know, Sire, and I'm quite at a loss as to what to make of it. The new weapons were nowhere in evidence during the attack on Goron's sector. None were seen; none were used. And we have still seen none in the camp opposite us. The terrain here – a flat plain – would make their presence – even their arrival – difficult to disguise.

Jasper

What game are the Teutons playing? And is Charles playing it with them or is he merely a tool in their hands?

And why no cannons? Surely they know we're not equipped with them, so deploying them would provide an enormous advantage.

Is my strategy with the ransom going to founder? Have I made a critical blunder from which a recovery may not be possible?

The answers to my questions come a week later in the person of a man who practically falls to his knees from exhaustion when he's shown into my private reception room. "I've been scarcely four days on the road, Your Grace. Sir Jasper said the most important thing I'd ever do in me life was to get this to you faster than a man could. So I never slept until I were on the ship, and then I could barely sleep for being seasick."

Taking the sealed message from him, I clap him on the shoulder. "Well done, my good man. I'm sure you'll be properly rewarded."

"Right now, Sire, the only reward I want is a soft bed."

"Then off with you and find one. You've earned it."

When the door closes behind him, I break the seal and open the message, which has another folded page inside.

Your Grace,

This was delivered yesterday under a white flag from the camp opposite us. A single man, who appeared to be no more than a camp follower, unarmed, and bearing his flag and this message. He came and went quietly with no change in activity on their side – not even the gawking I would have expected from something so out of the ordinary.

I can offer you no further clues as to how to interpret this. The entire border is quiet. There've been no further signs of military action from the Teutons. We've heard no news that the ransom has been paid or of any factional unrest in this kingdom. And Charles's captains have been quite well-behaved under my command. Perhaps you'll have more insight than I do.

Jasper

I quickly unfold the enclosure.

The time has come for us to return your king. He will be returned by way of the camp from which this message is delivered. There is one condition. He will be handed over only to King Alfred and no one else. Do not think you can trick us by sending another in disguise. Our captive knows King Alfred by sight, so such a ruse would be pointless.

We will know when King Alfred has arrived in your camp and will send further instructions then. It would be prudent not to delay.

Prudent not to delay.

Is it a trap? Of my own making? Or one long-planned by Charles and now being sprung? If the latter, then any thinking man would have to admire the ingenuity and the patience to wait until escape is nigh unto impossible.

For in truth, I have little choice. Though my fellow kings know treachery on Charles's part was a concern from the very beginning, there's a higher code of loyalty once pacts have been made and words have been given. In the absence of overt treachery, there are obligations. This could all have been avoided had Charles followed our example and refrained from taking the field.

But did any of us really expect him to do that? It would have been unusual, given that the play was being staged in his own kingdom – extraordinary for a man of Charles's temperament. So it's difficult to argue that his actions rise to the level of treachery.

Or did he do it all intentionally to lure me into checkmate? To finally take the revenge that's been denied him for so many years.

Could we infiltrate someone into the Teuton kingdom to either rescue Charles or assassinate him? That would take time – a lot of time that we don't have. Prudent not to delay. Delay could be the catalyst to unleash the full force of Teuton ambitions and weaponry.

Much as I'd like to circumvent this responsibility, I know that doing so would forever damage the unshakable trust we have with my fellow kings – would taint all my future dealings with them – and would likely shatter all the progress we've made with the Territories, not to mention Egon's dream. I feel the weight of the crown as I've never felt it before.

Rupert has no better answers for me. "However we got to this point – whether it's by Charles's design or the Teutons' – you're right about the choices – or lack of them," he says gently. "I wish I had an honorable alternative to offer."

When we climb into bed tonight, I show Gwen the messages. For a very long time, she says nothing, and I'm sure her thoughts are following much the same path mine did earlier. At long last, she sets the pages aside, slides closer to me, and takes my hand. "You have to go, don't you?"

"I wish I didn't."

"So do I." She caresses my hand with her thumb. "Take Tobin and all his best guards with you. Carew can look after us here."

She wraps her arms around me and we hold each other tightly, love and fear consuming us both. Then she whispers in my ear, "Come back to me, Alfred. Come back to us all."

It takes two days for Tobin to organize the journey. Two days for me to try to meddle in the arrangements. Two days for me to imagine every possible thing that could go awry. Two days for me to fret over whether all is in order for Geoffrey should I not return. As usual, Samuel is my savior.

He appears in my private reception room at midafternoon the first day. "Coliar says there's nothing more here that needs your attention. So let's go to the tavern. Richard's meeting us there."

When I hesitate, he adds, "Come on, Alfred. No excuses. Richard's buying."

As we walk to the town, he turns the conversation to the new de Courcy manor house. "The family quarters are complete, and Tamasine's last letter said the masons were promising to have the guest quarters done before the first frost if the rain holds off."

"I thought you'd have gone down by now to check on things yourself."

"Ronan's keeping an eye on the construction for me. He and Alienor finally agreed to move into the cottage we're vacating. Father gave him the tenancy the moment I got my title, but he wouldn't hear of moving until we had what he calls a proper lord's house."

"That sounds like Ronan." We both chuckle.

"Anyway," he continues, "we're leaving all the furnishings there for them – it's no less than they deserve after all Ronan's done for me.

So Tamasine's doing everything new for the manor house. Truth be told, Alfred, I'd much rather be here than in the midst of all that decorating."

At the tavern, Samuel and Richard keep the conversation far away from everything that's on my mind. And when Gwen and Richard's wife, Avelina, join us for supper, it's almost possible to imagine that there's nothing amiss in the world.

The next morning, Samuel's waiting when I arrive at the stable. "How about a ride to the monastery? Henry's been pestering me for a dog like Edward's so I thought I'd see if Brother Adam will have a puppy available around the time of Henry's birthday." Samuel's second son and mine do everything together, so this is no surprise. But I know it's not Samuel's real purpose.

Once we're well away from hearing ears, he turns to serious matters. "Tobin has everything well in hand, Alfred, so you can stop worrying. You'll sail with the first tide tomorrow. He's sending all the guards and supplies down this afternoon, so they'll be aboard before you arrive. They'll load the horses at dawn. You and Osbert and Tobin will ride down tomorrow morning, but it'll be an early start – it's a midmorning tide.

"You'll travel as an additional troop going to join Jasper's forces. No royal banners. No fancy tents when you camp. Nothing to draw anyone's attention to your presence. Alfred, I know you're going to be anxious to get there and get this done, but no forced march – the ordinary pace of a patrol. Listen to Tobin – do whatever he tells you – and you'll get there safely.

"And, Alfred?"

"Yes?"

"No hare-brained schemes. Do what you have to do, and then let Tobin get you out of there." The concern in my friend's voice is genuine and touching. We both know the danger I'm headed into.

"I think, my friend, this whole venture is hare-brained enough on its own."

Samuel finally smiles. "Just remember that . . . and don't make me have to come rescue you."

When we arrive at the monastery, Samuel heads to the kennel so that I can have some private time with the abbot. "A mission fraught with risk," Warin says when I've finished explaining what I'm about to do. "But God will be with you, Alfred. Just as He always has."

"I'm just as concerned for you, Warin. If this is a trap – if for some reason I don't return – the young viscount's fate will be entirely in your hands, and I never intended you should have to bear that responsibility alone."

"We have means, Alfred. There are places I can send him that you could not. Places where he would be safe. And the young man is remarkably amenable to whatever is required for his protection. So put that worry aside and turn your mind to completing your task and returning to those who care about you."

As always, Warin's manner and his words bring a calm that holds all other turmoil at bay. And in the afternoon, when I visit the tombs of my father and grandfather, I find the equanimity to embrace my task as the essence of what it means to be a king. I only hope I'll measure up.

We depart at sunrise. Just before we break our final embrace, Gwen whispers in my ear, "Come back to me, Alfred." Her eyes gleam with moisture, and I know the best way to help her maintain the demeanor of a queen is to mount up and be on our way.

The ship is ready and as soon as we're aboard, its captain orders the moorings released and we move into the channel. The winds are fair and the sea is calm, so the crossing is the most pleasant I've ever experienced. Let's hope that bodes well for the rest of the journey.

At our measured pace, its four days' ride to the southeastern province. Jasper must have given orders, for our arrival draws no particular attention, and his own greeting dispenses with protocol. As Tobin dismounts, he says simply, "Come. Let's talk in my tent." Then he gestures to me and says, "You too."

Once inside, he points to stools in a corner of the tent well away from the open flap. "Begging your pardon, Your Grace," he says, "I wanted no overt signs of your presence until Tobin has a chance to familiarize himself with the situation here and organize your protection."

"Don't fret, Jasper. I'm under Samuel's orders to behave myself and follow instructions." That gets a laugh from them both.

"Do you think he'll obey orders, Tobin?" Jasper asks.

"He has so far, sir, but I suppose we'll just have to wait and see."

"Well, you have the rest of the afternoon to make your dispositions." Jasper walks to the tent flap and beckons to someone who's been waiting outside. When the young knight comes inside, Jasper says, "Gentlemen, Sir Cedric. One of my finest captains."

"Sir Cedric?" I ask.

"At your service, Your Grace," the young man replies with a slight bow. "And to answer your question, the famous one was my great-uncle."

"So, Tobin, Cedric will show you the layout of this camp and point out what we've observed of the one opposite. He's at your disposal for any arrangements you want to make, including the location of the king's tent. Any changes we need to make to accommodate your needs, just ask."

"Erecting the king's tent will be the last thing we do," says Tobin.

"And if I might suggest," says Jasper, "let's not fly his banner until the morning."

"I couldn't agree more, sir. If you're ready, Cedric, let's go have a look around."

When they've left, Jasper offers me a mug of ale and pours one for himself before taking a seat on his camp bed. "There's been no change since my last dispatch, Sire. All the sectors remain quiet, and there've been no more arrivals in the camp here. It's unlike anything I've experienced or even read about. I've no better idea what's afoot than when I last wrote to you."

"It's like a peculiar chess game where the players wait weeks between each move. And I've been unable to work out whether Charles is the king or the pawn. Truth be told, Jasper, I'm more than a little worried that this is a trap that's been months in the making – perhaps even back to the end of the previous war."

"As am I, sir, but I've shared that with no one but Evrouin and Cedric. And I haven't told Charles's captains yet about the offer to give back the hostage. I told them that the last message was an ultimatum to expedite the ransom, and that seemed to satisfy them. Once your banner flies tomorrow, I'll have no choice but to tell them. If they were assigned any role in a trap, we should be able to tell if they suddenly start scrambling around doing one thing or another. If there's any sign of that, Evrouin has orders to detain them."

"Then I suppose there's little else to do but wait for the next move."

The wait lasts two full days. At midday on the third day, a nondescript man carrying a white flag crosses the border, makes straight for Jasper's tent, hands something to the sentry, and returns the way he came. Once the messenger has completely disappeared from view, Tobin and I make our way there unhurriedly. We find Jasper and Cedric seated at the map table. Jasper hands me the message straightaway.

A road leads east from the back of our camp. Follow it until the point where it veers south to go around a forest. Leave the road on the track that goes into the woods. Stay on the main track, avoiding side tracks or animal trails. The hostage will be waiting in a small clearing. If you leave your camp an hour after sunrise, you should reach the clearing when the sun is at its zenith.

Come alone.

I hand the page to Tobin, who reads it and passes it on to Cedric.

"There's one thing for certain." says Tobin "You're not going alone."

Knowing he probably expects me to object, I tell him, "Of course not, Tobin. You're going with me."

"There should be more than two of us, Sire."

"I agree," Jasper chimes in.

"Then only one more." Time for me to act like a king. "I won't have this all go wrong because we choose to blatantly ignore the terms of the handoff."

"And what if it's a trap, Sire?" asks Jasper.

"If it's a trap, we'll be so far outnumbered it would take your entire army to prevent our capture."

Tobin and Jasper look at each other, both unhappy but both, I think, recognizing the truth of my words. "Very well," says Tobin eventually. "But I want the entire troop of Guards at the ready as a rescue party if we're not back by the appointed time. So I need your very best swordsman, sir."

Jasper rests his chin on his hand and looks down at the table.

"I'll go, sir," says Cedric.

"There's no finer swordsman among all my men," says Jasper quietly.

"Are you certain, Cedric?" I ask. "We've no idea what we're riding into."

"It would be an honor, Sire."

We wake the next morning to a chilling site – the Teuton camp is completely abandoned – not a man in sight. Tents still in place. A few banners fluttering in the occasional light morning breeze. The remains of camp fires. Supply wagons still visible at the back of the camp. In the paddocks, horses munching contentedly on piles of hay left for them. But no sign of a knight, an archer, a foot soldier, a squire, a cook, or anyone . . . anywhere. How did they slip away so quietly in the night? Where have they gone? And why? Everything points to an intent to return, but why leave in the first place? And why on this day?

Will we find them lying in wait for us somewhere along the route to the rendezvous? Is giving Charles back just a ruse to capture me instead? Everyone's cautioned me repeatedly about that. Maybe I should pause now and listen to those voices. Tobin looks more worried than I've ever seen him. Osbert is uncharacteristically taciturn. If they intend to attack us along the route, then why would I assume they'd want me as a prisoner? If Charles has made a deal, then it's far more likely his intent is that I should die in the attack.

But if they intend to surprise us once we're alone in their kingdom, well away from any kind of help, why abandon the camp? Why not leave everything as it has been these past weeks? Is someone trying to make absolutely certain that nothing can possibly go wrong while we're in their lands? If so, why?

Nothing makes sense.

What if we don't go? What's at stake? Was that concentrated assault on Goron's forces a harbinger of what's to come if we don't play this out according to the Teutons' expectations? And if we do go and I'm captured or killed, would Jasper act in revenge? And would he turn on Charles's forces or the Teutons? Would our allies abandon us in the face of all-out war – possibly even a two-front war? Jasper certainly can't fight the Teutons alone with the forces he has here.

I once asked my grandfather how he made decisions in the absence of enough information. His answer seems somehow lacking in this situation, for I can't imagine an alternative outcome that would achieve our ends.

It seems there's nothing for it but to stay the course. And somehow I have to find it in myself to show a face of confidence, to try to allay others' fears, to help them channel their concerns into preparedness for whatever might happen. My father's last words to me were that I was as prepared as a man can be for whatever the future might bring. Nothing can prepare a man for something like this.

Altair is waiting outside my tent. Tobin and Cedric are already mounted. Jasper is here to see us off. Checking my horse's gear and climbing into the saddle, I put on my cloak of confidence. "I don't know what they're up to either, Tobin, but we've come this far. Let's go retrieve our hostage."

Jasper shakes his head slowly. "I wish you'd reconsider, Sire."

"I wish I had that choice, Commander. We'll be back before nightfall."

We ride out in absolute and total silence, through our own camp where every man has stopped what they were doing to watch us leave and then through the empty Teuton camp opposite. It's not difficult to find the road leading east from behind their supply wagons. The land is a treeless plain with the road marching in an absolute straight line across it. Surely an old Roman road, for if there's one thing the Romans learned from the Greeks, it's that the shortest distance between two points is a straight line, and their road builders doggedly followed this principle. At some distance to the south is woodland. The hiding place for the missing Teutons, I wonder? To the north, it seems as though the plain eventually gives way to farmland.

We've been riding for at least an hour when we spy a low ridge ahead, running north to south. "So much for hoping this plain would take us all the way to the forest," says Tobin.

"My thoughts exactly," echoes Cedric. "The back side of that ridge would be a perfect place to lie in ambush."

I suddenly realize these are the first words any of us has spoken since we left our camp. Such is the level of anxiety all three of us must feel. As we approach the base of the ridge, the road affirms its Roman heritage, going straight up from the plain to the peak. Tobin calls a halt before we start the ascent. "I'll ride up and see what's on the other side," Cedric volunteers. "If I signal you to leave, ride for your lives, and I'll try to catch you up."

Tobin and I watch as he climbs the hill. Every muscle of my body is tensed, ready to wheel Altair around and race away from here at the first sign of trouble. Well before the top of the hill – before anyone on the other side could see him – Cedric dismounts and gets on his hands and knees, crawling up the verge. As he nears the peak, he drops flat on his belly and slithers the rest of the way, barely raising his head to peer over the top. Tobin and I both hold our breath as we watch.

At last, Cedric jumps to his feet and begins enthusiastically waving at us to join him. From the top of the ridge, we can see three more hills, somewhat lower than this one, and, in the distance, the forest that must be our destination. "What do you think, Tobin?" I ask. "How much risk is it to just ride over those hills? We've no idea how deep into that forest we'll have to go and the sun is already well on the way to its zenith."

"I'd be happier, sir, if we approached each one just as we have this one," Tobin replies. "But something tells me you're of a mind just to ride over them together."

"I don't want to be foolish, Tobin. But I don't want to have something go wrong because we're late to the rendezvous." I glance up toward the sun.

"Very well, then. We go up single file with you in the back, sir. At least that way, if there's a trap, you have three or four lengths' advantage over any pursuit and Cedric and me between you and the pursuers."

"If we have to run for it, Sire," says Cedric, "ride north up the valley and try to get to that farmland. At least that way we can avoid being in a pincer if they've brought up another force back down there on the plain." He gestures to the bottom of the hill, where we've just come from.

"Right," I say with more confidence than I really feel, "let's go."

Once again, we ride in silence, each man with his own anxious thoughts, until we crest the final ridge. The forest now looks much closer, and we can see where the road veers to the south to go around it. It doesn't take us long to get there, and it's surprisingly easy to spot the deer track leading into the woods. I wonder if perhaps the old Roman road actually went through the forest and lies buried somewhere under centuries of fallen leaves and branches and underbrush, known only to the animals that live here.

The track is narrow and the forest more dense than any I've ever seen. We have no choice but to ride single file. This time Tobin puts me in the middle, with Cedric taking point. The shade of the forest after the open sky of the plain and ridges means our eyes need some time to adjust. Not far in, we come to the first place where an even narrower trail goes off to the left. "Let's mark the trees along the track," I say. "I wouldn't put it past Charles to have made a plan to lead us the wrong way as we leave and actually lure us into a trap."

"Agreed," says Tobin. "We'll mark them on the right as we ride in." Cedric has already taken out his dagger and is marking the tree just west of the side trail. "Then if we keep the marks on the left as we exit, we should be fine," Tobin continues.

It's slow going, and we pass several more trails leading right or left of the main track. Finally, we come to what passes for a clearing in this dense forest – a slightly wider spot on the track where a pony cart sits stopped, its driver dozing in the seat.

Charles is in the back of the cart, propped up in one corner. His face is swollen and bruised, and his head lolls on his shoulder, a bit of drool escaping from the enlarged lips. No doubt further inspection will reveal missing and broken teeth. His eyes are closed, and he makes no attempt to open them. His hands are bound in front of him and lie in his lap, twitching occasionally as if he's having a dream. There's no way to tell until his clothing can be removed what further damage may have been wreaked on his body.

"He's in no state to ride," I say. "One of us will have to ride pillion and try to hold him in the saddle. See if you can get him out of the cart." Cedric dismounts and approaches the cart, trying to work out the best way to move the inert form.

"That will not be necessary." The deep voice comes from behind us, speaking Charles's language with the guttural accent of the Teutons. "You may take the cart and driver as far as the border."

Cedric turns and draws his sword in a single, swift motion. Tobin wheels his horse around and reaches for his weapon as I turn in my saddle to see who has come up so quietly behind us. Three mounted men sit facing us. The one in the middle wears a small coronet and sits astride an enormous grey stallion. He appears to be a bit older than me, with piercing, almost-black eyes, a neatly trimmed beard, and a scar on his cheek from some prior fight. The men on either side of him are armed to the teeth, but have drawn no weapons. I turn my horse slowly around to face them and tell my companions, "Sheath your weapons." When they hesitate, I add, "We're in no danger." They look unconvinced, but do as I ask.

Switching to Charles's language, I reply, "That would make our journey easier. I thank you."

"I see," says the man on the grey, "that you have interpreted 'come alone' as loosely as I have. A wise decision, for one never knows what one might encounter on a lonely woodland trail."

"Especially one that's little more than a deer track."

"I chose this place because it would be safe. No one could mount an attack among all these trees. Archers could never get a clear shot. Horsemen could not advance at more than a walk, and maneuvering would be impossible. Even a foot soldier would not have room to properly swing an axe or a sword or a flail."

"And the empty camp this morning?"

"That was for your safety. It would not have served my purpose for some hothead to decide he could become a hero by killing the enemy king. I wanted to see the man who was able to inspire so much anger and hatred in that one." He nods his head toward Charles.

"I once disarmed him in a duel. It happened in front of his entourage and his father, and he considered it a total humiliation."

"I have heard you held his manhood at sword point but inflicted no wounds to his person nor did you kill him. Perhaps I can understand his feeling dishonored."

"The place and the audience . . . even the fact that the duel took place . . . were of his choosing. He's an excellent swordsman, so he no doubt expected to be victorious. But he underestimated the determination of a man fighting for the release of his kidnapped daughter.

"Since that time, he's put all his energy into redeeming his image of himself at my expense, but all his schemes have ended in miserable failure. His vanity and vindictiveness are like blinders on a horse. His vision is focused on his need for revenge, but he's oblivious to what's happening all around him."

No one speaks. The forest is both profoundly silent and yet filled with a gentle rustling high in the treetops and here and there the call of a bird. The big grey nickers softly and shakes his head. The man on his back strokes his neck to calm him.

At length, the deep voice sounds again. "I take you for a man of honor and intelligence. And so you deserve to know how we came to be here in this wood.

"That one . . ." Again the gesture toward Charles's sleeping form and the obvious refusal to call him by name. "That one came to me some months back with a proposition. He wanted my help to rid himself of two great thorns in his side – you and the Duke of Aleffe. He had a plan to lure you and your army here, but it required a small force of my men to provide the bait and to help him destroy your forces. You, he wanted killed or captured.

"In return, he would look the other way while my main force overran Aleffe province and annexed it to our kingdom. This was a prize I could not refuse. Not only is the province rich in and of itself, it is also the perfect place to launch a takeover of the port on the Southern Sea. And with his kingdom in disarray and his people terrified by our takeover of Aleffe, that one would have been unable to muster sufficient forces to stop us. As you say, he was so intent on seeking revenge that he failed to see the consequences of the bargain he sought to make." He pauses for a moment, and the distinctive call of a cardinal fills the quiet.

"But then you changed the plan," he resumes. "And though there was ample time, he did not see fit to tell me. I can only surmise that his arrogance was such that he thought it would not matter . . . that he could still achieve his ends."

"I agree with your assessment," I tell him. "In every encounter between us, he's allowed his arrogance to overcome his acumen. And always with disastrous results."

"Such duplicity could not go unchallenged. That is why I had him captured." He pauses once again, waiting, I think, to see if I'll question his motives or his actions.

When I say nothing, he continues. "He offered me a ransom. But his kingdom never paid."

"A side effect of a kingdom in disarray," I remark. "His adherents wouldn't pay unless the insurgents also raised money. The insurgents had no interest in ransoming a man they'd sooner be rid of."

"I suspected as much. While we waited for the ransom, I treated him as a proper royal hostage. He was comfortable and well fed, though I never admitted him to my table. When it became clear no ransom was forthcoming, I threatened to put him in my prison if he could not provide me with a better idea.

"By then, he was becoming desperate. He urged me to proceed with the invasion of Aleffe province. That sector was manned, he said, by a young, inexperienced commander who had a hodgepodge force with ten different loyalties. He was certain I could still take Aleffe and offered that as his ransom.

"So I decided to test his truthfulness and your resolve. I sent a substantial force against that section of the border. And they were met, not by a disorganized rabble with poor leadership but by a highly disciplined army under a brilliant commander.

"At that point, I had had enough. So I threw him in prison and let the guards do whatever they wanted with him. As you can see, they may have gone a bit further than necessary." He pauses before adding, "But he brought it on himself. I could have left him there to rot. But I preferred to give him back as an object lesson to his followers. And, as I said before, I wanted to see you for myself."

I don't respond immediately, silently acknowledging the accolade and assessing the man who I'm now certain is the Teuton king. When I do speak, I imitate his head gesture in reference to Charles. "He won't be fit to rule. And after this fiasco, I think we can be certain his nobles will force his abdication and crown his heir as quickly as they can.

"The heir is not yet of age, so there'll be a regency. But I'm confident the regent will be someone not affiliated with either side in the recent unrest. In fact, it *must* be that way, and I'll use whatever influence I have to make it so. The heir and the regent will both be popular, so the kingdom will heal quickly and things will be as they were in Goscelin's time."

"There was a wise ruler."

"Indeed. And to me, a man I could call 'friend.'" I pause. "We should go. I've no wish to induce anxiety in those waiting for me at the border."

"A wish that I share."

"Might I venture to make a request?"

"You may ask."

"The heir . . . the new king . . . is young, and all of this is being thrust on him quite suddenly. I ask that you let him be until he comes of age and gets his feet under him. Once he rules alone . . . once he can deal with you man-to-man – as an equal – king-to-king . . . then whether you have peace or conflict between you is up to the two of you to determine. Until then, leave him alone. I give you my personal word of honor that he'll make no move against you."

The Teuton king looks at me intensely from those piercing dark eyes. I fear I may have gone too far. And then, an ever so slight upturn of the corners of his mouth – just a hint of a smile. "I shall consider your words, King Alfred."

He and his men turn their horses and ride away into the forest. When I can no longer make them out among the dense trees, I turn back to my companions. Cedric is already mounting his horse. Tobin says, "I'll lead the way. You two follow the wagon." And our little party heads back down the track that brought us here.

I'm under no illusion that the Teuton king is anything but a fierce, warlike ruler. His vengeance on Charles leaves no doubt. And though it's unlikely we'll ever be friends or allies, some form of mutual respect was forged here in the forest. That's all I'll have to build on to protect my people.

As we approach the rear of the Teuton camp at the border, we can see that it's been reoccupied. Cedric and I ride forward to join Tobin. "You two ride ahead and get a litter to carry him to my tent," I say. "Tell Jasper to meet me there. If anyone asks, Charles is gravely ill. We mustn't give his forces any reason to go rogue and attack the Teutons."

"With all due respect, Sire —" Cedric begins.

But Tobin cuts him off. "As you wish, Sire." He's already seen the remarkable sight ahead of us. As we emerge from among the supply wagons, those in the Teuton camp stop what they're doing and step aside, making a clear path for us to follow.

"I'll be quite safe, Cedric," I add, nodding my head from side to side to acknowledge the gesture of respect being offered by our enemy. "Once we have Charles in my tent, Tobin, organize a guard of your own men. I don't want anyone here to see what's happened to him."

"Aye, Sire."

They canter away leaving me to continue at a walk with the cart and its occupant.

Jasper is waiting at my tent. "Walk with me," I tell him, giving Altair into Osbert's care. Unwilling to provide any fodder for camp gossip, I remain silent until we reach the open meadow behind the supply wagons. Then I tell him everything that happened in the forest.

"The only thing anyone is to know is that Charles is gravely ill, and that's why he was given back. I'm convinced the Teutons don't really want to engage with us at the moment and that if I can succeed with my plan, they'll start to dismantle their camps. So the last thing we need is to have Charles's men get wind of the fact that he was mistreated and decide to take their own revenge."

"So what's your plan?"

"In due course, Jasper. I want to leave tomorrow and take Charles to the castle. We'll put it about that the best healers are there. But for that I need a carriage."

"A carriage, sir? Where in *hell* am I going to find a carriage in the middle of a battlefield?" Then realizing he may have crossed a line, his shoulders tense and he bows his head. "With all due respect, Sire," he says more quietly . . . and then looks up to see the big grin on my face.

"I rather thought Samuel might have told you that hare-brained schemes are my specialty."

"He did, sir, but he never said just how hare-brained they might seem."

I laugh out loud and Jasper visibly relaxes.

"I admit it sounds ridiculous, Jasper. But Charles is no shape to make the journey in an open wagon, and having people see him as we pass won't serve my purpose. It doesn't have to be anything elaborate. Just something enclosed. I've discovered that squires can be resourceful in ways that would never occur to you or me. So what if I lend you Osbert, and he and some others can forage for something suitable in a nearby town or village?"

"Let's see what they can do."

And then I tell him in detail what my plans are. "If I succeed, you'll be organizing an orderly withdrawal to get all our armies back home. If I fail, then you'll probably have to withdraw fighting. But withdraw we will. We've done what we came here for, and I'll not have our forces embroiled in a wider civil war or an all-out conflict with the Teutons unless we regroup with our allies and make a different plan for dealing with the threat."

"Should I consider that an order, Sire?"

I understand why Jasper makes this a formal request. He needs absolute clarity about his mission and his authority. "You should, indeed, Sir Jasper.

"What I've told you is for your ears only, Jasper, because you'll likely have to make decisions here without our being able to exchange messages. I'll do my best to keep you informed, but I've no idea how possible that will be."

"I understand, sir."

We've walked quite a distance from the camp by now, so I turn to begin making our way back. "The first move is mine to make. But the next one belongs to the Teuton king. If I read him right, then you should see an orderly withdrawal and abandonment of this camp once he knows I've been successful. Unfortunately, I can't predict how long it will take for his spies to get word to him and for his orders to reach the commander here. If I fail, I won't be surprised to see hostilities escalate. Another thing I can't predict is his strategy. Take Aleffe province and the port first, then mop up the rest of the kingdom? Or begin the attack from here and wipe out as many of our forces as he can on an aggressive march north?

"If it were me, sir, I'd go after Aleffe first. That would cut half our forces off from a path of retreat, leaving the western port as our only option – and a really bad option, at that."

"Then be sure Goron is prepared. You can give him the rough outlines of what I'm attempting to do, just not all the details.

"Now, I have messages to write, and I'm going to need some things from you as well. Orders to the commander at the port to put his fastest ship at the disposal of my messenger. Three safe-conducts. No individuals named, just safe conduct for the bearer."

"Isn't that risky, sir? What if they fall into the wrong hands?"

"It'll be riskier if they fall into the wrong hands with the names of the individuals I'm sending them to."

"As you wish, sir."

"And then I'm going to need your three fastest couriers. You can, of course, order them to make their way back here as soon as they've delivered my messages. Men you trust completely, Jasper, so nothing falls into the wrong hands."

"Of course, sir."

"Finally, I'm sorry to do this to you, but I'll be taking Cedric with me. He's seen Charles, and he knows what happened in the woods. I can't risk leaving that knowledge here."

"Is that really necessary, sir? It sounds like I might need all my very best men." He pauses briefly, then adds, "Cedric is totally loyal. He'd never reveal anything he's seen if you order him not to."

"I don't doubt his loyalty or his discretion among our people. But I don't trust Charles's men. When they get curious about what really happened to Charles, they'll go looking for someone who knows. And I don't want Cedric to be forced to choose between loyalty to me and preserving his life. That would be a waste of a good man we might need later."

"Put that way, sir, I see your point."

"And I'll need to share your tent until we depart. Best we keep up the ruse that my tent is quarantined because of Charles's illness."

"It's at your disposal, sir. I can move in with my captains, if you wish."

"That won't be necessary, Jasper. Let's go get those documents prepared."

I start with the easiest one.

> To Gerart, Duke of Aleffe,
> Greetings.
>
> I write to tell you that my mission to retrieve the hostage from the hands of the Teutons has been completed successfully. However, he is gravely ill. I'll be taking him to the castle where the best healers and physicians can assess his condition and prescribe appropriate remedies.
>
> If, as I suspect, you have knowledge of the whereabouts of the duchess and are in communication with her, I beseech you most urgently to command her to come with haste to the castle to meet with me. You may assure her that she will not be turned away and that she will not be imprisoned. Further, the enclosed safe conduct will guarantee she can travel free from harassment. Nevertheless, she should keep quietly to herself until I arrive so as not to jeopardize the future for herself, your family, or the kingdom.
>
> As for you, sir, it is vital that you remain on your estate for now. You must be seen to be going about the normal daily business of managing your domain. I will send for you in due course and all will become clear at that time. But for now I call upon you to trust me and to heed these instructions.
> Alfred

The next message is also rather straightforward.

> My dear Petronilla,
> We've retrieved the hostage. He is, however, gravely ill, so we leave as soon as possible to bring him to the castle. Please have your most trusted

physician on hand to attend him as soon as we arrive. Due to the severity of his illness, he must travel by carriage, so we can proceed only at the speed of that conveyance. We will, nevertheless, make as much haste as possible, and I expect to be with you in the space of a few days.

You'll also be receiving an unexpected guest in the person of the Duchess of Aleffe. I've given my assurances that she won't be turned away at the gate or formally imprisoned. If she arrives before me, however, she must keep quietly to herself and make no attempt to draw together her affinity among those present at your court – or anyone in the castle, for that matter, nobles and servants alike. If she seems unwilling to exercise such discretion, then it may be necessary for you to confine her to her quarters until my arrival.

Lucia also must refrain from taking any action. There can be no good outcome from either of these ladies disturbing the status quo. I trust you to take whatever measures are necessary to maintain the usual order of things until I arrive.

Alfred

And finally the trickiest one to write, as I must be sure Gwen can infer my intent without actually revealing anything that could put my plans at risk if the messenger should be waylaid or my letter fall into the wrong hands.

My darling Gwen,

I'm back in Jasper's camp, having safely and successfully retrieved the hostage. At no time was I actually in any danger. But that's a story that must wait until such time as we're once again together in the same place. In the meantime, there's much for both of us to do.

As soon as a proper conveyance can be found for the hostage, who is gravely ill, I depart with him to the castle, where I must assess what's to be done next relative to our mission to secure this kingdom from the Teuton incursion. Our wounded from the skirmishes in the southeast and from the larger battle in which Goron's forces were engaged are being attended at the monastery just north of Aleffe manor. I'd like for them to have the benefit of the healing skills known to our monks. To this end, please ask Warin to send Brother Eustace and Brother Joseph with utmost haste. Since they will be in an unfamiliar land and an unfamiliar community, Warin should also remind *his brothers in the sternest of terms to whom they've given their vows and that only he who received the vows may release them.*

The man who brings this message has orders from Jasper allowing him to commandeer the fastest ship for his mission. The brothers are needed most urgently and so should come with this messenger as he returns. One of the safe conducts included with this missive is for their use to ensure travel from the port to the monastery is unimpeded.

The other safe conduct is for you, my dear. I'd like to have you and Geoffrey at my side as soon as may be. Also, Petronilla is most desirous to be reunited with her daughter once again, so I've given her my word of honor that Richenda will come with you. There's no need for delay for any of the trappings of a royal visit. Come in haste, as quickly as you can. I love you and can't wait to hold you in my arms once again.

Alfred

I read my words twice over, to be sure I've said enough for Gwen to know how to act – half of my plan will be in her hands, after all. Satisfied, I affix my seal and watch quietly as Jasper instructs the couriers and they rush off into the last, lingering bits of daylight to get as far as they can before darkness slows their progress. With everything in play and no going back, I'm sure I'll sleep as little as they do in the coming nights.

By midday, Osbert and the squires have come up with a carriage of sorts. Not so much a carriage as a cart that's had a tent-like covering attached to protect whatever or whomever it was intended to carry. "I be thinking it be better than a real carriage, m'lord," says Osbert, "on account of I dinna' think the person inside be able to sit fer the whole journey."

"Your thinking is right as always, Osbert," I reply, surveying the contraption.

"It be old, but it seem sound enough, and the farmer, he be right happy to get a handful of coins fer it."

"Very well, let's see what we can do about getting our passenger inside. Tobin's men have our gear ready and the horses saddled. I want to be away from here as fast as we can."

Alas, what I want and what I get are two different things. Just at that moment, Jasper walks up followed by four men I've never seen before. "Charles's captains," says Jasper. "They want to be sure it's really their king you've brought back and that you're not up to some sort of trickery."

It takes all my self-control to prevent exasperation from showing on my face and in my posture. I switch to their language. "There's no doubt, gentlemen, that the man we retrieved is King Charles. I know him well and would not mistake another man for him."

"That may be," says one of the men, who seems to be the leader. "But it's our duty to be sure."

"Your king is quite ill, my good man, and we've no idea what the illness is. For all I know, it could be the plague that ravaged my own kingdom not so many years ago. That's why I've allowed only two men to go anywhere near him until we can get him home and his physicians can determine what's wrong and what to do. Surely you don't want to go inside that tent and take the risk of contracting the illness yourself and then spreading it throughout this camp?"

They whisper among themselves, no doubt weighing the risk of contracting a deadly illness against how much they're willing to trust me. Finally, the leader turns back to me. "We must see for ourselves."

"Very well, here's what I propose. The four of you stand near the tent flap. We'll open it and you can look inside at the man on the cot. I'm told he's sleeping fitfully with a fever of some sort. Perhaps if you stay outside and don't go near, you can see for yourself. But if I were you, I'd still say a prayer that you don't contract the disease."

"Why are you not afraid of getting sick?" one of the others asks. They're still suspicious.

"Because I had the illness when it was in my kingdom and I survived. If a man survives it once, he can never contract it again."

They whisper among themselves some more and then follow the leader up to the tent flap. I pull it back for them to peer inside and am relieved that Charles is lying with his face toward us. The whispering begins anew, with a heightened tone of urgency. I drop the tent flap. The leader turns to me, his stance more aggressive than anything I've seen so far. Jasper's at my side in an instant. "That is King Charles," says the leader, "but he looks like he's been beaten. Did your men do this?"

"Calm yourself, my good man. We've done nothing but tend to him. What you've seen is why I fear he may have the terrible illness I survived. It can make the faces of its victims swell up so they look like they've been in a fight. I must get him to the healers quickly if we're to know for sure."

"Then one of us will go with you." Exactly what I'd dreaded from the moment they appeared and what I must prevent at all costs.

"Think, man. What would Charles's orders be if he weren't so ill? Would he not order you to return to your posts and be leaders to your men? As a king, that's what I would do. If one of you leaves, all your men will start talking among themselves, inventing all manner of stories about what might be happening. If you stay and things are normal, they won't have reason to doubt, and they'll follow your own orders without question." The leader still looks a little dubious, but has abandoned his aggressive posture. "Go back to your men. Look to Sir Jasper here as field commander. Let me rush your king to those who can help him. And I promise to send word immediately when we know his path to recovery."

They move a short distance away and huddle together again in conversation. I can't make out any of what they're saying, but from his gestures, it seems one of them is rather more agitated than the rest. Eventually, the leader says something that appears to calm them all, and he beckons to me to join them. "Will you give your word of honor," he asks, "to send a fast courier with news of the king's recovery?"

"You have my word of honor. And I also promise to use a messenger of the king's affinity to guarantee the news comes straight to you and to no one else." An easy promise to make, since I know there'll never be a need to fulfill it.

He looks to the others. "Are you satisfied?" Two firm assents and one rather grumpy one later, the leader seals the deal, "Very well, we'll return to our men. Be on your way, and take this sickness with you. But don't forget you gave your word of honor."

"A king's word of honor," I remind him. "And I've ordered Sir Jasper to burn this tent as soon as we leave to keep the sickness from spreading."

Having come to a decision, the four walk quickly away, in the direction of their section of the camp. Jasper comes up beside me. "That was a close call," he remarks.

"Aye. But perhaps better than *your* having to deal with it after we'd gone."

"Do you really want the tent burned?"

"Best do it. It'll buy you some good faith with those men. And if my plan succeeds, it'll be one thing less you have to bring back home."

We're on our way in less than half an hour, and, as I'd hoped, the lighter cart affords us a much brisker pace than we'd have been able to manage with a heavy carriage. On the final morning of the journey, Tobin sends a guard ahead to bring news of our arrival. I'm relieved when we find Petronilla waiting for us in the inner courtyard.

She gives me a sisterly kiss on the cheek. "Thank God you're safe, Alfred. I take it he's in the cart?"

"I want you to see him before we go in." She walks with me to the cart, where I pull back the flap enough for her to see inside without other prying eyes getting a glimpse. Despite the fact that we got him cleaned up and into a proper night shirt, there's been no change in Charles's condition since the moment we first saw him in the forest. "It's worse than I let on, but I needed the ruse to get here safely and forestall any premature action by either faction here."

"I have a room prepared for him and the physician is waiting there. Let me get some servants to take him up."

"Let Tobin's guards do it. I don't want anyone getting too close and starting to spread gossip just yet. Can your healer be trusted?"

"He attended Goscelin in his final illness. He'll do whatever I ask."

I beckon to Tobin. "Let's get him inside and into his room . . . with as little chance for anyone to see him up close as you can manage."

When the guards get the litter out of the cart, they close ranks around it. Petronilla takes my arm and says, "Follow me." As we make our way to the room she's arranged, she adds, "Tiece arrived yesterday evening. She hasn't left her quarters, so unless she's smuggling messages out through the kitchen maid that brings her food, she hasn't been up to any mischief."

"Good." We say no more until we arrive at Charles's room. "Send for Tiece and Lucia. I want them to be together when they see him for the first time, and I want them both to hear my conversation with the physician. There'll be a guard outside the door with orders to admit no one until all three of you are present."

She heads off down the corridor as I shut the door and take up a position to prevent anyone from entering while the guards get Charles into the bed. Their task complete, Tobin says, "Cedric, take the first watch while I organize a rotation for the rest of the men. No one enters until Lady Petronilla says that the right people are present."

"Aye, sir," Cedric replies as he closes the door behind him.

The physician has begun examining his patient. "This man is not suffering from an illness, Sire," he begins.

"I know that, but the ruse was necessary to get him back here. If you please, good sir, it's rather important that you conduct your examination and state your findings with the queens and the duchess present."

"Very well," he replies, stepping back to where he'd been standing when we first entered the room.

We haven't long to wait. Two strong knocks on the door, and Cedric opens it to admit the women. Lucia gasps. "Holy Mother of God, what's happened to him?" Tiece is stoic. No doubt her mind is already racing with possibilities, though she, too, is in for a surprise.

"Please, sir," I gesture to the physician, "please conduct your examination."

He pulls back the bed covers and examines Charles from head to toe. He then asks some simple questions, trying to elicit some sort of response from his patient. When nothing is forthcoming, he turns to me. "Does he take food and water?"

"He drinks if someone holds the cup for him. We've given him only broth and porridge for nourishment. He drinks the broth as he does the water. The porridge, he takes from the spoon and mushes it about a bit before swallowing some of it. I'm told only about half of it gets swallowed and the rest drools out of his mouth."

"As I suspected." He covers Charles back up and gestures for us to join him before the fireplace. "Your Grace . . . My Ladies . . . His Grace King Charles is not ill. He has been tortured. There is evidence that some bones have been broken, but also evidence that they were not set properly, for they are healing in unnatural ways. Since it seems he can eat and drink, it's likely that his organs have not suffered life-threatening damage. Without further examination, I cannot be sure if he has lost his hearing and doesn't know I was speaking to him or if he has lost his ability to speak and cannot respond. But as he showed no agitation nor any basic recognition when I tried to speak with him, I'm left to conclude that he has lost his mind."

I wait some moments for the women – particularly Lucia and Tiece – to fully grasp the import of what they've just heard before putting my next, crucial question to the physician. "I suspected as much, my good man. It appears to me that the damage is such that he will never again be as he once was – that he will not regain his mind or be capable of ruling his kingdom."

He steals a quick glance at Petronilla, who's sitting opposite me, and she gives the slightest nod in reply.

"It is said that God can work miracles when men least expect it, Sire. But in my opinion, a miracle from God is the only thing that could restore King Charles to any of his faculties. I served his father and am saddened to witness what has happened to the son, but it's best that you know – that all of you know – the truth."

"Will you stay and attend him, Gaspard?" asks Petronilla.

"If that be your pleasure, My Lady, though there's nothing I can do but see to his basic needs."

"That's enough for now, Gaspard," she replies. "The queen, the duchess, and I must consult with our advisors about the proper next steps, and it would not be helpful for Charles's condition to become known before we can assure the people that proper rule of the kingdom will continue. King Alfred's men will stand guard night and day and will be the only ones allowed to enter or leave this room until I say otherwise. I'll have your meals sent up along with food and water for Charles."

"As you wish, My Lady."

Now comes the trickiest part of this entire undertaking. "I needn't tell any of you what's at stake," I tell the women. "And you all have an important role to play if we're to keep this kingdom together and prevent a Teuton invasion. During the journey here, I've had ample time to think about everything that's in play and how best we can assure your future." Both Tiece and Lucia are showing signs of impatience at my intervention in what each of them, in a different way, perceives as the natural order of things. "To that end, I'd like to speak to each of you privately so we can consult on what's best to be done.

But as Lady Petronilla said, it does none of us any good to fuel court gossip or act on our own until we have a plan. If you'll give me your word of honor not to mention anything you've seen or heard here, you may return to your apartments. Otherwise, you must remain here until I send for you."

"And how long are we to remain your prisoners?" Tiece can hold her tongue no longer.

"You're not my prisoner, Duchess, but I must have assurance of your cooperation. I give you my word of honor that we'll speak before this night is over."

"Give him a chance, Tiece," says Petronilla. "Your father held Alfred in great respect. I think we can both do the same."

"Do I have your word, ladies?"

"Without question, Alfred." Petronilla's response is both immediate and warm.

"If you insist." Tiece can't mask the reluctance in her tone.

"I insist."

"Very well." She now sounds resigned.

"Lucia?"

"I'm queen here, Alfred. I can do as I please."

"Not if you want my help to avoid being ousted from your throne by invading Teutons."

She hesitates. "Very well. But we *will* speak before the night is over."

"I'll find each of you in your chambers. Now, if you will, Petronilla, please show me to my own room. I'd like to shed the grime of travel before we speak again."

When we arrive at the rooms that have been set aside for me, I invite Petronilla to stay. "No doubt Osbert has everything at the ready, so I'll only be a few minutes. And I want to speak with you first."

"In that case, let me order some supper to be sent up," she replies.

I emerge refreshed from the dressing room to find our plates have already been served and wine poured. Despite what she's just seen, Petronilla seems quite cheerful. "The moment I got your message and saw that Tiece was expected, I knew there was more to this than you were telling me. You *do* have a plan, don't you?"

I chuckle. "You know me too well, my dear. But yes, I have. From the moment I saw Charles at the rendezvous point and realized what a state he was in." Over the meal, I tell her everything, including all the details of my conversation with the Teuton king. "So you see," I conclude, "we have one opportunity to truly set things right. But I'm afraid it all depends on you." I pause. "And I'm also afraid there isn't time for you to think this over. If the plan is going to work, everything has to be put in train in my first conversations with Tiece and Lucia. If either of them has the chance to make any other move, nothing but chaos will ensue. I'm sorry to put this all on you, but I really can't see another path that would succeed."

She sips her wine, the expression on her face deeply thoughtful. Then she rises and makes a full circuit of the room, ending in front of the fireplace, where she peers into its depths, her hands clasped in front of her, as if hoping the wisdom of some oracle might emerge from it to guide her. At long last, she takes her seat again and once more sips her wine. Finally, she looks up at me. "You know, Alfred, how much I've longed to see Goscelin's legacy restored to this kingdom. And though you're right that this is a rare opportunity to do that – hopefully without bloodshed – it won't be easy. If I'm to do this, I must know that I have your complete support."

"That I will happily give."

"Your *complete* support, Alfred. Whatever that may come to mean as events unfold. And I must be able to make that known, should it be necessary to achieve our ends."

I think back to the days when Petronilla had the role of regent for Harold thrust upon her at a time when she was ill-prepared and expected to play only a ceremonial part. The woman putting her conditions before me now looks the same, but her political acumen has grown beyond measure . . . as has my admiration for her. Why, I wonder – not for the first time – does it take some kind of misfortune for a woman to be able to take on an important role in this world? Why is it that Gwen – who's even more capable than Petronilla – must play a lesser part just because life is progressing smoothly in our realm? Am I the one holding her back? Not by intent, certainly. But perhaps by failing to challenge conventional wisdom more aggressively? And what of Juliana's notion that women should be able to inherit and to participate in the running of the kingdom? Much for me to ponder.

But right now, I have to decide how deeply committed I really am to restoring this kingdom to its former state. Am I willing to commit my personal honor and the people and resources of my kingdom? There's no question, really. I made the commitment, intentionally or not, when I devised the plan and set everything in motion. Aside from wanting to honor Goscelin's legacy, I need this kingdom as a buffer against the ambitions of the Teutons.

"You have my complete support, Petronilla. My word of honor."

"Then I'll do what you ask . . . if you can get the others to do their part."

"Tiece is next. I expected her to be the most difficult to convince, but from what I've just seen, I think Lucia is not going to be as compliant as I'd hoped."

"You'd be right in that assessment. During the weeks that Charles was held hostage, she's developed an overblown sense of her role and her power as queen. I've been able to do things behind her back so far. But you'll have to bring her down to earth if this is to succeed. It will do no good to have her trying to undermine my efforts."

"Then let that be my first show of support to you."

"You'd best be off to talk with them. They'll both be getting anxious."

When she answers my knock, Tiece can't keep the impatience out of her tone. "Well, that took long enough." She steps back to invite me in and gestures toward the chairs in front of the fireplace. When she joins me there, she's still almost combative. "Let's not waste any time on pleasantries. There must be something you want, else you wouldn't have sent for me."

"There's no need to be so out of sorts, Tiece. In fact, I think we both want the same thing. I'm sorry for what's happened to your brother – I wouldn't wish that on any man – but we need to move quite deliberately if we're to avoid chaos, so I have a proposition for you."

Her demeanor changes – she seems somewhat mollified. "And what might that be?"

"I will put your son on the throne – "

"So you *do* know where he is. Tell me. Where is he? What he's been doing? Who's looking after him?" The angry duchess is suddenly a concerned mother. "Will you take me to him?"

"I will put your son on the throne," I keep my tone quietly determined, "but there are conditions."

"And what might those conditions be?"

"He will be crowned, but there will, of necessity, be a regent until he comes of age. That regent must be someone who has no connections to the conflict among the nobility here. What that means is that neither you nor the Duke can be regent."

"I don't see why not. Gerart has never wavered in his profession of loyalty to the Crown."

"That may very well be – and I have no reason to doubt it." I need to offer her some courtesy, especially as I'm going to be thwarting her ambition. "But those who opposed the king have done so in your name, which means the Duke is tainted with the scent of rebellion, whether he deserves it or not. And the widespread rumors that *you* have actually been leading the insurgents only serves to put your family squarely in the middle of the opposition in many people's minds."

While I was talking, she rose from her chair and began pacing about the room. Now she stops in front of the hearth and rounds on me. "Well, I'll not have *Charles's cow* as regent for my son!" The venom fairly drips from her tongue.

"I think perhaps you forget yourself, Duchess." My own tone is stern, my posture commanding. "The woman of whom you speak is, after all, my cousin."

Realizing she's gone too far in her zeal, Tiece returns to her seat. "Begging your pardon, Your Grace," her tone now contrite, "but I fail to see how the queen could be more acceptable as regent than my husband."

I relax my posture now that I have her attention once again. "Perhaps you didn't hear me clearly. The regent must have no connection to *either* side of the conflict. And for this reason, I've chosen the dowager queen. Surely you'll agree there's no one better to remind people and nobility alike of what life was like during your father's reign. I'm convinced she's the only one who would be trusted by both sides."

"Perhaps."

"There's nothing to prevent your husband from acting as one of the regent's advisors, but he must do so alongside those of Charles's affinity. If he truly is as loyal to the Crown as he professes, then his presence might help to heal the rifts and coalesce everyone behind young Denis."

Tiece is deep in thought. At length, she says, "But what about those determined to rally behind Charles?"

"I didn't say it would be easy. But so long as he retains his title and no able-minded or able-bodied man can take up the mantle of Duke of Lamoreaux, then perhaps their rallying cry will be less stringent. It remains to be seen whether they were simply loyal to Charles's person or if they have some deeper-seated opposition to their fellow nobles. Petronilla will need thoughtful and reasonable people – not zealots – to help her put the conflict to rest so that when Denis assumes rule in his own right, he inherits Goscelin's legacy.

"What I need from you, Duchess . . . Lady Tiece . . . is your word of honor as Goscelin's daughter that you accept my conditions and that you'll devote every ounce of your energy to reconciliation for your father's people . . . nay, for your *son's* people."

"What about Gerart? Do you not need his word as well?"

"We'll speak when I send for him. But you're the one with royal blood. You're the one who can and must speak for your family . . . and for your son. Without your agreement, my purpose here is at an end from this moment, and I'll take my armies and return home."

"What about Lucia? She gave a rather good impression of a haughty queen back there in Charles's room."

"Lucia's actually a gentle soul who's been dominated by others for most of her life, so I don't begrudge her a moment of savoring her position. But she's not mean-spirited, and I'm confident of being able to persuade her of the wisdom of this path."

She sits quietly for a very long time, staring at the ceiling. What, I wonder, is going on in her thoughts? A counter-proposal perhaps? I hope not. I've no intention of negotiating with her. Praying? Invoking her father's spirit?

At last, she seems resolved and returns her attention to me. "You have my word of honor, Sire. It's time to undo the madness my brother visited upon this kingdom."

"You won't regret it, Tiece," I assure her. "But I must bid you goodnight. There's another conversation that awaits me before all can be settled."

Lucia has me escorted to the monarch's reception chamber and makes me wait, apparently intent on reinforcing her position as Charles's queen. When she finally deigns to join me, her first words contain a note of condescension. "I'd decided you couldn't be bothered to keep your word, Alfred, and was preparing for bed. I hope whatever you have to say warrants my having to dress for a second time today."

I'd been thinking, during my wait, about whether or not it would be useful to change the approach I'd planned to take with her. Now, I'm convinced I shouldn't.

"Lucia, you saw Charles today and heard what the doctor said. We both know he'll never again be fit to rule."

"Then it will fall to me to rule in his name."

"Do you really think you're prepared for that?"

"I'll have advisors, just as any ruler would . . . just as you do. Surely that can overcome any lack of preparation."

"But think, Lucia. Do you really believe the rebellious nobles will rally to you? Or will they more likely see this as their opportunity to finish taking over the kingdom?"

"Then they would simply have to be suppressed."

"And while you're conducting this civil war, how do you prevent the Teutons from crossing the border and taking advantage of the chaos inside your kingdom?"

"Your army has the border under control, if what I'm told is correct."

"That army will not be there. We've done what we came here to do . . . what Charles asked us to do . . . ejected the Teutons from the southeastern province and restored the integrity of the kingdom. How long do you think it would take to convince your nobles to stop fighting each other and unite against the greater threat? Too long, I fear, if the Teuton king decides to seize the opportunity he's always wanted."

"Then what do you think I should do, Alfred? I'm sure you didn't come here without a proposal."

"I think you should do your kingdom one extraordinary service and abdicate in Charles's name so that his heir can be crowned."

"You mean the missing viscount?"

"I'm inclined to think that, once your intentions are known, the viscount will be missing no longer."

"And a king not yet of age could accomplish what you believe I cannot?"

"Despite his age, he's Goscelin's grandson. That counts for a lot in this kingdom."

"It didn't count for much for Charles."

"I think you understand the difference, Lucia. And I know that I'm in your debt because you have that understanding."

She's calmer now . . . the gentler, more insightful Lucia who tried to provide comfort and safety for her mother by marrying a man who would never share her bed . . . the Lucia who warned of the invasion of my own kingdom, allowing us to be ready to repel the threat . . . the Lucia whose heart I'm about to break once again.

"The new king will require a regent until he comes of age. Is it not logical that should be me?" she offers tentatively.

I take her hand, hoping to soften the blow. "At a different time, perhaps. But if this kingdom is to heal, the people and the nobility must be reminded constantly of how things were in Goscelin's reign. And there's none better to do that than Goscelin's queen."

The tears well in her eyes and, despite her best efforts, a few escape to roll down her cheeks. She turns away from me, trying to hide them.

"You'll remain Duchess of Lamoreaux," I continue, hoping this might provide some sort of consolation. "And with Charles incapacitated, the management of the duchy will be entirely in your control. You'll be wealthy, and I have a feeling the people of Lamoreaux will thrive in your care and come to love you. And eventually, I'm confident you'll be invited back to court. You could even bring Isabella to live with you, if that were your wish."

At the mention of her mother's name, she turns back to me, the tears flowing freely. "It's too late for that, Alfred. If only Mother could've accepted life as it is and not the way she wanted it to be . . . things could've been *so* different. I loved her once. But that's now just a memory. We're all better off if she remains in the convent." She takes a handkerchief from her sleeve and begins to dry her tears.

"Must you have an answer now, Alfred? I'd like to pray on this."

"The longer we wait, the higher the risk of something or someone thwarting our plans."

"Please, Alfred . . . as a repayment of your debt. When Petronilla told me you were bringing Charles here, I had a terrible sense of foreboding. So I wrote to Sister Constancia and asked her to come. She should be here tomorrow. Surely there can be no harm in waiting overnight."

Despite knowing that every hour – every minute, even – is a risk, giving her a way to find some comfort is a small price to pay for the gift she already gave to me. "Will you agree not to speak of this to anyone other than Constancia until you've given me your answer?"

"If that's what you require."

I take her hand again. "Know, Lucia, that I bear you no ill will. You've been blameless in all of this and deserve better. I hope you find that as Duchess of Lamoreaux." She makes no reply. "Send for me when you're ready, my dear." And I take my leave.

To my surprise and relief, Constancia arrives at midmorning and goes straight to Lucia. Over the midday meal with Petronilla, I lay out the next steps of my plan. "Once she agrees, you must summon all the nobles to court. No explanations, just a summons from the dowager queen."

"What if she doesn't agree?"

"I think, in all the world, Constancia is the only person Lucia truly trusts. And I trust my aunt to help Lucia find comfort in what she already knows she has to do."

"I hope you're right, Alfred. So much depends on it. But how does any of this work without Denis? We can't proclaim him king and just hope he reappears to claim his crown."

I hate withholding the truth from her, but until the crown is formally on Denis's head . . . "One step at a time. How many of the nobles do you think will respond to your summons?"

"There's really no way to know, but I rather suspect their curiosity will overcome whatever reservations they might have."

The afternoon seems to drag on interminably – as if every grain of sand has to struggle to find its way to the other side of the hourglass. It doesn't help that I need to stay out of sight so no one can guess I've any reason to be anxious. I spend part of the time pottering around in Goscelin's library. From my first gift to him of a book of Psalms until his death, he and I kept up an intermittent correspondence about the expansion of his collection. My real purpose, though, is to find a map – something that will be essential to the next step in my plan. I also collect the paper, quill, and ink that are the other necessary ingredients.

Finally, as the church bells sound for Nones, Osbert appears. "Ye be wanted in the chapel, m'lord. Ye be needing me to show the way?"

"Thank you, Osbert. I think I can find it for myself." Best everyone thinks I'm simply going to pray rather than being led to a rendezvous.

Sister Constancia and Lucia are side-by-side on the bench immediately in front of the altar. My aunt rises to embrace me but says nothing. There'll be time to speak with her later.

"Sit with me, Alfred," Lucia pats the spot on the bench just beside her. "You said last night that I had given you a priceless gift with my warning about the invasion. I realize now that your debt is long since paid. You gave me our dear aunt, who has become more of a mother to me than my own ever was. I should never have known her, were it not for you.

"Without her, I'm not sure I'd have been able to set aside my own disappointment and grasp the wisdom of what you're doing. I see now that it's up to me to set things right . . . that the fate of this kingdom is entirely in my hands. I won't condemn its people to a future of conflict or possibly even subjugation. I'll do what you ask, Alfred. But I ask in return that you be a good friend to Denis and to his people."

"That I can promise you without the least hesitation."

"Then tell me what I must do."

"Rest for now. Enjoy Constancia's company. Inquire after Charles's health once each day, to maintain the ruse of illness, but otherwise, keep to yourself. I'll come to you when everything is in place."

Sister Constancia rises to accompany me to the door. I give her my arm. "She's a lovely woman, Alfred, in a very unlovely position. Thank you for being kind to her."

"I only hope her legacy will be remembered . . . that the chroniclers will record that it was *she* who made reconciliation possible." I pause and turn to the still beautiful face beneath the veil. "Thank *you*, Aunt, for loving her enough to be here."

"We'll remain here for a time after you leave," she says, releasing my arm. "No need to fuel the servants' gossip."

Walking back to my room, I have to force myself to keep my pace measured, so strong is the sense of urgency I feel to put the next steps in train. Osbert seems to sense that urgency as I close the door behind me and make straight for the writing table. "What ye be needing, m'lord?"

"One of these days, Osbert, I need you to tell me how you always seem to know when I need something." He chuckles. "But for now, I need you to fetch Tobin and Cedric here."

"Aye, m'lord."

And while he's gone, I pen the final two messages that are the lynchpins of the plan.

To Gerart, Duke of Aleffe,
Greetings.
By now you will have received a summons to court from the dowager queen. Please do not act on this summons until you have in your possession something you will recognize as of immense value to both yourself and the kingdom. What this might be will become clear very soon. Once it is, I beseech

you to come here with as much haste as safe travel and protection of what you bring will allow.

Alfred

And the final missive.

Brother Eustace,

I hope you will forgive me for depriving you of Brother Joseph's services, but he's now needed elsewhere.

Please give him the following instructions. He's to proceed as quickly as possible to Aleffe Manor, there to reveal himself to his father . . . and only to his father. He's to tell his father nothing more than that he's been living with a community of monks in order to safeguard his life. Please impress on him most strongly that this is all he's permitted to say.

As for you, it's important that you get underway with the process of bringing our wounded home. Sir Cedric will remain with you to see to the logistics of arranging transport to the docks and securing passage on board whatever ships may be required. The army will begin its withdrawal soon, so there's some urgency to your task to permit time for the ships to return to collect the troops. Should you need to enlist the help of your fellow monks to tend the men, please assure them there will be no impediment to their returning on board our ships.

I trust you to protect the confidence of this message. Sir Cedric knows his assignment is to assist you but nothing of the other matters to which you are privy.

You have, in advance, my deepest gratitude.

Alfred

Tobin and Cedric arrive just as I finish applying my seal to the second message. "I'll get straight to the point, gentlemen, since time is of the essence. Tobin, I'm going to deprive you of Cedric's services, I'm afraid."

"Well, I suppose that puts me in Jasper's good company, sir," he chuckles. How I'm going to miss this man when he's replaced as captain of the Guard!

"And Cedric, I'm going to ask you to be my errand boy and general factotum to a monk."

"It's not the kind of duty I've had before, Sire, but I'll do my best."

Spreading the purloined map on the writing table, I point out where the messages need to be delivered. "Aleffe Manor first, then the monastery. I can't give you this map as I've temporarily liberated it from its home in the library, but I hope you can sketch out what you need."

Cedric studies the map. "Don't worry, Sire. It looks straightforward enough."

"And remember, Cedric. The message for the duke into his own hands and no one else's."

"Only the duke. If there's nothing else, Sire, then I'll be on my way."

"One thing, Cedric. You're to go home with the wounded. I want you on the last ship of wounded with Brother Eustace."

"But, Sire, I really should —"

"Be on that ship. I can make it an order if I need to." I pause. "Go home, Cedric. You've earned it . . . along with my deepest gratitude."

When they're gone, there's once again nothing to do but wait. Five long days. Five days punctuated only by the daily inquiry into Charles's status and a short ride – exercise for Altair and fresh air for me – ostensibly to clear my mind, though every waking moment seems devoted to imagining the myriad things that could go wrong. Tiece keeps entirely to herself. Lucia plays the role of dutiful wife to perfection, going personally to Charles's room each day to ask the guard, "Has there been any change?" and hear the predictable, "No, My Lady."

Petronilla's anxiety seems to grow by the day. Concerned by what this might mean, I join her for supper on the fifth night. "I've reached a decision on how this must be done, Alfred, and I'm not sure you'll like it."

"Then tell me. I might just surprise you."

"There can be absolutely no suspicion that this is some kind of power grab . . . nothing that can cast a cloud over Denis's legitimate accession and my authority as regent." She pauses, apparently expecting some sort of reaction.

"Go on."

"I want the nobles to see Charles. All at the same time and just before we go to the church. I want that image of his ruined state fresh in their minds so they're not inclined to object to anything that follows." She pauses.

When I offer no comment, she continues. "I want Richenda and Denis married straightaway. The last thing I need is for the nobles to start scheming to get one or another of their daughters married to the king. Besides, a celebration will be good for the people. And this one will be a signal to them of a return to Goscelin's wishes and his ways." She leaves unsaid that the marriage will also send a message to the nobles and the Teutons alike of my continuing interest in what happens in this kingdom. "They're both young, so I'll not permit them to live together as man and wife until Richenda is fifteen. That's about the time Denis will come of age, so they can step on the stage together, already man and wife, as monarchs in their own right. I'll prepare Richenda when she arrives. As with everything else, it's up to you to prepare Denis when he appears. Which I hope is soon, since everything hinges on him coming out of hiding."

When she finishes, I ask, "And what made you think I'd be opposed to your plan?"

"Only that I thought you had a different one. And the fact that I know if I don't get this right from the beginning, then all our hopes could easily be dashed."

"I wouldn't change a thing, my dear. And the fact that it's your plan and not mine means you're getting off to a very fine start indeed."

On the sixth day, the first of the nobles arrives at midday. Aleffe and Denis make their appearance after dark, Denis still in monk's garb. "We decided this was the best way to avoid drawing attention to his identity," says the duke. After a brief, emotional reunion with his mother, I take Denis to my own room, where he can share Osbert's quarters. Since there's already a guard stationed outside my door, we avoid the gossip that would necessarily arise from another guarded room . . . and Osbert can see to his needs.

Two days later, Gwen arrives with Geoffrey and Richenda in tow, precipitating another emotional mother-and-child reunion. Not to mention a joyful husband-and-wife reunion that continues long after all the candles have been extinguished.

•   •   •   •   •

Petronilla has decided we should wait no longer. The nobles at court are getting restless and all who intend to come have had enough time to travel. But even as she receives the court, she seems oddly ill at ease. "I'm pleased you've all come," she greets them. "This reminds me so much of our court gatherings when my dear Goscelin was alive."

"With all due respect, My Lady, I must protest." A voice from the front of the room. I can't see its owner as I'm trying to remain inconspicuous at the back. "You send an urgent summons for us to come to court. 'Make haste,' your message read. And yet you've shown no urgency whatever in receiving us."

"Your protest is noted, Robesson, but I'm confident that before this morning is over, you'll share my view that receiving all of you together was the best course of action."

"And where is the queen?" A different voice, but one I think I've heard before. Suidbert, perhaps?

"The queen is at prayer. An hour from now, we'll all join her for a short mass in the church within the castle walls. But first, there's something you need to see. Come with me, gentlemen."

My task now is to smuggle the viscount into the crypt of the church so that he's out of sight until his presence is required. Osbert has him arrayed in the finest court garb imaginable, complete with a fur-rimmed cap to disguise his tonsure. "I still can't quite believe this is real, sir," he tells me as he settles in to wait.

"It seems we were both born for similar things, Denis . . . restoring our grandfathers' legacies. And if you keep that purpose firmly in your mind, then your own legacy will be assured. Now, I need to be upstairs before anyone else arrives."

Lucia and Sister Constancia are praying before the altar as I emerge from the stairwell, and the bishop arrives within minutes. When the nobles appear, two or three are whispering among themselves. All look grim. Suidbert is ashen-faced. We take our seats in the choir stalls, royalty on one side facing the nobles on the other, Gwen and Geoffrey on my left, a vacant place for Petronilla to my right. "What was their reaction?" I whisper when she takes her seat.

"Horror. Dismay. Much as you see on their faces now. Robesson had the nerve to ask if you were responsible for the torture. Someone was bound to. It didn't take much to convince most of them you had nothing to gain by doing such a thing and that, in any event, you hadn't had an opportunity. I suspect, though, that Robesson himself may still be suspicious."

As the mass concludes – but before the bishop can begin his exit – Lucia rises. "My Lord Bishop, there's one more duty we require of you today."

"Of course, my child. And what might that be?"

"All in due course, Bishop." Then she turns back to face the nobles. "All of you have seen this morning the terrible state in which my husband, the king, was returned to us. If there is any doubt among you that he is unfit to rule – that he is even unfit to speak for himself – I invite you to give voice to your concerns." They all look around at one another, but no one utters a sound.

"Very well then, gentlemen. I've spent many days in prayer and contemplation, seeking to know the best path for our kingdom. I could choose to rule in Charles's name. But I fear that path leaves us vulnerable to the ambitions of our enemies. After all, the Teutons know what state Charles was in when they gave him back to us. I also fear that such a path would be an opportunity for a power struggle among my nobles . . . something we've already had enough of and yet another sign to our enemies that our weaknesses can be exploited.

"What our people need is reconciliation. And to that end, there are two things I will do in Charles's name. The first is to renounce all his claims to the throne and any claims I might make as his queen. Charles will be succeeded by the lawful heir, Goscelin's grandson, the Viscount Aleffe."

At the mention of his name, Denis emerges from the crypt and walks to Lucia's side. The gasps from across the aisle match the stunned faces.

"And as my final act in Charles's name, I choose our dowager queen as regent for the new king until he comes of age and can rule in his own right. And now," she crosses the aisle, "I join you as the Duchess of Lamoreaux. As soon as it can be arranged, I'll take Charles back to Lamoreaux where he can be cared for until his time on earth comes to an end."

The silence in the church is profound. Finally, the bishop speaks to Lucia. "And what is the service you require of me, my child?"

"To crown the new king, of course. From the moment I relinquished Charles's claims, this kingdom has been without a monarch. And that is a state of affairs we must remedy straightaway if we're to avoid the ill consequences I spoke of earlier."

"But, my child, how am I to know that King Charles is in such dire straits?"

"Gentlemen," she turns to those with whom she now sits, "perhaps you'd be so kind as to relate to the bishop what you've seen this morning."

The bishop seems easily convinced. I wonder if perhaps Constancia had spoken with him in advance.

"Very well," he turns to Denis, "My Lord Viscount, if you would kneel before the altar, we'll begin the ceremony."

Suddenly Suidbert jumps up and rushes into the aisle. "This isn't right, Bishop. King Charles named me as his heir. I'm the one who should be crowned."

The bishop turns. "Who here knows of this proclamation?"

Silence. Petronilla speaks, "I know of no such proclamation, Bishop. You may proceed."

Suidbert crosses to me. "You were there, Your Grace. You heard him say he'd name me his heir . . . even said it would serve people right for rebelling against him."

"I believe, Lord Suidbert, that what Charles said was that he *might* name you his heir. And it seemed to me at the time that he was merely mocking the insurgents."

He moves to Petronilla. "And how do you know, My Lady, that he didn't write such a proclamation? Has anyone searched his private papers in Lamoreaux?"

"Enough, Suidbert!" All eyes turn toward the resonant baritone voice coming from the back of the church. As its owner makes his way up the nave, Petronilla whispers, "Greville. At last! I had given up hope."

I turn to see a radiant smile on her face. "Greville?"

"The only noble who stayed completely out of the quarrel. He retreated to his estate and would have nothing to do with either side. Wouldn't let any of his affinity serve in either Charles's army or the militias . . . and his people are fiercely loyal to him, so they stayed home. I've come to believe he's the reason Charles never attempted to reclaim the castle. He couldn't know which way Greville would swing. If he went with the rebels, Charles's forces would have been hopelessly outnumbered. And if Greville insisted on staying out of it, then the choices for Charles would be to try to fight his way through Greville's domain and lose men in the process or to waste time and supplies going the long way around to the north. He's the one I want to head Denis's Council, and it was looking like I'd have to find some other solution."

By now Greville has made his way to the choir stalls. "You were once the favorite, Suidbert, that much is true. But then you were unable to find the missing viscount . . . and we all know how quickly Charles changed allegiances when he thought someone had failed him. Now sit down."

Suidbert can't give up that easily. "With respect, gentlemen," he gestures to everyone on both sides of the aisle, "how do we even know this is the real viscount? After all, he's been missing for so many months."

Greville walks to Tiece, brings her hand to his lips, and then turns back to Suidbert. "Don't you think a mother would recognize her own son?"

"*That* mother would say or do *anything* to get her family on the throne. Charles always said she wants the power for herself."

"If I'm not mistaken, her family has been on the throne since long before any of us were born. And if you were listening, you know that the duchess is not to hold the power. Now sit down and shut up." I can almost see Suidbert tucking his tail between his legs as he gives up and returns to his seat.

Greville goes next to Lucia. "What you have done today, My Lady, shows far more wisdom than any of us knew you had." And finally he bows to Petronilla. "My Lady."

"Perhaps, Lord Greville," she says, "you should see Charles – as the others have – before we proceed."

"That is my duty, My Lady, but a duty that can be postponed. I slipped into the church during the Mass and have heard enough to be convinced that Charles is unfit to rule . . . or to do much of anything, by the sound of it."

"Then we'll speak later."

The bishop looks thoroughly confused. Glancing first to Lucia, then Petronilla, then Greville, he asks rather plaintively, "What am I to do?"

"Why, crown the king, of course," Greville replies jovially as he moves to take a seat with his peers.

"But . . ." the bishop looks about once again. "But I have no crown."

Lucia takes the coronet from her own head and holds it out. "Perhaps this will suffice, Bishop. At the very least, it's symbolic of what's happening here today."

The bishop looks a little doubtful, but takes the coronet.

"We'll proclaim his accession to the people tomorrow, Bishop," says Petronilla, "but it's vital that the new king be properly and lawfully crowned immediately."

"This is all highly irregular . . ."

"But entirely lawful," chimes in Greville.

"Very well. Remove your hat, my son," he says.

"I believe, Bishop," replies Denis, "that the coronet will fit nicely on top of the hat."

"Be that as it may, your head must be anointed with holy oil, and I don't believe Our Lord would consider anointing a hat as a proper substitute."

Why hadn't I thought of this? God help us all if the bishop refuses to proceed. Denis reluctantly takes the hat from his head.

The bishop can't suppress his astonishment. "Holy Mother of God! This lad's a monk!"

"I'm no monk, Bishop," Denis is surprisingly calm. "I've taken no monastic vows. It's simply that I've been living with a community of monks, and it seemed that fitting in with them was the most practical way to ensure my safety."

Greville roars with laughter. "It seems, My Lord Bishop, that God works in wondrous ways to protect those he's chosen to be kings."

"But how can I be certain that he's not under some religious obligation?"

"Are you suggesting he's lying?" Greville.

The bishop is now totally befuddled.

"Besides," Greville continues, "even if he did take a vow, he's clearly renounced it in favor of becoming king. That seems like a good bargain to me. Now let's get this done so we can get on to the midday meal. I, for one, am getting quite hungry."

The bishop is left with no choice, and in less time than it would take to describe it, the ceremony is complete and the new king has donned his hat once again with his coronet nestled on top. He embraces Lucia and says, "God be with you, Duchess. You're a remarkable woman." Next he greets Petronilla with a kiss on the hand. "We have much to do, you and I." I wonder where Denis has acquired this regal manner? Did he learn from Warin and the monks how to be calm and magnanimous no matter what the circumstances? Or has he been taught by Tiece from the time he took his first step what it means to be a king?

The bishop makes to leave but Denis stops him. "My Lord Bishop, there's yet another service you can render here today."

"Another, my son? Haven't there been quite enough surprises for one day?"

"I don't think you'll find this one onerous," Denis chuckles. "Come." He walks to Richenda and takes her hand. "Lady Richenda. Despite the fact that I abandoned you . . . that I left you all those months with no word of where I was or even if I was alive at all . . . that you've had no hope of ever seeing me again . . . Despite all that has happened, I still want you to be my wife if you're not already promised to another."

I've never seen Richenda so happy . . . not even when her betrothal was first announced and her head was filled with dreams of being a bride and a life lived happily ever after. Petronilla prepared her daughter well, for instead of gushing, girlish excitement, Richenda replies, "I'm promised to no other, Your Grace, and would be pleased to renew our betrothal."

The bishop leads them through the betrothal vows, but it seems Denis has another surprise. "And now, Lady Richenda, would you agree to come with me before this bishop ten days hence to become my wife?"

Richenda looks to her mother. "Mama?"

"The decision is yours, my dear. You must wait until your fifteenth birthday to live together as man and wife. But if that's agreeable to you both, then by all means . . ."

Richenda's eyes, when she looks back to Denis, are pleading. "It's agreeable to me," he says.

"And ever so agreeable to me," she responds.

And then everything becomes very awkward. No one speaks. No one moves. Finally, it dawns on me what's happening. "Your Grace, if I might suggest . . ." Denis doesn't immediately realize that I'm addressing him. "Your life has just changed from one of deference to one of precedence. We none of us can leave here before you. So perhaps you might lead us all to the dining hall. Like Lord Greville, I'm becoming rather hungry."

Recovering himself, Denis asks me, "And is my bride-to-be permitted to accompany me?"

"I'm not familiar with the protocol of your court, Sire. Perhaps that's a question for your regent."

He turns to Petronilla. "My Lady?"

"As king, you can do whatever you wish. But if I may offer a suggestion?" She pauses, waiting for an answer, and quickly takes silence as consent. "It might be better not to spark any rumors that you're already married. I think the expectation and excitement of a royal wedding might be just what this kingdom needs to rally behind you and begin looking to the future. When you're proclaimed to the people tomorrow, you can take that opportunity to announce the upcoming nuptials."

Denis hesitates once again, still a bit unsure of himself. "May I walk with you, Your Grace?" I ask.

"Please."

As we make for the dining hall, Petronilla and Richenda fall in behind us, and Geoffrey offers Gwen his arm to join the procession. I clap the new king on the shoulder. "It all feels very strange at first, Denis, but with a bit of practice, you'll get used to it."

The following morning, after the royal procession is on its way to the cathedral where Denis will be proclaimed to his people, Tobin quickly organizes our traveling party to leave with no fanfare. The celebratory mood here will last at least through the royal wedding, but I want to be long away and my presence here just a vague memory before that mood begins to fade and someone thinks to ask questions.

As our carriage begins to move, I watch the courier depart with my message to Jasper. A single line:

Time to come home.

The port recedes in the distance while I watch over the starboard rail as our ship plows through the sea. Studying the wake it leaves in its path, I find myself contemplating the past few weeks and what I've left behind. I matched wits with the Teuton king and secured a truce, albeit an uneasy one. I put a boy king on Goscelin's throne – the legitimate heir, to be sure, but a boy nonetheless – and hand-picked his regent. And by marrying my cousin to the young king, I've bound our own kingdom more tightly to his than ever before. So much is in Petronilla's hands. But what I saw of Greville gives me hope for her success and Denis's future.

My son makes his way to the rail beside me and stares into the water, apparently wondering what I find so interesting there. "Something on your mind, Geoffrey?" I ask

"Mama said you might want to be alone."

"Not necessarily."

He turns to face me. "Papa, are you going to help Denis learn to be a king?"

"No, Son. That's the job for his regent."

"But Aunt Petronilla's never been a king."

"True. But she spent many, many hours at Goscelin's side and learned quite a lot from him. And he'll have advisors. And his parents."

"He could learn a lot from you."

"I'm glad you think that. But I can't interfere in another kingdom's affairs." His face falls and he looks back down into the water. "I'll tell you what I *can* do . . . what I *will* do." He looks back up, more hopeful. "Once our armies have come home and things have settled down a bit, I'll organize a grand state visit and encourage my fellow kings to do likewise. That will send a strong message to his people and will also signal any adversaries that he has our support."

"And Denis could talk with you then."

"And with other kings too."

He seems quite satisfied with that, but resumes his contemplation of the sea. There's something else. Some topic he can't decide whether to broach or not. The southwesterly breeze is strong, and the port is now just a speck on the horizon. At long last, he makes up his mind and looks back up. "Papa?"

"Yes?"

"Denis and I decided to write to each other. You see, we both like horses so that's something we have in common. And he has a lot of catching up to do on his training since it's been more than a year since he's had any, so he wanted to be able to ask questions about mine."

"I think that's a splendid idea." I can see the relief wash over him.

"And maybe if he has any kind of questions I don't know the answer to, maybe I could find out and tell him."

"It sounds to me like you two will have as fine a correspondence as I did with Goscelin." This is precisely why I'd wanted Geoffrey present at the coronation. I may not be able to help Denis directly, but correspondence between the lads is the perfect conduit. I couldn't be prouder that Denis worked it out and that Geoffrey understood. And even if Denis was guided by Petronilla, that, too, bodes well for the future.

·　·　·　·　·

As we sail up the river late on the afternoon of the following day, I get my first glimpse of how our new defenses will appear to friend and foe alike. Even though the cannons aren't yet in place, the fortifications to support them are nearly complete on the west side of the river. Once the weapons are installed, there'll be no doubt of our intent. When we could rely on the chains, our defenses could remain out of sight unless we were threatened, and this transit was far more welcoming. I have a keen sense of nostalgia for that view, combined with sadness that the burden of being the first line of defense for three kingdoms and the Territories has been thrust upon us by others.

Laurence is at the dock when the last of the mooring lines are made fast and we can finally disembark. "Welcome home, Sire . . . My Lady." He bows and then kisses Gwen's hand for the benefit of onlookers before leading us away from the ship. "Come with me. Your usual rooms are ready, and Estrilda's organized a cozy supper for this evening."

I glance up at the position of the sun. "Much as I enjoy your hospitality, Laurence, after the turmoil of the past few weeks, I'd really like to sleep in my own bed tonight. And it looks like there's time to get there before dark." I turn to Tobin. "Any objection?"

"None at all, Sire. Just let me get a couple of men and horses unloaded and we can be on our way."

"You can have a couple of my horses, Tobin," says Laurence, "and my people can sort the rest out once the ship's unloaded." Then he whistles and beckons toward the lads who hang around the dock hoping to earn a coin or two running errands or helping passengers with their belongings. "Here." He tosses half a coin to the lad who got there first. "Go to my house and tell them to get the king's carriage ready straightaway. And be quick about it." The boy takes off up the street at a trot.

"Half a coin, Laurence?" asks Gwen.

"He'll get the other half when he delivers the message. I learned long ago that's the best way to keep them mindful of what they're supposed to be doing rather than taking on some other task along the way if it looks like it might pay better and maybe never finishing my errand at all."

When we start to make our own way up the street, Laurence turns to Osbert. "Don't worry about the travel trunks and horses, Osbert. My people will get everything unloaded, and we'll bring it up tomorrow. I might even ride Altair myself," he chuckles. "Could be the only chance I'll ever get."

"Well, before you do, get your people ready. The armies are coming home, and it's going to get very busy around here," I tell him. "But *do* follow us up tomorrow. I've a lot to tell the Council and the rest of the lords – and you should hear it too."

As Gwen and I settle into the carriage, Geoffrey lies down on the seat opposite us. He's asleep before we've even left the town. "Like a little soldier," I chuckle. "Seems he can fall asleep anywhere, anytime."

"I don't think he slept much on the crossing," says Gwen. "Tobin told me he was on deck half the night getting the sailors to teach him how they navigate by the stars."

"Not a bad way for a lad to spend an evening."

We ride on in silence, neither of us wanting to disturb our son's sleep. When we pass the milepost that marks the halfway point in the journey, Gwen says softly, "I'll speak to Matthias tomorrow to begin planning the celebration for when the army returns. Is there anything specific you want to have?"

"I'm not sure a celebration is even in order. This certainly doesn't feel like a grand victory. It's more like an interrupted chess game. And with no way of knowing if the players will abandon the game entirely in favor of other pursuits or if they'll return once they've dealt with whatever distracted them."

"But don't you think Jasper deserves some recognition? After all, it was *his* strategy that succeeded in holding the Teutons at bay."

"And it was our good luck that the Teutons turned on Charles."

"I'm not sure luck had anything to do with it. From what you've told me about your meeting in the woods, I'd say Charles was the author of his own fate."

"Perhaps you're right." I pause. "And you *are* right that Jasper deserves credit for getting this done with so few lives lost. So plan something fitting."

"I'll talk with Samuel too. He'll know what awards should be given."

The silence returns. At long last, she takes my hand. "You're pensive tonight."

"I just can't shake the image of the interrupted game. And then there's the matter of what to do about Hugo that's waiting for me. Not to mention the looming question of Juliana's choice of husband."

She squeezes my hand then brings it to her lips for a kiss. "My poor darling. These past weeks have been more taxing, I think, than even the war over the bastard boy." Another squeeze of my hand. "As for the game, the players may, as you say, move on to new pursuits. But even if they return to it, you've reset the pieces, so the play would have to start afresh – different moves in an entirely different game. Your father and grandfather would be quite proud." Another kiss of my hand. "And as for the rest, after a good night's sleep in your own bed, I'm sure none of that will seem so daunting."

Just then, the driver makes the turn onto the road leading to the castle, and through the carriage window, I catch a glimpse of the sentry towers looming through the gathering twilight. From that first time when Samuel brought me back from captivity, these homecomings have become milestones in my life. I hope Gwen is right about this one.

Author's Notes

The *droit du seigneur* – the lord's right to be the first to have intimate relations with a vassal's bride – is a practice that may or may not have existed in the Middle Ages. Though mentioned frequently in literature, some scholars now question whether it was a legal right, a custom in some locales, or even a practice at all. The lord certainly held much sway over the lives of his vassals, including, in some places, the right to choose the vassal's marriage partner. The supposed lord's right is entangled with "marriage taxes" of the time, known variously as the avail or merchet. A payment to the lord would permit a vassal to choose their own marriage partner, for example. The merchet might also be paid to exempt the bride from the lord's "attentions" on her wedding night. And things get further confused when one considers that the Catholic Church sometimes prohibited couples from consummating the marriage on their wedding night – but they could pay the Church for an indulgence to circumvent the prohibition.

Those who argue that the practice is largely a myth cite, among other reasons, the fact that the literary references generally are from much later periods and may be simply the use of a legend to create narrative interest. Others point to mention of the practice in a fourteenth-century French epic poem and a tenth-century biography of Gerald of Aurillac (who eventually became a saint) as evidence of its existence in some form and/or some places.

Some of the better known literary references are Beaumarchais' play *Le Marriage de Figaro*, from which Mozart's opera *The Marriage of Figaro* was adapted, and Sir Walter Scott's *The Fair Maid of Perth*. Scholars disagree over whether Jack Cade's line in Shakespeare's *Henry VI, Part 2* – "there shall not a maid be married, but she shall pay to me her maidenhead ere they have it" – refers to the lord's right or to the payment of merchet.

The term *droit du seigneur* used in this context appears to date from Voltaire's 1762 comedic play *Le droit du seigneur, ou L'écueil du sage*. In Alfred's time, the practice would have been known by the Latin phrase *jus primae noctis* (right of the first night). Though Latin would still have been the universal language then, I chose the more familiar term – which could very well have been used in ordinary conversation.

Throughout this series, there have been occasional references to the daily religious observances of monastic life. The monastic day begins at 6:00 a.m. – the first hour – and the names of the services correspond to the names of the hours, one service every three hours. Prime for the first service of the day. Terce for the service at the third hour – 9:00 a.m. Sext for the service at the sixth hour. Nones for the ninth. So when Charles made his foiled attempt to discover Denis in hiding at the monastery, the brothers were gathering for the noon service.

I've tried to be diligent about linguistic anachronisms, but sometimes concessions are necessary for modern understanding. In Alfred's time, people would have used "wain" to refer to what we now call a wagon. Since "wagon" came into common usage in the mid-1500s, I've opted for the more recognizable word. Another is "catch at a straw" – "grasping at straws" didn't actually come into common usage until the eighteenth century. Even "catch at a straw" is a bit late for Alfred's time – it dates from the 1500s – but I decided to use it because it has such a nice, period feel.

When it makes sense, I've adhered to historical spellings and usage. Examples include "potage" rather than the more modern "pottage," "alright" rather than today's preferred "all right," and "cannons" for the plural of "cannon," though today we don't use the "s." Some might take me to task for using "pottering," considering that to be the British spelling rather than the American "puttering." But the so-called American form didn't come into use until 1878. Similarly for "cannon-balls," which is a single word in the modern American form but was hyphenated during the Renaissance.

And occasionally, there just isn't a period-appropriate word or phrase that is "fit for purpose" for the modern reader. One set of such words: "diplomat," "diplomatic," and "diplomacy." They came into the language much later than Alfred's time – nineteenth century for the first two, slightly earlier for the last. I simply couldn't find suitable synonyms that instantly convey all the nuances we understand today from these terms; and writing an elaborate, period-appropriate explanation seemed an unnecessary distraction from the narrative.

Names of characters (both forenames and surnames) are mostly authentic for the period, the exceptions being Boskren, Durrus, Korst, Narth, and Nerrick, which I made up.

This novel is a work of fiction that tells the story of what might have been in a world that doesn't precisely correspond to the one we know. Readers will note similarities with northern Europe, but my decision to fictionalize the setting was a matter of practicality for my characters. European history from this period and its major actors are too well known for it to be plausible that a different set of kings and nobility might actually have existed. The fictional setting also gave me the freedom to embed the allegory of our own times within Alfred's story. *The Weight of the Crown* explores international relations (trade, mutual defense, and espionage), abuse of power (including abuse of women), the impact of the emergence of new weapons of war, and the burdens of leadership.

For those who prefer to read the *Second Son Chronicles* solely as entertainment, I hope you get as much enjoyment from immersing yourself in Alfred's world as I've had in bringing his tale to life.

COMING SOON

Destiny

Was Alfred's grandfather wrong? Could all that Alfred has accomplished be brought down from a completely unexpected quarter?

About the Author

Pamela Taylor brings her love of history to the art of storytelling in the *Second Son Chronicles*. An avid reader of historical fact and fiction, she finds the past offers rich sources for character, ambiance, and plot that allow readers to escape into a world totally unlike their daily lives. She shares her home with two Corgis who remind her frequently that a dog walk is the best way to find inspiration for that next chapter.

Note from the Author

Word-of-mouth is crucial for any author to succeed. If you enjoyed *The Weight of the Crown*, please leave a review online — anywhere you are able. Even if it's just a sentence or two. It would make all the difference and would be very much appreciated.

Thanks!
Pamela Taylor

We hope you enjoyed reading this title from:

BLACK ROSE
writing™

www.blackrosewriting.com

Subscribe to our mailing list – *The Rosevine* – and receive
FREE books, daily deals, and stay current with news about
upcoming releases and our hottest authors.
Scan the QR code below to sign up.

Already a subscriber? Please accept a sincere thank you for
being a fan of Black Rose Writing authors.

View other Black Rose Writing titles at
www.blackrosewriting.com/books and use promo code
PRINT to receive a **20% discount** when purchasing.

Printed in Great Britain
by Amazon